Blood Ties

About the Author

Peter Taylor-Gooby is a leading sociologist with a strong international reputation. He has advised Lloyd's of London, UK, European, Chinese and Korean government departments, the European Commission and the Prime Minister's Office, and been awarded an OBE. He has written thirty-five academic books and two novels. He comments: 'research may analyse our changing world, but it is our feelings and our beliefs that drive modern politics. That is why I write novels.'

Blood Ties

Peter Taylor-Gooby

Matador
9 Priory Business Park,
Wistow Road, Kibworth Beauchamp,
Leicestershire. LE8 0RX
Tel: 0116 279 2299
Email: books@troubador.co.uk
Web: www.troubador.co.uk/matador
Twitter: @matadorbooks

ISBN 978 1838594 169
British Library Cataloguing in Publication Data.
A catalogue record for this book is available from the British Library.

Printed and bound in the UK by TJ International, Padstow, Cornwall
Typeset in 11pt Minion Pro by Troubador Publishing Ltd, Leicester, UK

Matador is an imprint of Troubador Publishing Ltd

I am very grateful to Sue Lakeman, David Ewens, Tim Armstrong, Nick Riding, Simon Wroe, Helen Barham, Kate Belshaw, Cass Bonner, Alex Chai, Liz Chettur, Imogen Crimp, Julian Dobbins, Anwen Hayward, Mark Henstock, Alicia Kirby, Emma McDonagh, Rachel Mendel, Ed Moustafa, Terry Pratt, Curtis Brown Creative, and to many others for guidance, support and advice.

London,
a couple of years from now

Ritchie Morlan

I'm Ritchie Morlan, ex chief creative at Dance and Fitzhugh, the top-flight advertising agency. I joined twelve years ago and left yesterday. I took the job because it was something I could do. Myles Fitzhugh mentored me. He seemed to like me, and people listened when I made suggestions. The agency looked after me, and at that time I needed looking after. In any case, the children were still in school and I had to earn some money.

Elsa, Elsa Dance, was never my friend, I knew that. Then we went public and Elsa was CEO and Myles was on garden leave. We moved very fast in a political direction. Soon we were the number one agency in the field. Well-groomed young people, sleek as seals in Dolce suits, crowded into the top-floor lift every morning. I took to going in late.

Things came to a head yesterday. I found myself standing at my desk, my hands trembling with anger.

I wrote out a letter longhand, and twenty minutes later I was in Elsa's office. Floor to ceiling windows and London laid out like a garden with the river snaking through it. The air tasted of nothing.

She looked up at me. Her eyes are the grey-blue of deep water on a dull day and she looks directly at you. It's not a challenge, it's not empathy. She just looks directly at you.

She smoothed out my letter on the oak desk.

'Ritchie, you're our leading creative. We need you.'

'I can't be part of this.'

'But you are. You're an adman. You'll always be an adman. It's what you do.'

I shake my head and she drops the letter into the attaché case by her chair.

'Let's talk this through.'

'There's nothing to say. I'm finished.'

'Think about it. Without you, Dance and Fitzhugh would still be middle rank. I can offer you a salary review. Maybe your own division.'

'Goodbye.'

'Ritchie, if you leave here, where are you going to go?'

The door closes behind me, cutting her off. I've chucked in my job and I feel as if spring's come early in Canada Square.

I walk past the lift and take the stairs three steps at a time. Peters is in his usual place at the lobby door.

'Good evening Mr Morlan.'

I shake his hand and leave him staring at the five twenties in his palm.

That was yesterday. Now the air chills my face and the streetlights are still on. So many people on the street this early, all huddled in overcoats or fleece jackets. They're mostly headed west between the glass and concrete blocks, more glass and less concrete as you get nearer the tube station. I check my mobile. There's an energy in me that makes my fingers itch.

It's not spying. They're my children and I'm on their side. I can help them, I'm going to help them. Nothing can go wrong.

I spot Jack ahead of me He's wearing a charcoal woollen overcoat and a scarf, and has a leather satchel slung over his shoulder. I wish I'd brought a hat. I can't see Nic anywhere. It's good he's come along for her.

I hear a shout from behind and my chest tightens.

'Dad! You shouldn't be here.'

She's striding towards me with her knock-kneed walk. She wears her red hoodie and she's got her hands pushed down in her pockets as if she's trying to get her whole body in. I'd buy her an overcoat like a shot if she'd let me.

I stand waiting for her.

'I've got to talk to you.'

She has to understand. I'm no longer that other Ritchie, the one who thought the money made up for everything.

'I'm busy.'

She's looking further down the street, at Jack, but she doesn't push past me.

'I've quit the agency. I should never have worked there. I told myself we needed the money. You get drawn in.'

She pulls the hood back and stares directly at me.

'Twelve years with the agency and you've quit? You're not just saying it?'

'Burned my boats. I told Elsa what I thought of it.'

She's considering, moving from one foot to the other.

'It's not just the job. It's Mum.'

5

'I think about her every day. The coroner…'

She fixes her eyes on me and shudders. She speaks as if she can hardly force the words out.

'Fuck the coroner. I think about her every day too, and I can't even remember what she looked like. You … What's the use?'

She shoves past, shoulders hunched and head down.

'Wait. I did my best. We needed money. I had to get a job.'

I'm walking as fast as I can. My right knee aches and she's already way ahead of me. Nic, who never needed anyone, restless in day-nursery, sailing through school, flying through Oxford, out into the world, out of control, hurtling onwards, anywhere, away from me, and I was so proud of her. Nic, giving her money to the homeless guy by the station and hitch-hiking home. Nic with her law degree, and her training contract at Clifford Chance, then she walks out and sets up *Refugee+*. Nic with her shared room in a shared squat somewhere (she's never told me where) on the Leyton Grange estate. Nic, with her black hair, same colour as Jack's but close-cropped, and her sudden gestures. Nic, always too jerky, uneven and reckless where Jack is neat, symmetrical and ordered. Nic with her bi-polar disorder, no problem as long as she remembers the pills.

Nic and Jack, my main reasons for living.

I blink and rub my cheek.

Twelve years in advertising and what have I got to show for it? A dicky heart and my children despise what I do. So I quit. I can help them now, they must see that. I'm still Ritchie Morlan, ex chief creative at Dance and

Fitzhugh. I know how to promote things, how to make people listen. Nic and Jack are campaigners. I'm good at campaigns. It's going to be OK.

The *Refugee+* website mentioned a leafleting campaign out here first thing, and here I am. Doesn't look like anyone else turned up. Nic says you find a lot of casual labour on building sites, they're a good place to contact immigrants who don't know their rights.

Nic touches Jack on the shoulder and walks on past him, from lamp-post to lamp-post into pools of light, then darkness, then light. He calls out and hurries after her but she doesn't answer.

They go down a side road onto the Olympic site past one of the new blocks, lights in the windows, to the area where work's still going on, turning the athletes' accommodation into flats. Vans with tradesmen's logos and a few cars are parked along the kerb.

The clouds to the east are pink and golden. It's going to be a fine day. I'm shivering and my knee hurts every time I put my foot down.

A van roars past, too fast, I swear the wing mirror brushes my shoulder. I step back onto the pavement.

Three metre high hoardings surround the block, with the logo 'Coral Reef Homes' and a red lattice-work of girders and scaffolding reaching up behind them, some of the wall sections in place with black holes where the windows will go. A fire glimmers inside on the ground floor. The only person in sight is a bearded figure in a denim jacket and a yellow helmet, standing in the site entrance, like a guard. He glances at us, steps back and pulls the gate shut behind him.

Nic shoves a wad of leaflets through the letter-box slit in the fence. I read "Shit Government! Shit Jobs!" across the top and under it bullet points in English and another language I can't understand.

I touch her arm.

'Let me give out some leaflets. I can talk to people.'

She ignores me.

Jack catches sight of me and sighs.

'Dad, please go home. This isn't an ad campaign. You'll catch cold.'

They set off past the row of vans. I don't really feel anything, just a bleakness as if none of it is worth doing. This can still turn out OK. They stop and Nic points to a van parked some way up the street with the engine still running. It's slightly larger than the others and reminds me of a Tesco delivery van, except it's a dirty white and the sides are blank. There's a banging noise from inside it. The rear doors are padlocked shut.

'Something's not right.'

She starts towards it. Jack moves fast to catch up with her.

'Take it easy.'

The passenger door is thrust open and a sandy-haired man wearing a black T-shirt and denim shorts gets out. His work-boots reach halfway up his calves and are laced tight and polished. Muscular shoulders, buzz-cut hair and a drinker's face. He looks like a boxer, out of condition.

He brushes something off his shorts and smashes his hand against the side of the van. The noise stops.

Nic walks forward holding out one of the leaflets.

He spits and glares at her.

'Who are you looking at?'

'Wondered what you've got locked up in there?'

'Fuck off, sweetheart.'

He snatches the leaflet out of her hand, screws it up and chucks it at her. She catches it one-handed. Jack's next to her and I'm half running, half stumbling towards them, as if I could help. My head feels thick with blood. The big guy smacks his fist into his palm and takes a step towards Nic. The van driver shouts at him and he hesitates, then laughs.

'Gotta go.'

He stoops and gets back in. The van drives off. Jack holds his phone up, filming it. He wraps his other arm round Nic.

'You OK?'

Neither of them looks at me.

It's half an hour later, my knee's throbbing and I'm trying to keep my weight on my other leg. We approach another site, a derelict warehouse in the development zone south of the Olympic Park. Corrugated iron creaks in the wind and the windows are smashed in. One end has already been demolished and the roof is sagging, a broke-back whale. A long strip of fencing has rusted through and been forced back. A wooden gate with barbed wire on top stands half open, the paint peeling off it. I'm still tagging along somewhere behind them. I want to be part of it, to be of some use to them.

We pass no-one, except a man in a stained mackintosh with a shuffling walk and a mongrel on a length of string.

He keeps his eyes down and crosses the road to avoid us, muttering to himself. I look round. No-one else in sight anywhere. I'm chilled to the bone.

As we get nearer a white van drives up and parks ahead of us. The driver, a small man with dark hair, gets out. Jack would look a bit like him if he went to the gym more. He bangs on the side of the van, ignoring us, fiddles with the padlock and yanks open the rear doors. It's the van we saw earlier. My mouth is dry. I want to shout at Nic and Jack. Why don't we go somewhere where there are people on the street?

A brown-skinned figure in a dirty boiler-suit swivels his legs round and stumbles out, supporting himself on the door. He flexes his knees to get the blood flowing again. The driver goes over to the wooden gate, heaves it open with his shoulder, and goes through.

A group of Asian men, six or seven, step down from the van. They're dressed in worn-out jeans, T-shirts, one in a denim jacket, one in a grey jumper with a hole in the sleeve. They stay close together, looking round as if they don't feel safe here.

Nic and Jack walk over to them. Jack says:

'Hi. How are you doing today?'

They stare at him. No-one responds.

Nic holds out a leaflet with both hands, as if it were an offering. The man in the boiler suit takes it and starts reading, tracing the words with his forefinger. The others keep their eyes on the passenger door, none of them talking. We should go.

The big guy we met before gets out. My skin prickles and I start towards him. He ignores Jack and scowls at Nic.

He hesitates for a moment, as if he's trying to work out what to do. He walks round the van, slightly bow-legged, grabs the leaflet out of the man's hand and smacks his cheek, as if punishing a schoolboy. The man staggers back towards the gate. The big guy turns to face Nic and thrusts his head forward. He's a good six inches taller than she is.

'I told you to fuck off.'

She offers him a leaflet.

'Better rights for workers. You should read it.'

Jack taps at his phone and holds it up.

'Leave her alone. It's a public street.'

The thug doesn't even look at him, just flips up one of his bricklayer's hands and shoves him backwards. He trips and falls to the ground.

I've nearly caught up with them.

'Please.'

I'm panting. I lean forward.

'It's OK. We'll get going.'

Jack gets to his knees, blood smeared across his hand. He shakes his head and glances at Nic. She stands very straight, takes a bag from her pocket and offers it to the thug.

'Jelly baby?'

He knocks the packet out of her hand. Multi-coloured sweets scatter across the pavement.

'You can fuck off, both of you.'

He stamps hard. His boot misses Nic's trainer by the width of a raindrop.

'Now. Get lost.'

Nic winces and her face is pale as paper. She stays where she is. He seizes her arm.

Jack shouts:

'Behave yourself. The police are on their way'

I stumble and clutch the thug's shoulder. He whirls round and grabs at my face. My gut clenches and I retch, lurch backwards and vomit. The acid burns my throat and over it I taste the sweet tang of the Paradise Bars I ate earlier.

The driver rushes up. He slams the van door and grabs the thug by the arm.

'Cool it, Syker. No trouble.'

The big guy shakes him off. The padlock is in his other hand. He holds it like a weapon. He slams his fist into the side of the van so hard that it rocks and the men shrink back. He swears and cradles the fist in his other hand.

The worker who took the leaflet shouts something. The thug bellows and punches him in the stomach. As the man folds forward, like a discarded puppet, the thug jerks his knee up into his face. The man falls to his knees and gasps for breath. Blood spills from the corner of his mouth. He claps his hand across his face. The thug roars and the men flinch back, silent. He drags the man to his feet and herds all of them through the gate. It crashes shut behind him.

'God, Dad. Are you alright?' Nic's holding my head.

I spit to clear my mouth and try to sit up.

'I'll be OK. Water. Get my breath back.'

Jack squats and wraps his overcoat round me. Nic slips an arm round my shoulders. She opens a water bottle and holds it to my mouth.

'Take it easy, Dad. Just rest a minute. We're calling an ambulance.'

I lean back and close my eyes and drink.

The Emergency Response Unit arrives in four minutes. I sit in the back seat of their car and feel better than I have for a long time. An efficient young woman with green hair and a pale freckled face sticks tabs to my chest, wires me to a black box like a Bakelite radio and checks my pulse.

'Not too good, not too bad.' She takes a white gadget like a mobile phone out of her bag. 'Now this is the Dracula bit. You OK with needles?'

I feel a prick on my middle finger. She stares at the screen.

'Your blood sugar is in the top half per cent. What did you have for breakfast?'

'A couple of Paradise Bars. Keeps me going.'

'Explains a lot.'

She fiddles with the black box and glances at her colleague. He points at the messages scrolling up on a screen in the centre of the dashboard.

'We have to crack on. We'll drop you off at A and E. Bit of a queue I'm afraid. It may be six hours before the registrar gets round to you.'

'I'm OK. I just need a rest.'

'You really should have a check-up.'

I glance at Nic and Jack. The police have arrived and Jack's showing them the video of the attack on his phone.

'My kids will look after me.'

The other medic says something to the one who's dealing with me. She doesn't look at him.

'You will see the GP won't you? Today?'

She looks me full in the face. It's as if we're making a pact, just between the two of us.

The kids are still busy. I nod.

'Shouldn't really do this, but we must get on. Make sure you get round to the GP – and listen to what she tells you.'

The other medic's already putting his seat belt on. I climb out of the car and they drive off.

The policewoman hands Jack his phone. She's older than I first thought, slightly-built, neat and formal.

'Was a knife involved?'

'I didn't see one. That man, the one who was beaten up, needs hospital treatment.'

'I'm very sorry to hear that.'

I want to join in and back him up, but this is their business.

'Did you see any indication of hate crime?'

Nic joins in. She's talking too fast, it's hard to make out the words.

'It's not only that, it's forced labour. They're terrified. They were locked up in that van I don't know how long.' She jabs her forefinger at the policewoman. 'You've got to do something.'

Jack moves in front of her. I take hold of her hand, but she shakes me off.

The policewoman steps backward.

'We will investigate and make a report. We are strongly concerned about such crimes.' She sounds as if she's reading a statement to a group of reporters.

'I'm very glad you came so quickly,' Jack says. 'I hope the film of the attack will be useful.'

'Of course. Please email the video to this address.'

She gives him a card and settles her bowler on her head.

'Thank you for all your help. We take these accusations very seriously. I see your father is much better.'

She nods to the other cop and they walk across the road and bang on the gate. She shouts: 'Police.'

Someone inside drags the gate open and they enter. Nic tries to follow, but the cop says something and the gate slams to in front of her.

She turns and holds her arms out wide, and includes me in the gesture. I'm filled with love for her.

'Same as last time – press don't turn up. If we could get a journalist here maybe we'd get somewhere. I hate all this.'

We sit in the kitchen back in Jack's flat – living room, kitchen, one bedroom and a view of Stratford shopping centre. It always feels warm, the walls are buttermilk and saffron and the doors stripped pine. I helped him buy it. I'd help Nic if she'd let me.

The photo of the three of us, Jack and Nic as teenagers, and me on that holiday in Arcachon, suntans, seafood and Bordeaux white, hangs above the sink. Always makes me think of the photo I don't have any more because I tore it up: Margate sands, the children much younger and everything easy. Seven year old Nic races away down the beach, Jack staggers after her on his chubby legs, clutching at his sun-hat, the sun streaming golden under ice-cream clouds. I remember taking it, kneeling on the beach, stunned that such glorious people are my children.

Jack glances at me and stirs two spoonfuls of sugar into my coffee.

'Shock,' he says and grins.

Nic's on her mobile, gesturing with her free hand as if the other person could see her.

She puts the phone down and Jack hands her a mug of coffee. He puts the packet of pills next to it.

'Any luck?'

She frowns and her nostrils flare but she speaks calmly.

'At least that guy, the one who was beaten up, is in hospital. The thug calls himself a gang-master. He says it was a fight between workers and he broke it up. No-one else will talk. Waste of time. Cops say the film's not admissible unless it's corroborated. They're grateful for our help and they're sorry. They'll keep an eye, whatever that means.'

Cat flashes into my mind. Cat in the hospital, white as the bedsheet, with Jack on her breast, one arm cuddling Nic. Cat on the steps of the High Court with the reporters buffeting round her, the day she won the Stevenage Seventeen deportation case. Cat on the platform at the Human Rights Watch annual dinner, laughing.

'That thug's taken their passports. It's slavery.'

'Yup, but the police won't start anything unless they know they'll get a conviction. Everyone's too scared to talk.'

'Slavery in plain sight. No-one knows. No-one cares. No-one bothers.'

They sit on opposite sides of the table, just looking at each other. Jack touches her arm.

'You tried.'

She gives her lop-sided smile.

'No-one turned up. Not the press, not the council, no-one off the supporters' list.'

She slips two of the pills into her mouth and swallows.

I'm not part of this. I want to be, but I'm not. I'm angry too, I'm shocked, of course I am, but what use is that? I've been in advertising all my life, I know about publicity, I know about changing people's minds.

'I've got contacts. Next time, I'll chat them up for you. They'd come.'

Jack shakes his head.

'Don't do that.'

'But I want to help.'

Nick frowns.

'It's not some advertising stunt to con people, this is real.'

Neither of them looks at me. I finish my coffee.

'I guess I should be going.'

Jack gets to his feet.

'Dad? You'll be OK, won't you? Keep in touch – and don't do anything stupid.'

He hugs me.

'Take care.'

Nic's still sitting at the table. She raises her hand to wave and I grip it and there's something twisted in my smile. That makes two of us.

Crossing the Road

London, where justice stands blindfold on a pinnacle and stockbrokers jostle money-launderers in the fat lands of the City. London, mother of parliaments, where tourists shove against anti-terrorist barriers in the shadow of Big Ben, where wealth is smeared over poverty like jam on stale bread.

It's no good preaching at people, it's no good telling them other people are wretched when they aren't, and it's not fair. Nic and Jack don't understood that. In my world everybody knows what to do: make it fun, make it theatre, make it new, and people will listen.

It only took two weeks to set everything up. I assembled the gear, checked it out with some of my contacts and found the right phone numbers in the Parliamentary Security Department. I hired the van and Tim dropped me off. He said he'd make the call and I gave him my phone for them to trace. I didn't want his name in it. I let him think it was a stunt for a TV programme on security in our top institutions. I should have told him the truth. He joined the agency when I did and he told me the first week that he'd always wanted to be a journalist.

I wait by the crossing at the Parliament Square end of Whitehall. The sun's hot on my neck. I lick my lips.

The lights change and the green figure strides forward. Jaunty bugger. I shuffle out, head down. The iron collar chafes at my neck, my arms stretch out to the cuffs that clamp my hands to the yoke and the chain between my legs clatters on the tarmac. People are already taking photos. A group of Americans, their backs to me, snap selfies with the weirdo. Performance art – you get a lot of that in London.

My knees are already bowing but I keep going, the breath harsh in my throat. The green man's flashing and I know I'm not going to make it. I feel sweat running down my back. My trousers are sticking to my legs and my feet ache. The last of the crowd streams past, a woman in a yellow jacket drags a child who stares up at me, an ice-cream fast to his mouth.

Engines rev up and a motor-bike shoots in front of me, followed by three cyclists, two in pink and white lycra and one in a pinstripe suit, with the whirr of an electric motor.

'On your bike,' he mutters out of the side of his mouth.

I take another step and the iron ball on the chain between my legs rumbles after me, the anklets scraping at my skin. A car hoots and I catch the uneasy howl of a siren. I'm doing well, nearly half-way and the taste of rust in my mouth, but I'm still moving. Vehicles squeeze past in front of me, a taxi, a dustcart, a bus. The sweet smell of biodiesel keeps me going for another stride. On the other side of the road a man with a London Dungeon sandwich board cheers. People line the pavement, pointing at me, holding up mobile phones, laughing. They think the chains are plastic. They aren't.

Big Ben chimes the hour and all the faces jerk upwards. Five pm on a Tuesday in early September. Rush hour, start of the parliamentary term – maximum impact. I catch sight of Nic in the crowd, a huge grin on her face, her hand raised in a thumbs up. I try to grin back, but it's not Nic, it's someone else, holding up a placard to the cameras:

"Kill the Bill. Welcome to the World".

I drag myself forward another pace, lift my head up so everyone can see my face and fall to my knees and then flat out, my chains crashing onto the tarmac on both sides. For an instant I feel an immense luxury, lying there. The wrapper from a Paradise Bar blows past, right in front of me, absolute colours, black and white and red. I could do with one right now.

I force myself up off the road and start dragging my body forward, my knees scraping on the tarmac.

'Stag night was it, sir? Don't suppose you've got the key?'

I twist my head sideways. A helmet, blue eyes and a moustache. I shake my head and the iron collar bites at my neck.

'Alright, get his other arm, someone take his legs. We'll get you out of everyone's way and then we can have a chat.'

More camera flashes, and the crowd makes way. About time someone showed up from the real media. A woman I nearly recognise in a blue suit with neat blonde hair leans down towards me, holding a microphone.

'Why are you doing this?'

A younger woman in jeans stands behind her, a TV camera clasped to her shoulder.

Brilliant! I told you I've still got contacts.

Another policeman in a flak jacket with a submachine gun slung across his chest is forcing his way through the crowd towards the camera. He's not your ordinary copper and he's going to slap his hand over the lens. One chance.

'Britain needs immigrants!' I shout and start coughing, my throat as sore as if I'd run five miles.

I spit.

'Making immigration illegal promotes modern slavery!'

Another officer, this one wearing a steel helmet, with goggles pushed up on it and a mask like a visor across his mouth, stands between me and the interviewer. He pulls the mask down under his chin with a gloved hand and grasps the interviewer by the elbow.

'Madam, you are obstructing the pavement. There will be a statement later.'

Tim timed the call just right. They've sent the terrorism squad and Parliament's in lock down. My heart's pounding but I haven't blacked out. Everything is going splendidly.

'Mr Morlan. What exactly did you think you were doing?'

We're in a windowless room with four chairs and a table, but it's not the same as you see on TV. There's no one-way mirror, no recording device and no surveillance camera. The furniture is scratched and the air smells clammy, as if it's been breathed too many times before. It reminds me of an all-night café at 4.00am. My shoulders are as sore as if I've been carrying a sack of cement. Pain stabs at me like a blade whenever I shift position.

The officer who brought me in sits across the table. He's wearing a grey-blue pullover with three-star epaulettes stitched onto the shoulders. His hand clenches into a fist, relaxes and clenches again. Next to him is a large balding man in a grey suit with a Brasenose College tie. He stares directly at me for the entire interview and says very little. They've taken my shackles.

I get in first: 'Modern slavery flourishes, now, here in London, hidden in plain sight. The anti-immigrant bill plays into the hands of the people-traffickers.'

'I see. Time-waster.'

'I have a right to protest.'

'Not near parliament. Not without telling us first. You're looking at a five thousand pound fine. Minimum.'

I could argue with him. I have a right to see my MP.

'I'm sorry. I don't want to waste police time.'

'First one I've had in here who's said that.' He lays his hand flat on the table and looks down at it. 'I get demonstrators here every day – "Real Jobs with Real Pay"; "Kick Out the Illegals", "Britain for the British", "Welcome to the World". Half of them want to start a fight and blame the others for it. Somewhere among them, hidden in plain sight, the shy young woman with the suicide vest or the schoolboy with the knife.'

He lifts his face and stares at me.

'We've got riots in Dagenham and police officers injured. Britain is a divided nation and it's my job to police it. You don't make it any easier. Get it?'

Someone raps on the door. The man in the suit opens it and goes out. When he comes back he looks at me, as if memorising my face, and says:

'OK. You're out.'

'I'm free to go?'

The terrorism officer looks at him for a moment, shrugs and stands up. He grasps me by the upper arm and escorts me from the room.

'Good-bye. Come back and I'll … don't come back.'

He slams the door and the glass in it quivers. I rub at my arm and look round. I'm in a large tiled lobby, rather like the entrance to my school, with the bustle of the reception area off to the side.

A figure in a pinstripe suit strides in through the street doors in a gust of cold air. He holds out his hand, then hugs me.

'Jack!'

'Dad! Sit down for a minute.' He pauses. 'You know you really shouldn't be doing these things.'

'Thank you.' I hold him. He's my son. I don't care about the ache in my shoulders. He's wearing his City suit and I smell the aftershave. 'It's wonderful to see you. Let me buy you lunch.'

'It's Adam you should thank. My solicitor. He's a friend of Thomas's.'

A lean man who can't be more than twenty-five stands next to him. His suit is immaculate and his tie smells of Oxford. I thank him. He does not return my smile.

Jack takes my arm.

'Thomas?'

He grins.

'Tell you later. Now listen. We can't be linked to extremists and we don't do stunts. Why on earth did you do it? They might have shot you.'

He's got his eyes fixed on my face, as if he needs to know my answer.

'I want to help. Get you and Nic some publicity.'

'Well you did that alright. Listen, I have to get back to the House, it's the Immigration Select Committee. Can I drop you somewhere?'

He raises his hand and a taxi appears as if it had been waiting for him. I'm about to say 'yes' when my phone rings, so I wish him good luck. I'd rather sit in a café, anyway. Preferably the all-day breakfast, maybe leave the fried bread.

I shout:

'Thanks again – you're a star,' after him and thumb the button on the phone.

'Mr Morlan? I'm Adeline, BBC *Overview*.'

I sit down where I am, on the steps of New Scotland Yard, and give her my full attention. *Overview* gets five million viewers on a good day and I'm going to tell them the truth about modern slavery. I'm feeling good.

Makepeace

I take a deep breath. My arms ache but I have clean bandages on my wrists and the padded leather chairs feel like swansdown. I relax into the warm hush after the confusion of the phone call and the dash to Langham Place.

A young woman with cropped hair, white shirt and black trousers and jacket comes up. She's Adeline and she's the first person today who actually asks me if I'm OK.

'Are you up for this? You've had quite a day.'

'Fine.'

'I need to check a few details. You're Ritchie Morlan and you're an adman from Dance and Fitzhugh, with a new fashion angle that's caught people's attention. I'm sure I don't have to remind you, no reference to any commercial product on the programme. Don't you usually get the interns to do this kind of thing? You're lucky you're not in a cell right now.'

'I've left the agency. I'm not trying to sell anything. I'm protesting about this government's anti-immigrant policies. Forced labour – modern slavery – here in London, right in front of you. No-one takes it seriously and a clamp-down on immigrants will make it worse.'

'Slavery.' She grimaces. 'Bit of a turn-off, it's the style issue that people are talking about. Protest fashion. Excuse me.'

She talks into her mobile and listens, nodding.

'You're in luck, we can get you on. The Home Secretary – Henry Makepeace – is the star interview. Jobs riots and his Immigrant Repatriation Bill. I see you've got a new suit for us.'

She points and the price tag is still hanging from my jacket. I rip it off. They'd been very formal in Selfridges when they saw my knees through the rents in my clothes, but softened when I showed them my credit card.

'It was a bit hectic getting here.'

'Sure. Zahira will do the interview.'

Everyone knows Zahira, anchor-woman of *Overview*, the BBC early evening current affairs programme. Most people trust her. She has a friendly smile, wears little make-up and doesn't take powerful people seriously. *Overview* is the number one target programme, get it on there and everyone will pick it up.

We're in front of the cameras now with the lights glaring at us so it's hard not to blink, and the clock ticking down the seconds on the monitor screen at our feet. Zahira's talking to me but her brown eyes are on the studio door.

'There's something very special about what you've done, don't you agree?'

I do. But I know it's going wrong.

'Thank you. This is about the immigration ban and modern slavery.'

She holds up her hand. 'Of course. Trouble is, no-one's really interested. What's special about you is the way you protest. That's what's got everyone's attention. Some people think you're making a fashion statement – like bondage trousers.'

'People need to know that there are now more slaves in London than there were at the time of William Wilberforce. They don't wear chains but someone's got their passport and they're frightened to go to the police.'

Nic would be proud of me. I've been listening.

'Of course, but jobs and immigration are what people want to hear about. We've got Henry Makepeace. I'll squeeze you and your plastic chains in as an "And Finally". OK?'

'They aren't plastic.'

There's a bustle of well-dressed young people by the studio doors. A figure I recognise as the Right Honourable Henry Makepeace MP is escorted in and takes a seat on the other side of Zahira. He wears a suit with a waistcoat and looks like a bishop. He greets her with a handshake and ignores me.

She inclines her head.

'And here's Ritchie Morlan from Dance and Fitzhugh.'

He gives me a sharp look, then smiles and reaches over to shake my hand,

'I do apologise, for a moment I couldn't place you. Of course. I've heard much of your work.'

It's like shaking hands with a tailor's dummy.

The hands sweep round on the monitor clock and the title sequence cuts in, strange to see it without the music.

Zahira turns to the camera, her face serious.

'Good evening. We have the Home Secretary, Mr Henry Makepeace, in the studio.'

Makepeace looks into the camera. He doesn't smile.

Zahira continues:

'Last night: riots here on the streets of London.'

The screen flashes into life. People jostle past the camera and the picture's unsteady. I see violent movement, shadows and flashes of light. Car headlights, full beam, flare in from the side illuminating everything.

A line of riot shields pushes forward, military-style helmets visible behind them. People, mainly men, in hoodies and face-masks, some with sticks, crowd in front of the camera, blocking the picture.

Someone shouts and the chant comes back:

'Jobs, Jobs, Where's the Job?'

The rioters come to halt and a Jack Russell runs out from among them. It stands for a second in the space between rioters and police, panting, and runs back. Someone's on the ground, his face in his hands, the light glinting off shards of broken glass all round him. A young man crouches over him and pulls at his arm, gesturing to people to help.

I relax in my chair and then lean forward as a bottle shatters against a riot shield right in front of the camera and someone tosses a burning rag. A gout of flame roars up and suddenly you see the faces of the officers, none of them older than twenty. The police line jerks back and another bottle smashes but the fluid doesn't ignite.

Someone barks out a command. The police start drumming on their shields with their batons. The crowd hesitates, for a moment you can hear the traffic on the North Circular. A whistle shrieks and the police surge forward, batons raised. Someone screams, the camera lurches sideways and the screen blanks out.

Zahira addresses Makepeace.

'Home Secretary. The riots are a disaster for London and for your government. What is being done?'

Makepeace nods as if agreeing with her. He speaks slowly, like a teacher instructing a child in whom he has no confidence.

'We are doing everything possible to bring this disorder to an end. I am sure our thoughts are with the two policemen who were injured in Dagenham last night and with the innocent people and the local businesses caught up in the disturbance.'

'No doubt. But what is being done?'

'If I may answer your question, I have already set up a compensation fund for business. But we must remember, immigration is at the heart of this. The last government let in people we don't want and we don't need. Now our own countrymen cannot find jobs. Immigrant Repatriation is the answer and that is what the Bill I am bringing before Parliament will achieve. Every immigrant entering this country is another British citizen out of a job.'

'Many people say we need immigrants to do the jobs British people won't do.'

He smiles.

'British people can do most things when given the chance. Our government will give them that chance. First we must send the immigrants home.'

'And people-trafficking? Forced labour? Modern slavery?'

'Forced labour is the dirty end of immigration. Our Immigrant Repatriation Act will stop all immigrants of whatever kind entering this country and stealing jobs from hard-working Britons. We will root out slavery and send so-called slaves back where they came from.'

'Thank you. And finally, a different kind of demonstration brought Parliament to a halt this afternoon.'

Another film-clip: I'm lying in the road, stripped to the waist, my arms manacled to the yoke. Wish I'd remembered the spray-tan. The cuffs bite into my wrists and my knees are smeared with blood. My face turns to the camera. I mouth 'Britain needs immigrants', but you can't hear what I'm saying. I sag back, spittle running from the corner of my mouth and the film ends.

'Mr Morlan. You created quite a stir with a very unusual protest outside parliament this afternoon. Why?'

'Modern slavery. A least one hundred and fifty thousand people are forced to work against their will in Britain, now, all round us. The Repatriation Bill gives people-traffickers more power over their victims.'

'Perhaps, but your politics has style. People want to know about your costume. Who designed it?'

My chest tightens. I speak calmly. Nic, Jack, this is for you.

'Modern slavery is a ten billion pound plus industry. No-one enforces the law. The Immigrant Repatriation Act will drive immigrants underground, into the hands of the gang-masters.'

'What good do you think your stunt will do?'

'It isn't a stunt. I want people to think about what the Act means, about forced labour. Modern slavery is there in plain sight, on building sites, in nail bars, in car washes, in fruit-picking. Young women, children forced into prostitution and drug trafficking ...'

But the microphone is dead.

'I'm afraid we are out of time. Mr Morlan, thank you.'

Someone plucks at my sleeve.

A young man with a *News Behind the News* T-shirt leads me out of the studio. Makepeace stands at the entrance with his aides, glossy young women and men in expensive business suits. A woman with tightly-curled black hair holds out a tablet to him and points to the screen. As I pass he glances up and walks over with his hand held out.

'Mr Morlan, allow me to congratulate you. Quite an impact for an afternoon's work.'

'Thank you. Will you throw Zahira out of the country when your anti-immigrant Act is on the statue book?'

He smiles and wrinkles his eyes. His hand feels cold, and his grip is like a child's.

'Come now, we're not on camera. Have you ever thought about a career as a policy adviser? You won't earn so much, but you have the chance to make a difference.'

I shake my head and follow the young man past him into the Langham Place lobby.

'Thank you so much for coming.'

He waves me through the turnstile and turns back through the swing doors into the studios.

The lobby is crammed with people. Some of them pass through, some cluster round the reception desk. Four young men with guitar cases and skin the colour of whey are arguing with a young woman in a suit. A giant screen hangs on the wall above the desk and on it Makepeace is talking as if he thinks his listeners are slightly deaf.

Someone shouts 'Dad!' The crowd parts, and Nic, my daughter, is standing in front of me. Her hair is cut short, and shaved back on one side, but still looks untidy, and her jacket and trousers don't quite match. She grins her grin and holds out a cappuccino in a reusable cup and a giant chocolate chip cookie, all for me.

'I just heard. Thought you might need this. Henry Makepeace is a notable bastard.'

'Thanks, Nic.' The coffee warms my throat. 'That's great.' My eyes fill with tears, I wrap my arms round her and hug her against me.

'Careful, you're spilling it.'

'I'm sorry, I'm so sorry about everything. I'm proud of you and I'm proud of Jack and I wanted to help and all that happens is you get ministers mouthing rubbish and idiots who think fashion's more important than people-trafficking.'

I break the cookie and give her half.

'Let's get something to eat.'

An eddy runs through the traffic of people. I hear someone singing.

'What's that?'

The crowd steps back and the music grows louder. People start swaying to the rhythm. I recognise the tune – it's the Conga chorus.

A Conga line of neatly dressed young people enters, side-kicks rippling along it. A young woman, her hair cropped, leads them – the researcher, Adeline, the one who asked how I was feeling. A chain of paperclips links her ankles and other chains stretch across her shoulders to tie her wrists to those of the person behind. She stops and shouts out:

'Modern slavery! We're the interns. Twelve-hour days, no security and they take on one in ten of us. What do we want?'

The chorus comes back:

'Real Jobs with Real Pay!'

They're off again in a volley of yells and hoots and whistles, the chains shimmering, the kicks becoming less regular, more flamboyant:

"Ay Yi Yi Yi Yi Conga,

We Are Just the Interns,

We Slave All Day,

For Rubbish Pay,

Ay Yi Yi Yi Yi Conga".

A girl in skinny jeans trips and lurches backwards and the boy behind her stumbles into the reception desk. Papers fly up into the air and they're laughing and shouting and singing all at once.

Nic's in front of them, her arms stretched wide.

'Stop it! This is about real slavery and immigrants' rights, not the bloody middle ...'

Adeline reaches out and grabs her by the shoulders and whirls her round. All you can hear is 'Conga ... Conga!' and people clapping in time to the rhythm. Nic's arguing with them, I can see her mouth open and close, but the words are lost in the hubbub.

A security guard comes round the end of the desk, his hand out to stop them. The Conga line swerves round him, through the swing doors and out into the darkness. Nic's left behind, sitting on the floor in the middle of the lobby. Everyone stares at her.

'Don't you see?' she shouts. 'People trafficking, forced labour, that's what matters. Not the bloody middle class with their contacts and their internships and the safe jobs at the end of them!'

The guard lifts her to her feet and marches her over to the doors. When I catch up with her, she's sitting on the steps of All Souls church, staring at the paving stones in front of her.

'Nic, you OK?'

'What is the fucking point?'

I can hardly hear her. She's the other Nic, the one who sometimes comes and takes the real Nic away. She won't look at me.

'It's no good. You're still an advertising executive. Protest, that's what Jack and I do. Can you just leave it alone?'

Something clenches in my chest.

'I'm sorry. I just want to help.'

'Help.' She gestures. 'It's a stunt. Take it back to the agency.'

The security guard stands with the lobby door half-open, watching us.

My phone rings.

'Hallo? It's Rayanne Maurice, fashion editor, *Today* magazine. We're really excited about your new concept. It's brilliant – chain-gang style. We always love to see an amateur out there. Can we do a shoot? Do say yes, we'll send a limo. We'll use a model of course, but you'll get a credit.'

'Sorry. I'm fully booked.'

I put the phone down on the steps beside me. The guard holds out a pack of tissues. He's short and thick-set, with big shoulders. Gurkha, ex-soldier.

'Saw you on the big screen. You didn't do bad.' He points. 'You've got coffee down your front.'

'Thanks.'

He nods and heads back. Nic and I set off down the street, past a wine-bar. The door swings open and a couple come out, laughing. It sounds as if everyone in the place is singing along: 'Conga, Conga!'

I glance back at the steeple-spire of All Souls. It's starting to rain. I take Nic's hand in mine and hold it, tight. After a while she takes her hand away.

Jack and Thomas

My mobile rings. I glance at the number on the screen and jab the wrong button and have to ring him back.

'Jack! Really good to talk to you. I've been thinking.'

'Someone I'd like you to meet. My friend Thomas Caldor. I mentioned him the other day.'

'Yes. I owe him. But I want to talk to you…'

'Marco's? 7.30 – tomorrow? Nic's coming.'

He rings off before I can ask about how he is and about Thomas. Thomas matters to Jack. That's good enough for me.

Later there's another call. It takes me a few seconds to recognise the voice. He sounds much younger on the phone.

'Makepeace here. We crossed swords on the *Overview* programme the other day.'

'Indeed.'

'I believe we got off on the wrong foot. We should meet.'

'I have nothing to say to you.'

'Wait a moment. I have a proposition you might find interesting.'

'Good day.'

I ring off. He wants something from me. What's he offering in return?

A few hours later I find a letter in a Home Office envelope in my letterbox. It's hand-written in a clumsy cursive script.

'Sorry not to have an opportunity to talk … a great admirer of your work … very strong recommendations … we really must have a conversation …'

I sit at the kitchen table and wonder. I'm very good at my job and I love doing it – I used to love doing it, before I packed it in. The last sentence decides it:

'My friend Elsa Dance mentioned you to me.'

I tear it to fragments.

Good choice, Marco's. The service is adequate, the food excellent and the tables are reasonably private. It's a bright airy room and the noise gets lost in the space above the diners. We used to bring clients here, long lunches with men and women in business suits, courteous, cautiously effusive, weighing the next offer, nudging towards a deal. Maybe we'll talk about Jack and Nic's campaigns, the Repatriation Bill, the jobs demonstrations. Maybe they'll ask my advice on how to handle the media, how you get a prime slot on *Overview*. I'd be honoured to help. No-one will mention advertising. Maybe Nic'll grin her lop-sided grin and squeeze my hand when she gets here. They'll drink too much and we'll make plans to meet up again, and we'll all know we have to tread carefully, take our time. We're going to build something together, step by step, as if we were making a matchstick model of Notre Dame.

I'm sure Carlo, maître d', remembers me, but he pretends not to. News travels. A slight delay before he takes me to the table.

'How have you been, Carlo?'

He holds the leather-bound menu in front of his chest, like a breastplate.

'Never better, sir.'

Jack and Thomas arrive bang on time. Jack hugs me. His shoulders are tense as an athlete's. I pat his back. Thomas shakes my hand as if he wants to include the room in the gesture. He's one of Jack's university friends. His dad was an A and E consultant in Glasgow who went on to become deputy chief executive of Public Health England. His mother is a Harvard professor.

He's tall with wavy fair hair, regular features and a slight echo of East Coast America in his accent. The port-wine blemish on his cheek saves him from being handsome.

'Good to see you,' he says. 'I've heard a lot about you.'

They don't want wine. No problem. Fizzy water. Jack waves to the waiter.

'About ready when you are.'

Thomas folds his menu.

'Wait for Nic?'

'She can be unpredictable. We'll tell her later.'

Jack glances at Thomas. He raises his glass.

'To what's been achieved. And to us. Thomas is a very close friend of mine. He's director of policy at *Inside Track* – you know, the Great George Street think tank.'

'I'm delighted to meet you. You're a man of influence.'

Thomas grins.

'Hardly, but I know people who are.'

Jack and Thomas exchange glances for a second time and their eyes sparkle.

Jack places his hand on the table. He's holding Thomas's within it.

'More news. I've been selected.'

'Selected?'

'You know. Dagenham West. I'm the candidate!'

'Wow – you've done well, and so has Dagenham West. Here's to the member for Dagenham! You'll be the youngest MP in the House.'

I raise my glass. Jack, my son, tottering down the beach on chubby legs twenty years ago, and now sitting opposite me, self-assured and chockful of excitement at the same time. An absurd pride rises in me, as if it were my achievement too.

Thomas looks at me. 'Yes. Definitely winnable.' He hesitates, then adds: 'And we're partners. We wanted you to know. It's a sort of announcement.'

They lay their hands side by side on the tablecloth, identical silver bands on their ring fingers.

'Goodness.' I shake both their hands at once. Thomas's feels softer this time. 'I'm delighted, for you, for both of you! Great news. Twice.'

'We wanted you and Nic to know. Before anyone else.'

Jack turns to Thomas and they hug each other, and, there in the restaurant, kiss. I applaud, and people look up.

I test the little empty space in my breast, as if my tongue's probing a cavity in a back tooth. Surprising how small they are and how big they feel, dental cavities that is.

What difference will it make, after all? He wanted me to know first. I'm so pleased for him, for both of them, and I mean it. Dagenham West too. He had mentioned it, I guess it slipped my mind.

'Champagne?' I say. God knows how much a bottle it is here. Who cares?

Jack grins and Thomas murmurs: 'Special occasion.'

Time for another toast. I'm just getting to my feet when I become aware of movement at the other side of the room. People look round. Carlo's at his post by the entrance. He's holding out the menu folder to bar the way and two of the waiters have come up behind him.

A voice calls out:

'But Dad invited me!'

The group by the door moves backwards and a figure dodges past them. Nic! She waves and makes straight for us, ignoring the staff and the other diners.

Carlo follows on behind, as if Nic's his pilot fish.

Someone calls: 'Watch out!'

Jack twists round in his chair. 'Oh Nic. Take it easy.'

I'm on my feet, between her and the table. Her cheeks are red, as if she's been running. She flings her arms round me.

'Dad! Classy place.'

I can smell it on her breath, pungent, bitter, and I relax. Just a beer or two, but she's flying.

'Take a seat. We're ordering.'

She spots the champagne and grabs a glass from the next table. A tall scholarly man rises to protest. I apologise, hand him my glass and assure him I haven't touched it. I can't see Carlo anywhere.

'Sit down Nic, you need to eat.'

Nic's got the bottle by the neck and is splashing it out to both tables, half host, half small child eager for respect. Love for her, pointless love, fills me.

'Nic. Sit down and stop talking. Jack's got something to say.'

She doesn't hear.

Jack takes the bottle and Thomas places a hand on Nic's shoulder and pushes her down into a chair.

'What would you like? Have the braised aubergine.'

Nic chuckles.

'Let's have more bubbly.'

She waves to the waiter for another bottle.

'Could you get her some food?' I say. 'Whatever's quickest. She really needs to eat.'

Nic leans across the table towards me.

'Didn't do so badly, did we at the BBC?'

'Pretty good. Do you have your pills with you? You should eat something.'

'I've stopped the pills. They slow you down.' She looks sly and continues: 'Didn't get anywhere though, did we? No one really believed you.'

I bow my head.

Thomas intercepts the second bottle of champagne and presents it to the chap at the next table. The waiter helps to shift the table further away from us. Carlo himself places the roast vegetarian special in front of Nic and withdraws. He ignores me.

Jack sits back in his chair, his eyes on Thomas.

'Nic, eat something. Soak it up. We've got things to tell you. Thomas and I... you know Thomas don't you? Thomas Caldor?'

Nic waves her knife.

'Yes, of course. Hi, Thomas, how are the Whitehall lobbies?' She turns to me. 'We've got to make a plan.'

Jack raps on the table.

'You're fizzing this evening. Slow down. Are you OK with those pills?'

He holds out his hand and the silver band gleams on his finger. He pauses while we look at it and says.

'Thomas is very special to me. We're partners. And I've been selected for Dagenham West. '

I stop thinking about the tip.

'That's wonderful news!' Nic's mouth is full of roast parsnip which she's trying to swallow without chewing. 'I want to talk about what we do next. You and Thomas can help. We'll make a great team.'

Thomas lifts his glass.

'Nice meal. Very reliable, the kitchen here. What's the pheasant like?'

Nic jabs a spoonful of yoghurt sauce at me and spills half of it on the table-cloth.

'No good just telling people about modern slavery. Only hear what they want to hear. Keep telling you that.'

She scrubs at the stain with her napkin. Carlo is standing right behind her, the bill folder in both hands.

'Excuse me, sir.'

He gives the 'sir' exactly the same stress as the policeman in Parliament Square did. I stare at him for three seconds and flip open my wallet. Time to take Nic home, so Jack and Thomas can have their meal in peace. Best I can do for them. I smile but it doesn't ease the heaviness behind my eyes.

I pay, get to my feet and put my hand on Nic's shoulder.

'We'll talk about it tomorrow. You must be exhausted. Let's get you home, check your medication is OK.'

'I've got a better idea. You know where half of them end up? In the kitchens of places like this – cheap labour, no questions asked.'

She brandishes her spoon in an arc of gravy droplets. Carlo steps back.

'Yes, we should get going.' I lean across. 'I'm so sorry Jack, Thomas. I'll catch up with you tomorrow. You can tell me about your plans, and about Dagenham West. Nic was in good form yesterday.'

'Yup. I thought for once we could… no matter.' Jack squeezes Thomas's hand and lowers his voice. 'At least you know what you're getting into. Nic can be a bit bipolar. Understatement.'

Thomas laughs. 'You should see the Member's Bar at 11.00pm. Time for some cheese.' He waves away the handful of notes I'm offering. 'Don't worry, I'll sort this. My boss comes here quite often.'

Nic

Nic swivels round, but my arm is across her shoulders. A waiter who looks as if he could carry her bodily in one hand comes up on the other side.

We're halfway to the exit, trying to keep away from the other diners. Everyone glances up as we pass.

She hiccoughs.

'Just a mo'. Don't feel good.' She leans sideways, taking us towards the toilet. The waiter stands back and I reach out for the door handle.

'Fooled you!'

Nic ducks under my arm, feints towards the exit and is off the other way, back to the serving door. She brushes against a chair, it clatters to the ground and the room hushes.

I glance round at them all, busy with their plates. No-one meets my eye.

'Please! Enjoy your meals.'

Nic's through into the kitchen with Jack and Carlo right behind her. Thomas remains at the table and apologises to the diners next to us.

I ignore the babble in the restaurant and push through the door. The glare of strip-lights bounces up from the steel counters. I'm overwhelmed by sultry heat and the jangle of odours – gravy, garlic and rosemary. Sweat breaks out all over me. The staff in their chef caps and aprons are gathered round a taller woman whom I'm sure I've seen on TV, all staring towards the back of the room. No-one says anything. A fan hums somewhere overhead.

A tea-tray clangour of metal on metal beats at my ears. Nic's shouting over it all.

'Come out, come out wherever you are. You've got rights in this country.'

She's at the back of the room, next to a young woman in white overalls and a hair net who's chopping carrots at a sink. The woman's focusing hard on the knife blade, slicing into the orange and purple roots in front of her.

Nic bangs a ladle against the sink next to her and shouts:

'Out you come!'

Jack pushes past me and grabs Nic's wrist. The racket ends abruptly.

'Come on, Nic. You shouldn't be here. I've got a taxi coming.'

He gestures flat-handed to Carlo and tugs Nic towards the exit.

'In plain sight.' Nic twists round. Her eyes are burning. 'I'm right. You know I'm right.'

Jack is busy telling Carlo how the Shadow Minister loves this place. She will definitely bring a party here next week. I keep my eyes on Nic. She scoops something out of the bin with her free hand and stuffs it into her pocket. Jack shoves at the fire door and we're outside. The cold grips at me, Jack waves and headlights swing along the brick wall in front of us. A taxi draws up, its engine throbbing.

Thomas follows us through the fire door.

'You need any help?'

He shakes me by the hand. Jack hugs me and steps back.

'We'll catch up with you soon.'

'It's all under control. Thanks very much. Good to meet you, Thomas.'

Nic's already getting into the taxi.

'Come on. I've got the address.'

Nic pulls a piece of paper from her pocket and sits hunched forward on the seat of the taxi, trying to read it in the streetlights. She waves it at me:

'That's it: they outsource.'

It's torn off some packaging. The label reads: *Summerson's Prepared Meat* and the address is N18. She's already thumbing her mobile.

'Driver. We need to get to Argon Road. Where the Lea Navigation crosses the A406 – quick as you can.'

It's late and the lights hurt my eyes.

'No. It's OK. We'll go where I first said.'

The driver pulls up in the middle of the bus lane and looks round at us.

'Make your mind up.'

'Where I said, please. I'm paying.'

'You been drinking? Read the sign.' He taps the glass: *£100 Clean-up Fee. No Exceptions.* He has a round fleshy face and dark marks under his eyes. A miniature plastic crib is stuck on the middle of the dashboard with a snapshot of a baby in pink, both arms reaching towards the camera, propped up in it.

'Your little girl?'

'Yeah.' He touches the crib and it sways in its mounting. 'Little Louie.' A bus horn blares out behind us. 'Gotta go.'

Nic snatches my wallet.

'Argon Road, follow the trail. This is important.'

'Nic – give that back.'

She's got the window open and the wallet's half out, flapping in the slip-stream. She clings onto the tiny strap and watches it as it sways backwards and forwards.

'Nic, you need your medicine.'

She falls back against me, so suddenly it almost winds me.

'I never wanted to be like this, never, never, never ... no way I can tell you what it's like. Why can't I just be someone like Jack?'

She fixes her eyes on me and she's twelve years old and school is too easy for her and I'm telling her to be patient.

'I know I'm right. We can't not go there. You've got to trust me.'

I didn't ask for this, any of it. I just wanted kids.

I slip the wallet back in my pocket and tap on the glass.

'Like the lady says, can you take us up to Argon Road?'

'Right you are. You know it's double fare up that way after ten?'

Argon Road slants off the North Circular to the trading estate behind Ikea.

'You'll wait for us? Ten minutes?' I hand over an extra £20.

'Sorry.'

The door locks click and he's off.

I pull my coat tight and look round. The air's damp from the river and smells of diesel fumes and tarmac.

Two-storey corrugated iron sheds line the road, each with its compound, behind a three-metre metal fence. Harsh yellow streetlights clustered in fours on forty metre poles cast midnight shadows. I feel like an intruder in a giant's world. A huge lorry with blank sides like a moving fortress glides past, the driver invisible in the cab. In the background the roar of the A406 is continuous, here there's the pulse of solitary engines and the occasional shout and clatter of iron crates, but no movement I can see.

I shift closer to Nic but she's concentrating on the torn packet, holding it out in front of her as if it's a map and she expects to see landmarks. I shade my eyes to look for numbers on the buildings.

'That's it.'

The letters *SPM* in lime-green neon, superimposed on a golden bullock, shine out from a scaffolding above a one-storey shed at the end of the row.

Nic's ahead of me, I half run to keep up with her.

I can't catch my breath.

'Slow down, we've got to keep together.'

'That's it,' she says again. 'Don't you see – they outsource. No forced workers actually in your restaurant.'

'Nic, it's just a business. Come on, you need to get home. We'll sort out your pills.'

The windows along the side of the shed are ablaze with light. I smell the sour salt smell of blood and see people moving around inside. The fence is higher than the one for the next compound, and the gates are locked. Nic stands back, checking it where it turns a corner. The air's chill on my face and I start to shiver inside my overcoat. She doesn't seem to notice the cold.

She hooks her fingers into the wire mesh above her head and hoists herself up. I grab at her belt.

'Don't be a fool. That's razor-wire on top.'

'Lend me your coat.'

Her shoes are too broad to get a foothold. I catch her as she slithers down. She stumbles backwards against me and I get my arms round her.

She pauses for a second, leaning back into my chest. She's so cold. I open my coat and wrap it round her. For a few moments neither of us moves. I could stand there, like that, forever, they'd find us frozen in the morning. She stirs and rattles the fence.

'Thanks Dad. Let's go.'

I take her hand.

'I'll see if I can get a cab on the main road.'

We're back at her place, a room in a shared house off Roman Road. She leans against the sink, watching me, the grin back on her face:

'I was right, wasn't I?'

I pause in checking through the desk drawers for the pills. First time I've been in Nic's current place, she seems to move every other week. Someone's tried to force the Yale lock, you can tell by the marks round the door jamb. Two new hardware store bolts are fitted inside. I pull the sheet up on the bed, and she collapses onto it.

'I'd always help you get somewhere with a bit more space.'

She doesn't answer.

I gather the papers off the floor and sort them into two piles on the desk either side of the laptop – letters on one side, reports and longer documents on the other. A file headed "SALMA: Appeal Hearing" in typescript with a date two days off lies under a stack of envelopes. The cover's open and a photo of a young black woman in a nurse's uniform, with braided hair and a thoughtful expression, is clipped to the inside. I close the folder and place it on the keyboard where she can't miss it.

The air's stuffy but without cooking smells, just the earthy odour of sour beer. Empty cans are piled up under the sink, no bottles. I slide the window up six inches and take a deep breath. Someone's playing opera – the 'Provence' aria from Act II of *La Traviata* – across the court-yard, but otherwise it's quiet. I listen for a moment and remember when we used to go to the ENO and Holland Park in summer, Cat and I.

The only other furniture is an oak wardrobe. I tug at the door and it opens with a jerk. Something heavy and soft tumbles out onto me. Zephaniah Ted! I haven't seen you in years, I remember Nic choosing you in Harrods, third birthday. Ted's actually a panda, almost threadbare now and one of his arms is loose. Nic carried him everywhere, he was nearly as big as she was.

Still here are you, Zeph? I smell him. Nursery smell, warmth and milk, and coffee and a whiff of beer. Still here, still on duty.

I cram him back and find the pills under the bed. A beer-mug rests on the draining board. I smell it, rinse it out and fill it with water.

Nic grunts and takes a couple of pills from my hand. She gulps at the mug.

'I was right. Did you see that padlock?'

'Those places always have padlocks, razor-wire, CCTV, everything.'

'Not the outside gate. Didn't you see? The door to the hut. Maximum security padlock. In plain sight. On the outside – just like that van. No CCTV, they don't do CCTV – don't want records.'

Nic's nobody's fool.

She's asleep. I smooth back her hair and tuck the cover round her shoulders. Her skin's the usual colour now, pale and as smooth as when she was three years old. Sat up with her all night once, Cat and I, when we thought she'd swallowed a dishwasher tablet. I woke on the sofa at four a.m., grey light seeping round the curtains. Cat knelt next to the cot, her hand on Nic's forehead.

'You're tired,' she said. 'Get some sleep.'

'What about you?'

I kept awake after that by biting the inside of my cheek. Cat slept next to me on the sofa, her head on my shoulder and my arm round her.

That was the best time. We found the tablets next morning. They'd slipped down into the bucket under the sink.

Guess I'd better stay here tonight, I can tidy things up and check she's got enough pills for tomorrow. Buy her a better duvet, maybe some smart clothes. Help her go through the papers for Salma's appeal. Do something useful for once.

Tribunal

It's the first time I've been to the *Refugee+* offices, a couple of rooms at the back of a social housing block off Brick Lane. Salma waits for us at the door. She's slender and black and her hair's braided with something that sparkles blue and red in the sunlight coming through the top pane of the window. Nic greets her with a hug and introduces me.

'My father. Here to support us.'

'Good morning,' says Salma. She speaks with a slight accent, carefully pronouncing all the consonants, as if she had learnt the language from a text-book. 'Thank you.'

She doesn't look down, she faces us as if we're all equals meeting to discuss a business decision.

Nic opens a padlock to let the three of us in. Someone's tried to force this door recently too, there are scratch marks from a knife blade all round the lock.

I count six reusable coffee cups on the filing cabinet. Someone's crushed a party-size pizza box into the waste bin. The air feels stale, as if someone sleeps in the other room. Music filters through from the flat opposite. Posters with images of marching people, women and men, black and white, cover the walls: "Welcome Week!"; "World Solidarity Day!"; "Empire Day: Payback Time" and behind her "Kill the Bill! Immigrants Enrich Our Lives!" and "Shit Government, Shit Jobs!" white on black. I'm not the only one who does tag lines.

'Salma, you came to the UK as a refugee from Eritrea. They want to send you back. We will help you appeal against that decision.'

Salma holds out her hands, palms upward.

'My son. He has Ariam.'

'You were forced to work in a sweatshop and give all your earnings to the people-trafficker. Now he wants you to become a sex-worker.'

'He says the money is not enough. He is a serpent.'

I look at her and I believe every word she says.

'This is terrible, we must help you.'

'They kill my husband. If I go back, they will kill me – and my son.' She raises her voice for the first time.

Nic nods.

'I am ashamed for my country. I will do my best.'

'That man, he has my passport. We ran away but they caught Ariam. I am frightened.' She fixes her eyes on me and speaks with emphasis. 'You are a father.'

My cheeks grow hot. I don't say anything.

Nic glances at me and touches her arm.

'We understand.'

'You cannot understand.' She clenches her fist, then lets her hand fall into her lap. 'How can you?'

She takes an envelope from her pocket and pulls a photo out of it and shows it to Nic.

He's young, about 14, and he's smiling a bit skew-whiff, like Nic does. He wears white Arsenal shorts and a T-shirt with a USAID logo, just so you know who to thank. Brand placement. He's standing on a dusty road with a one-storey building behind him. Nic used to love football, even though she was no good at it.

Salma gazes at the photo and I bend forward, close to her, to see it.

'Your son? He's a footballer?'

She nods and wipes at her face with her hand, but she does not cry.

I want her to look at me. For some reason I want her to like me.

'He's a good-looking boy. Reminds me of my son when he was that age.'

What else can I say?

'Thank you. He is a good boy.'

I want to ask her more about Ariam, but Nic hands her the photo.

'He's a handsome lad.'

'You must help me. You must find Ariam.'

Salma stands erect, but she can't keep her mouth straight. She holds the back of the chair in front of her with both hands. Nic's next to her. She reaches out and puts her hand over Salma's for a few seconds and I remember how soft her hands once were, how they fitted in mine. Her hair is in a plait and she's wearing a new dark-coloured jacket and a white silk shirt.

I'm right behind them, with the folder of notes on my lap. The Home Office representative on the other side of the aisle doesn't look at us. He leans back in his chair and taps at his mobile. No-one else has come into the room and we're already half an hour after the time in the letter.

The asylum appeal is being heard in a concrete office block with a glass foyer somewhere north of Rosebery Avenue. The receptionist is seventeen and jolly and hopes we have a good day. We're in a large chamber with upright chairs and a table on a raised platform at one end. It reminds me of a 1950s school-room I once saw in a documentary. A Union Flag droops in a stand to one side and dust-motes hang in the air. Metal-framed windows fill most of one wall and you can see an identical office block next door.

A meeting is taking place in the room opposite us, mostly men, round a big table. They look across from time to time and the older one at the end of the table stares at us.

Salma glances back at me. Her eyes are large and fearful.

I murmur: 'Nic knows what she's doing.'

I wish I could say something that helped.

The clerk enters, wearing a grey trouser-suit and carrying a laptop. She stands at the front, hands clasped, until she is sure she has our attention.

'All rise.'

The door opens and the three tribunal members take their seats behind the table. We sit down. The chair is an older man. He reminds me of my first head teacher. He gazes at Nic for a moment and opens the file in front of him. The trade union and lay representatives, both women, are busy with their laptops.

'Good morning. I hope you are at ease. We wish to conduct proceedings with as much informality as possible. Ms Morlan?'

Cat flashes into my mind, but of course he's talking to Nic.

'Thank you for the documentation.' He taps the file. 'This case hangs on the issue of whether Ms Surafel will be in immediate personal danger from the authorities if she returns to her home country. Please summarise the grounds for appeal on form IAFT-5. As briefly as possible.'

He takes a fountain pen out of his pocket and uncaps it.

Nic stands.

'Thank you.'

Her voice is louder and clearer than I've heard it before.

'Ms Surafel, a trained nurse, is a citizen of Eritrea and has a real fear of persecution by the government of that country. She comes from one of the leading families in a small Christian minority group in the north. Her husband is, or was, a member of the banned political party, the Eritrean People's Democratic Front. He refused to serve in the militia. Just over a year ago Ms Surafel received a call from her uncle at the hospital where she works to say she must not return home. The police had arrested her husband. She has no knowledge of his whereabouts.'

She pauses. Salma is hunched forward. I move to sit beside her and offer my handkerchief. She doesn't look up, but takes it and dabs at her cheeks.

The chair moves his hand.

'We understand how distressing this must be. Please proceed.'

'Ms Surafel has a real and well-founded fear for her life. The uncle hid her and her son, Ariam, and arranged with an agent whom Ms Surafel has never met for them to travel to the UK. The agent took their papers and forced them to work as modern slaves in a sweatshop. He threatened to force her into sex-work. She escaped but her son is still held. Her initial claim for asylum was rejected.'

'How did they enter the UK?'

'By Eurotunnel.' Nic's voice is less confident.

'Be more specific.'

'In the back of a lorry.'

'Thank you.' The chair makes a note. 'In other words it is a case of illegal entry using a people-smuggler.'

'That person separated Ms Surafel from her son. He is now fourteen. She does not know where he is.'

'Thank you. You do understand that we cannot consider unsubstantiated claims?'

'I have submitted Mr Surafel's party membership card. The party is illegal in Eritrea. Members and their families are treated harshly, as the recent US State Department report – copy in the file – attests. Ms Surafel has a well-founded fear of arrest, detention, torture and possibly execution if she returns. She is a victim of modern slavery. She is desperate to find her son.'

The chair takes a plastic wallet out of the folder in front of him and shows it to his colleagues.

'Thank you. Nothing else? No police or newspaper report on her husband's disappearance? No statement from the uncle? No UK evidence from the Enforcement Branch or the police on the traffickers? Nothing to support the claims about prostitution?'

Nic's voice grows more resonant, as if she's addressing a public meeting.

'All Eritrean media are rigidly controlled. It is impossible to obtain reliable statements from within the country.'

The chair glances at the Home Office representative: 'Mr Emmet?'

His jacket's too small. When he stands I see an ink-stain on his shirt cuff. He looks straight ahead.

'One can encounter difficulties.'

'And the police?'

He shrugs.

'They visited the address where Ms Surafel claims she was held. It is a warehouse near Tilbury. It is empty. Their report is in the file. The alleged people-trafficker cannot be traced. There is no evidence that he exists.'

Nic is already on her feet.

'Of course it was empty. These people don't wait in for the police.'

'Thank you, Ms Morlan, you may sit. Mr Emmet? The Home Office view?'

'My Minister believes the claim has no merit. Ms Surafel entered the country illegally and worked under an assumed identity, using a false address. We have no confirmation that she has a son, nor of her assertions about her family and her husband's arrest, nor of the alleged people-trafficker, nor that she was forced into prostitution. It is worth noting that the claim for leave to remain is dated one year, by her own admission, after she entered the country. It is our belief that she has worked illegally, lost her job and claimed asylum in order to receive Asylum Support Benefit.'

I offer Salma my hand, but she wrenches herself away from me. She shouts something in a language I don't recognise. Everyone stares at her. The words become clearer.

'Ariam! Ariam!'

She holds the photo in her hand. Nic talks softly to her.

The chair glances at the clock above the door.

'We will take a brief recess. Five minutes.'

Salma drops back into her chair.

'Salma,' I say, but she doesn't look up. Her tears fall on the photo, on Ariam. The panel members talk among themselves, ignoring us. The Home Office representative taps at his mobile phone.

The clerk comes over and offers Salma a glass of water. She takes it and hands it to Nic.

Exactly five minutes later, the chair raps on the desk with his pen. 'I am afraid we have a busy schedule. Ms Morlan.'

Nic stands, her back straight:

'Ms Surafel did not claim earlier because she was held as a modern slave. She was frightened for her son's welfare.'

'Evidence?'

'Please refer to the photograph of the son in the file. Also details of his schooling in Eritrea.'

The Home Office representative raises his hand.

'All this shows is that someone with the name Ariam attended secondary school in Asmara.'

'What would you do if violent criminals had kidnapped your son?'

'Ms Morlan. Please remember where you are.'

The woman on the chair's left coughs, takes something from her pocket and lays it on the desk.

'Here is an Eritrean People's Democratic Front party card.' She sounds as if she's apologising. 'Blank. It was purchased on the Tottenham Court Road for two hundred pounds a year ago.'

No-one says anything.

The chair taps on the desk.

'We will break for lunch.'

We find a sandwich bar and eat something, I forget what. Nic keeps saying:

'Don't lose hope. We'll appeal to the next tier if we get knocked back. We'll go to the High Court.'

Salma nods to her but her eyes are on the photo. She presses the handkerchief against it gently, then wipes her eyes for the last time and hands the handkerchief back to me. She doesn't eat.

The clerk enters followed by the three tribunal members.

'Ms Surafel, the tribunal has every sympathy with your circumstances. We hope you make contact with your son, wherever he is, in the near future.'

He pauses, takes off his glasses and fixes his eyes on her.

'I regret that we cannot support your appeal. The only undisputed fact in this case is that you left Eritrea and entered this country illegally. There is no independent evidence that your supposed husband and son even exist and none of a real threat to you in Eritrea. As to the claim of being forced to work as a modern slave, there is again no evidence. The view of the Independent Advisory Group is that,' he glances at his notes, '"the fact of illegal exit is not of itself enough to place an individual at risk." Appeal dismissed.'

Nic starts forward into the area between the chairs and the tribunal's platform.

'This is monstrous. Ms Surafel's husband was a member of the banned EPDF. The card proves that. She faces the certainty of arrest and probably torture if she is returned. She has lost her son. She has been forced to work under degrading and inhuman conditions.'

The chair glances at the clerk.

'Please. Do I have to remind you again of where you are? We have other cases to adjudicate.'

Nic remains standing. The clerk claps her hands.

'The hearing is now concluded. The case returns to the Home Office.'

'One moment. The card.'

'It's worth nothing as evidence.'

'Mr Surafel died for it.'

The chair stares at her and inclines his head. The clerk hands the plastic envelope to Nic. Salma receives it in both hands, as if frightened she'll drop it. Nic takes her by the elbow to lead her from the court-room. Salma shakes off her hand and walks out in front of her, her head held erect.

The Home Office representative is waiting outside the door. There's a flabbiness about his face and he's beginning to lose his hair. He seems pleased with himself, though he only spoke twice. He addresses Nic.

'Eritrea. Always tricky. Your client has my sympathy. Ever think of doing a legal qualification?'

'I've got an MA in Human Rights from UCL and an LPC from the College of Laws. Ms Surafel is not my client. She is my friend. I don't do this for money.'

The lawyer pats Nic's shoulder, like they're school-kids and he's Nic's older brother.

'Good luck with that. Well, onto the next case.'

He closes the door behind him.

Salma doesn't say anything. She's pressing the nails of her left hand into her wrist. I touch her arm and take my hand away. Nic purses her lips. She won't meet my eye.

'You're right, it's monstrous. You did so well in there, you're impressive.' I don't say: 'You remind me of your mum. You'd make a great human rights lawyer.'

That's what I should have said five years back, when she told me she had a place on the Human Rights MA and I told her how much more she could earn in commercial law in the City.

She takes Salma's arm.

'I'm afraid they'll make a deportation order and pass the case to the Enforcement Division. We'll try for a judicial review. You mustn't lose hope.'

Salma looks at her but says nothing. Nic shakes her head.

'I am ashamed for my country. We must keep trying. I will make the appeal, I must do that now before the Home Office Enforcement Team take action. Go with my father. I will contact you later.'

She's off, walking fast. It's ten past two. The appeal took exactly one hour.

I take Salma to a café and she eats a few mouthfuls of pasta and a yoghurt. She spoons sugar into black coffee.

Jack would know what to do. So would Nicola.

'Salma, I am so sorry for what happened. Nic did her best, her very best.'

I want to put my arms round her.

She's saying something I can't make it out. At first I think it's his name:

'Ariam, Ariam.'

Then she says quite clearly:

'I lied, I lied.'

'I'm sorry?'

'I lied.'

She looks up at me.

'There is another address. Larkhill. I saw it once on a letter.'

'But ... why?'

'That man, the one who brought me here, the agent. They call him Yasir. I do not meet him, but everyone fears him. He is a serpent. He has my son. You tell the police, he will hurt Ariam very much. I know he will. The police took my husband.'

'You can trust the police in this country.'

She speaks slowly as if explaining something to a schoolchild.

'No-one from your church has been taken by immigration police on the street and you do not see them again. I must find Ariam, it is my task.'

She stares at me and I say nothing for a while. Then I start to speak and I tell her the truth.

'I did something very bad long ago. I lost someone

63

who was precious to me.' For a moment I can't look at her. 'There was a time I thought my children were lost to me, too. All through my own stupidity.'

'You are a rich man.'

'I want so much to help you, to do one good thing. Please trust me.'

'You cannot understand.'

'Don't be frightened.'

She shakes her head as if she does not know which way to turn.

'You must not tell – not police, not Jack, not Nic?'

'Of course not, we will be careful.'

'But…'

I hold my hand up.

'I promise you.'

She looks at me with no expression and nods her head.

My mobile's in my pocket and Nic's on speed-dial. I will help her, whatever she says. I'm on her side. Besides I know it's what Nic wants.

I put some money on the table and we set off. Someone shouts after us, but it's only the woman from the café. I've left my scarf behind.

A Respectable Address

It's a detached house on the Larkhill Park estate in South Lambeth. Low-rise walk-up flats with individual concrete balconies which people use for barbecues, living space or bike storage, a few glassed-in for greenhouses, the light glancing off them. Built in the nineteen-fifties, I'd guess, brick construction with pitched roofs. Not much litter, just a Red Bull can on a low wall by the bus stop. It's a respectable area, no people-traffickers or sex-workers round here. Early afternoon, bright sunshine and the wind whipping leaves round the street corners. Like Nic says, here, now, in plain sight, so obvious that no-one notices.

I'm beginning to shiver. Salma hasn't bothered to do up her overcoat. She doesn't seem to feel the cold. She hangs back a couple of paces behind me.

School's not out yet and the streets are nearly empty. That's good, I've got the feeling that everyone's staring at me. The only person who passes us is a young black woman with a child in a blue woolly suit and a rainbow bobble-hat. He's in a pushchair, flopped sideways, out for the count.

'Nice day.'

She smiles at me, not at Salma, and hurries on.

I wait at the corner:

'Not a bad neighbourhood.'

Salma halts.

'You go. I will stay here. Please. Go now.'

I walk past a three storey block, 214 to 225, same as those that surround it and all but one of the flats in private ownership I'd say. You can tell by the differences in the double-glazing, only one of them still has the old metal window frames. Wonder what the neighbours think?

227 is set back. A driveway leads round behind a Leylandia hedge. It's a house, late Victorian I'd guess, left over from before the estate was built. Double-fronted, large bay-windows with the blinds drawn down, grey slate roof and high gable echoed in the roof over the porch. The trees extend on all sides, it's always in shadow.

I'm not going down that drive.

I stroll across the road and take a seat at a bus-shelter that acts as a wind-trap and check the weather on my mobile, surrounded by the sour smell of privet.

After a while a car glides by, a gleaming black limousine the size of a cabin cruiser with a double logo, Mercedes star and Maybach shield, on its bonnet. Not many of those in this part of London. The windows are tinted and I can't see the driver. The car turns a corner. A few minutes later it returns, sweeps up the drive and parks. A burly man, built like a distance swimmer, gets out of the front passenger seat. He has a crew-cut and wears dark glasses and a navy blue suit. He looks up and down the street and stares directly at me for a second. My heart skips a beat, but his gaze passes on and he opens the rear passenger door of the car.

A sandy-haired man in T-shirt, shorts and work boots gets out. A shiver runs through me. I know you. I huddle into my overcoat and look down at my mobile. He bends down and picks something up from the gutter, holding it with his finger-tips. He beckons to the other man and hands it over. It's a drinks can, crushed by the car. He unlocks the front door and enters the house.

The bodyguard remains by the front door keeping his eyes on the street, the can in his hand. He flips it round the corner of the house, where his boss won't see it. The sandy-haired man returns carrying a stack of envelopes and nods to the bodyguard. They return to the car and it drives off, making no more noise than a breeze in a spinney. The phone's in my hand and I snap the number-plate.

I hurry round the corner and nearly run into Salma. She has her scarf wrapped round her face like a fugitive.

'Did he see you?'

'No. It's OK. You're sure that's Yasir?'

She frowns.

'No. That man is Yasir's jackal.'

'I'll ring Nic. We can end this now.'

She grabs my sleeve. She's stronger than I am.

'No. You promised.'

'What can we do?'

'He has Ariam.'

'It'll be OK. You have to trust me.'

'You promised.'

I can hardly hear her. I bend forward and she has the phone out of my hand before I see what she's doing. She stamps hard with her heel, twice. I stand there, witless, watching the shards of plastic skip across the pavement. Last link with the office that phone, top of the range, folding screen, we all had them.

Nic'd know what to do. Salma would trust her, people do.

She steps back, away from me. 'You promise! I thought you…'

'This is crazy. You want me to fight them myself?'

'You cannot fight these men.'

'I'm sorry. I really am.'

Sorry. I said that to Cat twenty years ago, on the Margate road, when Nic was seven and Jack was three and it was too late anyway. Sorry. I've been saying it ever since.

Salma jabs her hand at me. She's angry and she's crying at the same time.

'You people know nothing.'

I sit down on the garden wall. She's rocking from side to side, her hand thrust into her side pocket. I know she has her fingers on the photo.

She takes a deep breath and expels it slowly.

'Mr Morlan, you … Thank you. I will find Ariam.' She looks directly at me. 'I will do that work.'

She walks away from me, as fast as she can, almost running. I want to go after her, to help her, to make things right. Cat fought people, sometimes she won.

Everything happened too fast. A lovely day right at the end of summer. It was my idea to take the kids down to Margate and it worked brilliantly. We're all together, singing along to Bob Dylan on the CD-player, silly words to make the children laugh. I pull out for the cattle truck in front of us, one hand on the wheel, pretending I'm an expert.

'How long will the journey take? No time at all.'

The sunlight flares in my face and there's a green bus coming the other way, and the other car pulls out round it, a sports car, it comes straight at me, accelerating, down the middle of the road. I see his face through the windscreen, he's so young, his mouth wide open. He's singing to a disc-player too, and Cat screams and doesn't stop screaming …

'Alright? You want me to get someone?'

It's the young woman with the child in the pushchair, still asleep. She's looking down at me, her hand in that of a school-girl perhaps ten years old. The girl has her finger to her mouth. Her hair's in plaits with pink clips at the front and she's wearing a mauve cardigan and a pleated grey skirt.

'I'm OK. Thanks.'

I rub at my cheek.

'So long as you're sure.'

The girl tugs at her hand and she moves on.

I look round. They're some way down the street and the woman has bent down to pick up a lost glove. The girl's staring back at me. I wrap my jacket tighter against the cold.

I find a phone box on the corner but the receiver dangles on the cord and the earpiece is smashed. Someone's put a jam jar with winter pansies in it, blue and white and yellow, on the shelf. This time of year they had to pay for those flowers, and carry them back here and arrange them and top up the water. The fragrance hangs about me as I place the receiver back on the rest. There's a card behind them: "Real Jobs, Real Pay" and a website.

Someone's waiting outside the kiosk.

'Sorry,' I say. 'Phone doesn't work. Nice flowers.'

It's Salma.

'I'm sorry for what I said.'

She holds her hands together in front of her.

'I lost my husband. I must not lose my son.'

I want to put my arms round her.

'I understand,' I say. 'I lost someone too.'

We're both silent for a moment. Then she takes my hand and places her mobile in it. It's as thick as a phone book and half of it is keypad. I give it back to her.

'Do you need somewhere to stay for a bit? Away from those people?'

She starts to speak, then hesitates and shakes her head.

'It's OK.'

She touches my hand again, very gently, and turns and walks away. I take one pace after her and halt. She does not look back.

I find a café with a phone, ring Nic and tell her what's happened.

'I really thought we stood a chance,' she says. 'If we could get some evidence on this Yasir, we could win, I know we could.'

'She doesn't trust the police, the courts, any of it.'

'I know. She's right.'

'She doesn't trust us.'

Silence.

'You did your absolute best. You know you did.'

'Didn't get anywhere.'

'You were good in court. That lawyer thought so. I'm proud of you.'

'Yeah, well, not really a court.'

The warmth is coming back into her voice.

'I should report that guy. I've got the car number.'

Silence. Then she says.

'Yasir. We've come across him before. On paper he runs an employment agency. He also has a contract with Summerson's, all above board, all checks out. We need more.'

'He drives a very pricey car.'

'That's not a crime.'

'Doubt if he pays business rates.'

I read her a story once about a child in a red jacket who stood up to a playground bully. All the other children helped her. They tripped the bully up with skipping ropes and poured jam on his schoolroom seat and put spiders in his gym shoes and in the end they found he really wanted to be friends with them but he didn't know how.

She kept wanting me to read it. I should have told her: people love stories the same way they love adverts, because they're not real life.

Workforce International

So I track Yasir down. Takes two days and it's not as hard as you think. I wait near the house, sometimes round the corner, sometimes up the road, once pretending to make a call from the phone box with the broken receiver. I wear different clothes each time, in case.

Following him in a car like they do on TV, in plain sight and somehow invisible, is out, so I use the bike, the one Jack got me twelve years back. I could have given it to Oxfam but I didn't. Tyres need pumping, the mudguards rattle when you hit a bump and the brakes are rubbish but it still works.

I hate bikes. Doesn't matter what I wear, I can't get warm, and everyone's trying to kill you. First time I wear a brand new helmet, second time a woolly hat.

Don't really know why I'm doing this, I'm no good at it. I just know I have to. I should go to the police and be laughed at and take myself on holiday somewhere warm.

I lose him at traffic lights after about a mile. My lungs are burning and I'm coughing so much I'm half-choked. I hang about near where I lost him at the same sort of time for a couple of days and the car glides past, so silently I don't hear it coming. After that it's only half a mile. He turns off a bit south of Burgess Park and when I get to the corner, I can't see them. The car's parked in a side-street, the engine ticking as it cools. There's no sign of Yasir.

Another quiet area, this time because the flats are all empty with chipboard across the windows and steel shutters on the doors. Posters for pop concerts, jobs with "average earnings £1,000 a week" and payday loans are stuck to the chipboard. Someone's sprayed the "World Solidarity" and "Immigrants OK" slogans with the *Refugee+* thumbs up logo (that one's one of mine, I did it for Nic when she started for them) on the wall in black paint, and "Shit Government, Shit Jobs!" in red. Good for you.

I lean the bike against the wall and step round a broken push-chair, all four wheels missing.

A Victorian terrace with tiny front gardens still survives among all the modern flats. The one on the end is larger, with a shop front and a sign reading "Workforce International" above the window. The glass is filthy and you can't see much inside, just a wooden counter and a computer with someone sitting behind it. Nowhere else to go.

I pull off the woolly hat and cross the road.

I know what Nic'll say if I tell her: 'Thanks Dad,' and she'll pat my arm, as if she thinks I want a reward. Then she'll sit on the bed and look thoughtful and sad and maybe do something stupid as soon as I'm out of the room.

Jack'll say: 'You did good, Dad.' He'll talk it through with Thomas and they'll call the police and it'll be filed away and go nowhere.

Salma. She'd say: 'You are rich, you do not understand. He is a devil.'

Ariam is two years older now than the child in the photo, I don't even know what he looks like.

I push the door open and somewhere a bell jangles, the room smells of nail varnish.

'Yes?'

She's about twenty, her hair's been straightened and she's got a yellow fleece jacket on against the cold and wears pink mittens. She's still holding the varnish bottle.

'Good afternoon. I wonder if you could help me. I'm looking for someone with general secretarial skills.'

She doesn't say anything, just dabs a couple of times at the keyboard. Six box-files stand on a shelf behind her. They have typed labels "Construction", "Labouring", "Domestic" and "Services". I can't read what's on the end ones.

'We haven't got anyone.'

'Are you sure? Typing, answering the phone, that sort of thing?'

'I've checked. No-one.'

I lean over the counter.

'Kind of thing you could do. Sure you'd be good at it. Our office is a lot warmer than this place.'

'I like it here. Leave your details, I'll ask around.'

She pushes forward a card.

I glance sideways at the screen.

A green background with two playing cards centre screen, a two of hearts and an eight of clubs and another one, face down. Numbers at the corners, bets placed, and a large red flashing question mark with a pound sign next to it.

'You should maybe fold?'

'Thanks.'

She types in the number five. I stand up.

'I'll drop the form in next time I'm around.'

The computer beeps and she frowns and taps rapidly. Not sure she heard me. I glance up at the shelf. The labels on the end files are hand-printed in uneven capitals: "Summerson's N18" and "Paradise Dagenham". I let myself out.

I should go back and tell Nic and Jack. I'm feeling good, like I did the day Myles Fitzhugh offered me the job. I'm not number one at this kind of thing but I'm not the worst either. My nose drips. I've lost my handkerchief.

Wind gusts round the corner of the shop. It's a side-street, a dead-end, with weeds poking up between the paving stones. There's a noise of water splattering on stones and someone singing. It's beginning to get dark, but the streetlights aren't on yet.

I take a stroll to the gates at the end. Why shouldn't I? They're reinforced with corrugated iron, with a chain and razor-wire on top. You can see through the crack: the shop's been extended into a cobbled yard, which opens out into a larger area. A square white van is parked on the other side of it, in the shadows, with the rear doors open.

How many white vans in London the same as that – ten thousand?

Beyond it stands a low building, a Portacabin with the lights on. There are others behind it, in darkness. I smell diesel fuel and above it the spices I recognise from Salma – mostly garlic and ginger.

Water splashes down. Someone's standing at the end of the Portacabin clad only in jeans, washing himself, rubbing at his naked flesh with a cloth. Brown skin, black hair, muscles working at his shoulders, his ribs showing. He needs a good meal.

He's singing in a language I don't recognise, but the song sounds sad. He towels himself and pulls on a white T-shirt and opens the hut door. I hear a babble of voices. The room's packed with people, all men, mattresses on iron bedsteads down one side. Maybe they like living there. Maybe it's the social housing crisis. Maybe Yasir's got their identity papers and tells them the cops hate them and they'll be on the next plane back if they make trouble.

A door crashes open across the yard and light spills out towards the cabin. The men go quiet. They're grouped at the far end, their eyes fixed on the doorway. I shrink back, gripping the gatepost. A thickset man lumbers across, swears at them through the open door and slams it shut. He's got a padlock in his hand and he's doing something with it. He slams a fist against the door and I know who he is.

I press myself against the wall. He's looking this way, he must know I'm here. I don't move, frozen, my heart thudding in my chest. He swears again and tramps back towards the shop. I breathe out. I'm exhausted.

The bike can stay where it is. Last time I ride one. I walk up past a recreation ground, another padlock on the gates, this one broken, a dark figure moving among the bushes at the back, away from the streetlights. I come out on the Old Kent Road. A police car roars past, siren wailing, and there's that moment of silence after it's gone. The number 63 bus is just drawing up outside Asda and I hop on.

I'm upstairs on the bus, front seat, where I used to sit with Nic and then with Jack. I look down on all the shiny cars, the businesspeople driving home, thinking of the first drink of the evening, the women and men on their way to the shops, taking children home from school, sitting in coffee bars and sending emails and going to the pub. The people on the street, hanging around, hoping to meet someone they know, someone who'll talk to them, and on the edge of it all, the beggars and the homeless people, huddled back from the thoroughfare, not looking up, scribbled cardboard signs at their feet. I love this view, you're like the lookout on the *Cutty Sark*, you see everything and no-one ever thinks to look up at you.

An old man in a raincoat bends over a rubbish bin, rooting through the contents, mumbling to himself. An Asian kid in grey running gear with a Fitbit pulls a sandwich out of his backpack and holds it out. The man stares at it as if he doesn't know what do with it.

Street-life on the Old Kent Road, and, cheek by jowl, Salma's world and Elsa's world and Jack's world and Nic's world and the world I've glimpsed hidden away in plain sight, behind *Workforce International*.

The bus stops and the doors hiss open. I look down and through a shop-window to the row of women reclining in leather armchairs, chatting and reading magazines while younger women crouch at their feet, their heads bent over, working away at the fingernails. Do they choose to work here? Do they like it? Are they forced to work for nothing, by a gang-master who's stolen their passports or tricked them with stories about how much they owe him and how the police will rape them and beat them and send them back? The young woman at the end of the row looks up, catches my eye and smiles. She looks fourteen but maybe she's older. The hand she's holding shakes and she ducks down and the bus jerks forward.

Those men lined up, tossing bricks between them and stacking them on a wagon this time of night, what about them? No gloves, no safety helmets. The one at the end, muscles like a weightlifter, catches the brick on his fingertips, flicks it over his head, catches it behind his back and drops it onto the pile. The lad next to him shouts something and braces his skimpy biceps like a circus strongman and they all laugh. How can you tell? Everywhere round you. The car wash at the garage, the kitchen hands I glimpse through the open door at the back of the pulled pork take-away, and, out of sight, who digs up the potatoes for the supermarket, in the wet mud all the hours of daylight? Who slits the pigs' throats for you in the shit and blood and muck in the slaughterhouse?

I need a decent meal, so I get a real steak, guaranteed free range, from the butcher on Fortress Road. Jerry laughs at me.

'You need building up, Mr Morlan. Haven't seen you for a while. Pork pie like you usually have?'

Jerry's got dewlap cheeks and the belly of a contented bison. He's been in that shop, man and boy. He's proud of his pies and he should be. 'Me dad's recipe'. He wraps everything in greaseproof and ties it with string.

Not far home now. I head back to the main road. The chap in the greasy sleeping bag with the plastic sheeting over it sits under the railway bridge with the "Real Jobs" slogan sprayed on the brickwork above him. I hand him the pie and he thanks me and starts eating straight away. OK by you, Nic?

Some people accept that the world isn't fair and get on with it. Some don't. They're the fighters and Nic's one of them. So is Jack. So was Cat. I don't know why, that's how they are. I'll drink to that. No I won't. Because I've just had an idea. It's simple. I don't tip off the police about the Portacabins behind the shop, Jack and Nic do – and get their faces on all the front pages.

Best Idea Yet

Nic's sitting on the edge of the desk at *Refugee+*, grinning like I've told a joke that's made her laugh out loud and she can't believe I've done that. I'm in an upright chair in front of her. It's as if I'm back at work, pitching a campaign to Myles, only now there's no carpet and no picture window and it's too cold to take your coat off and our knees are about six inches apart. Nic's laptop is on the desk, with documents and letters, some of them still in their envelopes, stacked in piles, and the "Salma" file open on top of them with papers spilling out of it.

'Brilliant,' she says. 'You're on a roll, Dad.'

That's what Myles would say, except he'd miss the Dad out. Then he'd take it to Elsa and she'd thank me and do something different.

'You tracked them down. It'll help Salma, that's for sure. And Jack. Big court case, lots of publicity. It'll make people see what's right under their noses, make them look at it. Maybe we'll get an immigrant amnesty, maybe a new law.'

'Do my best.'

My heart's swelling. I can't stop myself grinning. I'm good at publicity.

She hesitates and bites at her lip.

'Dad, I'm an arsehole, I get carried away. Sorry.'

She flings her arms round me and my face is full of short black hair with a white streak across it, and I love it.

'Careful, I'm not that strong!'

She's grinning back at me. 'I'm sorry, it's just, that poster... I didn't think.'

She holds out her hand and I grasp it but I can't grip as hard as she does.

'You're not the only one. I didn't think either.'

Twenty years, I didn't think. I messed around a bit, I was going to write a novel and then I just found something I could do, because we needed money. I ended up at Dance and Fitzhugh. Myles seemed to have faith in me. I showed him the novel, what I'd got of it. He read a bit and put down his drink and looked up at me. 'You'll do,' he said.

And Catherine? I take a breath so I can speak clearly.

'Mum and me, she said once you were the best thing that ever happened to us, you and Jack. She was right.'

That day at Margate, the bottle of wine at lunch-time, when we'd found a pub that had wine, and driving back. Cat had got the job she wanted at Birnberg Pierce and I'd got the Beamer (second hand but shiny) because everyone in the office had them. The sun was warm on our backs. We'd swum and built sandcastles and had ice-creams and fish and chips and the future opened up like an empty road in front of us and ... I screwed up.

It should've been me. She only undid her seat belt for a minute to lean round and check on the children.

My voice wavers, I can't find the end of the sentence.

'You and Jack. I'm so sorry.'

Later, back at my place, after I've served (one-pot chicken chasseur, you can leave it on low in the oven for when people turn up) I give her the news.

'Talked to Jack. He's done everything he can, he's taken it to the shadow Secretary of State. The police say they've got better things to do than harass someone running a legitimate employment agency, especially a major figure in the local Rotary Club, and donor to charity, like Mr Yasir.'

'Makepeace is the problem. He can't let anyone see what the clampdown on immigration means.'

'I don't know.'

I feel desolate, as if I'm looking at her through a glass wall, and she won't look back at me.

'I'm sorry, Nic.'

I touch her shoulder, but she shakes off my hand and takes a swig of wine.

'No problem. Now listen: here's my idea.'

Her eyes gleam and the tension flows out of my body.

'It's people that count – real people, their dreams, their suffering. Facts don't work anymore, no-one believes in experts. You have to get human beings, people like Salma, like the guys on that building site, real victims of forced labour, talking.'

She's leaning forward in her chair, gesturing with both hands at the same time.

'They're not "illegals", they're people like you and me. They've lost their homes, their lives and we have to help them. We use the real mass media, Facebook, Instagram, YouTube, everything.'

She's right of course. I'm getting old for this.

I get the cheese out.

'So how do we do it?'

'We've got Salma, we could get to some of the people in Summerson's and in the Portacabins, interview them on film. Maybe get someone to take a camera in.'

Something else strikes her.

'You know what? If we could get Yasir to talk, and his side-kick? Real live people-traffickers, get them talking. That would really work.'

'That's crazy. They'd never do that.'

'Maybe they would. Everyone wants to tell their story – especially if the alternative is someone else telling it, someone who isn't your friend.'

'Nic, slow down. What about libel?'

She claps her hands together.

'Great. Always wanted to do a big case in the High Court. The Burgess Park One.' She looks at me. 'Sorry, Two. More publicity.'

I shake my head.

'We can't do this – lovely idea but it's just not possible. We have to keep working at the police.'

But she's already cleared her plate. She's excited about the film idea.

'Docudrama. This could be a turning point. Great cheese. What is it? Goat?'

Later. We're sitting in the car outside her flat. I don't want her to get out, I like her being there. I tell her more about my idea.

'A Grand Debate. We'll get big names, it'll focus on immigration. Someone to put the government's case. Thomas will help. You lead the pro-refugee side, main speaker. I know you can, the way you talked in that Tribunal.'

'You think so?'

She smiles, her unexpected brilliant uneven smile.

'You'd convince anyone who wasn't biased. It'll really take off, it'll go onto TV, newspapers everything. Then the police will have to act.'

It's there in my mind's eye, both of us, primetime TV, father and daughter. Silly idea. I wish Jack had been with us. He's got some common sense, he might have talked us out of it. Instead I tell Nic and she can't keep still, she has to get out of the car and stand there, hopping from one foot to the other.

'We could start on it now.'

'Maybe sleep on it.'

'The Bill comes up when the session resumes. Next week.'

'Let's meet tomorrow evening, talk it through.'

'OK. I guess we need to get it right.'

Maybe I'm not too old. Maybe she'll be calmer then when she's thought it through.

'I'll come over, cook you a decent meal.'

She needs feeding up. I enjoy cooking for her. I never expected that.

But of course when I drive over to Roman Road on Wednesday with the salmon steaks, honey, garlic, lemons and soy sauce all ready in a shopping bag, there's no light behind the curtains and she doesn't answer the bell.

Seventeen minutes later I'm in Burgess Park. The street's dark but the light's on in the shop and the Mercedes Maybach's parked outside. I take the food with me.

My mouth's dry. I lick my tongue across my lips.

'Cat, this is for you.'

I check the speed-dial on my mobile, take a deep breath and push at the door. The bell clatters and I can hear someone inside, not the young woman, someone who stamps when he walks. The door's wrenched open.

He's a hand's span taller than me. Close up I can see a scar like a pale crease running back across his face from the corner of his mouth. A ring with a green feather in it dangles from his ear-lobe. The weather's turned but he's still in T-shirt and shorts, and he's polished his boots.

We've met.

Yasir

My heart is clumsy in my breast. He whips the bag out of my hand and gives me a push. I stumble past the counter and through the door behind it. The light's too bright and I can't see properly. I'm in a small room that smells of cigarette smoke with an oak table in front of me that wouldn't look out of place in a city board-room. It's too large for where it is and so well polished that it reflects everything that happens round it.

Nic sits opposite me.

'Nic! Are you OK?'

I want to rush round and hug her.

Her back's straight and her shoulders are square, but her face is paper-white. She doesn't get up. The table's been shoved into her chest, pinning her chair against the wall.

A tall man I haven't met before comes towards me, his hand held out.

I push past him and seize the table to pull at it. Syker smacks my hands away. He's standing very close to me, gripping my wrists so tight I can't move.

'Seen you before.' His breath smells of fried chicken and ketchup.

'Sykes. Leave him.' The other man speaks sharply. To me he says 'I am Yasir. I am a businessman. I do apologize for my associate's behaviour. He has made a mistake. Sykes, move the table.'

Nic stands up, rubbing at her chest. A tremor runs through her shoulders but she keeps her back straight. 'I'm fine,' she says, her voice high and uncertain. 'Thank god you came. Let me handle this.'

Yasir links his fingers.

'Good evening. Please excuse Sykes here. His manners are imperfect.'

'My name's Syker. Mr Syker to you.'

He doesn't look at Yasir, who seems amused.

'Sykes is loyal but he is not well-read.'

Syker peers into the bag, pokes at the fish, seizes the honey and tosses the rest into the corner. I take Nic's hand.

'Come on. We're going.'

'Please sit down.' Yasir points to a couple of chairs. Syker stands in front of the door, his arms folded.

We remain standing. Yasir smiles, the smile I remember on the client's face (and mine too) at the start of every meeting. His suit is immaculate, his shoes polished, his face spare with vertical lines at the corners of his mouth.

'I'm truly delighted to meet you.'

'Pardon?'

'Ritchie Morlan from Dance and Fitzhugh. We have been discussing you. I believe you understand persuasive communication. We should talk.'

Nic steps towards him. Syker leans back against the door, glaring at us.

'It's me you should talk to. Don't trust him, Dad.'

'We're leaving.' I pull at her hand. I can hardly breathe.

'Stay here.' Yasir inclines his head. 'Please, let us all sit down. I wish to put a business proposition to you. There have been misunderstandings.'

Yasir has a tenderness (no other word for it) in his eyes that makes you want to trust him, whatever you know about him. When he looks at you he gives you his complete attention. I feel as if he values me.

'You hold my daughter against her will and you expect me to sit down and talk business with you?'

'I apologise unreservedly. A misunderstanding. First, let me offer you refreshment. Tea, coffee, water, fruit juice? I do not serve alcohol.'

'Two coffees.' Nic has her voice under control. Yasir nods to Syker who slips through a side door. We sit down and listen to him, I don't know why. I flex my fingers.

Yasir sits there contemplating us. It's as if he's judging us and a decision that will affect things I don't even understand is being made.

I shake myself.

'Nic. Come on, we have to go.'

'Please, all in good time.'

Syker puts white ceramic coasters on the table. Is he the one who polishes it? He brings a tray and places three small cups of black coffee and a bowl of white sugar in front of us.

Yasir claps his hands together.

'Good.' He lays his hands on the table. His fingernails are perfect.

'Mr Morlan, your daughter has made a number of misleading, I do not say slanderous, claims against my organisation.'

Nic cuts in. 'You're nothing but a crocodile in a business suit. We've got the evidence to prove it. I challenge you to a Grand Debate.'

Yasir raises his hand.

'Please. Allow me to finish.' He ignores Nic. 'You may find this hard to believe, but the young woman suggests that I use compulsion in my organisation. She shows me pictures of my business-partner' – he gestures at Syker – 'and our associates. I am told the police find them of no interest. You will understand how hurtful such allegations are. I must ask you, Nic, as one businessperson to another, to withdraw them.'

'You're a people trafficker. I can prove it.'

He frowns.

'Please, do not be childish. I hope you do not seek to blackmail me. I am happy to accept an apology in the interests of mutual goodwill. Syker!'

Syker stands very close to Nic, his right fist gripped in his left hand. I grasp a chair by the back. I can hardly lift it. I fumble for my phone.

Nic doesn't move. She speaks as if she has difficulty with the words.

'You're nothing but a slave-driver.'

'I am a businessman. We can speedily resolve this. You may find it helpful to meet my associates. You will not need your phone. Remember, these are people for whom life in your country is not easy. Sykes will escort you.'

The thug mutters 'Mr Syker' under his breath. He takes a torch from a corner cupboard and opens a door at the back of the room.

'Please follow Mr Syker. Be careful. The cobbles are uneven.'

Yasir remains by the door. Syker precedes us, lighting the way. I keep close to Nic.

The van is parked to one side, hardly visible, with others behind it. The only other light is from the windows of the Portacabin. Someone is singing the same melancholy song, rich with memories of home. Syker is already at the door. He makes no more noise that a cat.

Yasir calls out across the yard:

'Knock first.'

Syker taps on the door and jerks it open. The song is instantly cut off. I can't see the padlock anywhere.

'Not locked. Everyone is free to leave or enter, as they please.'

It takes a second for my eyes to adjust to the light. We're looking into a large room with a door opening off at the side. By the smell of it, this leads to the kitchen. About fifteen people are packed into the space, all men, all short, brown skin, black hair, most of them need a haircut. They're all staring at the door, arrested in whatever they were doing, like a still-life. From somewhere in South Asia, I'd guess. Nic'll know.

Syker glares round at them.

'You got visitors.'

No-one says anything and we enter the narrow space at the end of the room. The men glance at us for a moment but it's Syker they watch.

Some of them are in working clothes, some in T-shirts and jeans and one in his underpants. He's older than the rest, his hair greying and his shoulders stooped. He's sitting on his bed, sewing at a pair of jeans. The others are standing, grouped round a slight man with a beard, his face pocked with small-pox scars, at the far end, the singer.

I wish I'd brought some cigarettes. I offer the nearest man my last Paradise Bar. He rips off the paper, keeping his eyes on Syker, takes a bite, and passes the rest to a younger man, almost a boy, standing next to him. I smell the sweetness and my mouth waters.

The beds, iron bedsteads, made up with grey and red blankets, are crammed together along the wall, metal lockers between them. The door of one of the lockers hangs open and more work clothes spill out. I'm reminded of the hospital except there's no disinfectant in the air, just turmeric and body-sweat and stale air.

Nic moves into the room. She smiles round at them.

'Good evening. May I talk with you?'

No one responds. Nic stands before one of the men.

'Please help me. I want to know. Are you well treated here? Do you get paid on time? Who has your passports?'

The man shakes his head. He stares at Nic with doubtful eyes and gestures to his mouth and looks away.

The next man repeats the gesture. He flicks his eyes to Syker who's leaning against the door post.

Syker laughs.

'Don't understand, none of 'em do. Yasir looks after their papers, does everything for 'em. He's their friend.'

He says something in a language I don't understand, addressing the room. The men nod and look down.

Nic works her way round the room. Everyone shies away from her, shaking their heads.

'If only I'd brought some leaflets.'

She bites at her lip and I see her again as a baffled ten year old at the edge of the playground with no-one to play with.

Syker turns to go.

'Seen enough? There's your evidence. My workers are contented.'

Evidence. Salma had the party card. Her husband died for it, and no-one believed her.

I take a pace forward and shout out:

'Salma! Ariam!'

Everyone's looking past me to Syker. Someone, I can't see who, shouts out, a single word. It sounds like 'Paradise.'

Syker glares at them all, his face like a furnace door. No-one replies. He smirks.

'Ariam. No-one's heard of him. Maybe he's in Paradise.'

'Sorry?'

'Paradise. It's what they say. Means he ain't here.'

The door to the kitchen half-opens and a face appears, a man wearing metal-rimmed glasses. He stares directly at me. He moves back, into shadow, and my stomach tightens. The building site. Syker's boot slamming into the pavement half a centimetre from Nic's foot. The same glasses.

Syker pushes the door open. Nic's standing behind him. She looks straight at me and, for some reason, nods.

He ignores her.

'Come on. You're wasting time.'

Syker leads the way into the courtyard. Nic follows, head down. She trips on the step and grabs at the door. Syker catches her arm and sets her on her feet.

'Easy.'

He stands very close to her and pats her shoulder and doesn't take his hand away. She moves further into the yard. The door swings shut.

Someone plucks at my sleeve. It's the man with the glasses. He keeps glancing at the door. He meets my eyes and he's pleading with me.

I take his hand and it trembles in mine.

He's making a writing gesture. I offer him my biro, the good one that Jack gave me for my birthday a couple of years back, and he scribbles something on my palm and closes my fingers over it.

Someone bangs on the door. It's Syker.

'Hurry up.'

The man next to me winces and steps back. I remember when Jack gave me the pen. I've still got some of the special refills for it.

Syker holds the door open by the top corner, so I have to duck down to pass under his arm. Nic's in front of us, walking fast, holding herself straight. Syker follows me out into the yard. I hear his breathing right behind me.

The light from the boardroom door casts shadows across the yard. There's a dark patch on the cobbles over by the tap. The others are some way ahead. Syker catches my wrist and grips it tight.

'Don't fall over. You'll hurt yourself.'

He turns my hand over and opens my fist with his other hand. The two words "Paradise Dagenham" are written on my palm in copperplate script.

'Like I told you. Paradise. It's something they say.'

He closes my fist in his and squeezes so the pain lances up my arm and I stagger.

His face is very close to mine.

'Best take no notice.'

Nic stands just inside the door to the boardroom. I take her wrist. A tremor runs through her arm.

'You OK?'

'Sure.' She doesn't look at me. 'Let's sit down.'

Yasir sits at the head of the table and smiles round at us, as if presiding over a board meeting. Syker stands over by the door. He doesn't take his eyes off me.

'I hope your visit was satisfactory. My associates are not well-educated. They desire to work and I help them. They prefer to live cheaply.'

'Who holds their papers?'

'I do, naturally. Your immigration procedures are challenging. I manage everything for them. They are grateful.'

Nic's voice quavers.

'How much do you pay them? Can they leave this compound?'

'Ah, you British. So many questions. Have you not heard of business confidentiality?'

'You must tell us.'

'It is hard to forget that once the dark-skinned races were your subjects, is it not? Now, my proposition. Nic, I believe your slogan is 'Welcome to the World!' Do you really believe that, in your heart?'

He pauses. Nic doesn't answer. Then she says

'Of course I do', but she seems diminished in saying it.

I reach out and touch her sleeve with my fingers. Nic, I'm here. Please turn to me, smile at me, your lop-sided smile.

'We agree, the two of us. You believe in a more open world. There are many jobs that British people do not wish to do: in the fields, on building sites, in kitchens, in warehouses. Simple work, but it must be done.'

He reaches inside his jacket and lays a passport on the table.

'I am British. I help my country by bringing to her people who want to do those jobs. People who wish to insult me call me a trafficker. I accept the title. I am a true patriot and a true global citizen.' He inclines his head. 'Excuse me. I am an enthusiast. I wish to be recognised for the contribution I and those who work with me make to our great country.'

Nic is breathing very fast.

'Pinochet was a patriot. Your proposal?'

'Simply this. I agree to speak in a debate on the motion "Britain Needs Traffickers". But we must do this on my terms. Mr Makepeace calls the people I help illegals. The police want to destroy my business. They will arrest me if I argue my case in public. I offer a new business model. Perhaps one day I will trade openly, to the benefit of all.'

Nic braces herself as if she expects to be slapped:

'No-one will trust a people-trafficker.'

Yasir replies, his voice smooth as oil.

'Let us find out. Let me argue my case. Not in a public hall but where they cannot silence us, the new media, live streaming on Facebook. I will arrange an ... an anonymous account. I ask you: do you believe in what you say?'

Nic nods. I pull at her sleeve.

'No. You can't trust him, you said that.'

Nic looks at me, her face pale as curdled milk. She's speaking slowly, her voice flat.

'Real people talking on video. It's what we want.'

Yasir raises a finger.

'Very well. I think we agree. You oppose the Immigrant Repatriation Bill? So do I. You are against bringing immigrants into this country by any means possible? There we differ.'

Nic's eyes are fixed on his.

'Yes. A debate. We stream it live, then upload. No editing. My father's big idea.'

I slam my hand down on the table.

'No!'

They both look at me as if I'm interrupting a conversation. Yasir smiles his broad, impenetrable smile and turns to Nic.

'We must trust our fathers. Now let us be practical. In two days' time? Not here, of course. I have a number of properties. I will arrange the equipment. You see? I trust you. We are partners. We may become friends.'

He rises to his feet and holds out his hand. I'm on my feet too.

'Nic, you can't do this.'

Yasir holds a finger to his lips and nods to Syker.

'A mature debate. This is an advance for democracy.'

Nic nods her head.

'Deal.'

She doesn't shake his hand.

Yasir bows.

'It is growing late. I look forward to our next meeting. One thing.' He points at Nic. 'You will remain here. My guest.'

The blood pounds in my head.

'No! She comes with me.'

I'm right next to her, I don't know how I got there. I seize hold of her arm.

Yasir shakes his head.

'We must be realistic. You came here with serious accusations against me. I am not a fool, I need a guarantee. I promise you the young woman will be well looked after. She will not be required to work for her keep.'

He motions me to the door. I don't move.

'If you want a hostage, it's me.'

'An ugly word. I am afraid that would not be satisfactory.'

My throat constricts and I can hardly get the word out.

'No.'

'It's OK, Dad.' Nic tries to smile. 'Don't you see? This is my big chance.'

Yasir holds the door open.

'Do not think of going to the police. That would be unwise. I will look after her mobile and your daughter will call you once a day, and in two days, she will return to you.'

'But …' I step towards him. He shakes his head.

'It is for the best.'

He turns to Nic:

'You agree?'

She doesn't look at me. She hands him the mobile and reaches up and disengages my hand from her arm.

'Sorry, Dad.'

I open my mouth but the words don't come.

Yasir nods.

'Our visitor is leaving.'

Syker seizes me by the wrist and forces my arm behind my back. A jolt of pain burns into my shoulder and I cry out.

'Nic!'

She starts towards me. Yasir grips her arm:

'Until we meet again.'

Syker pushes me through the door and kicks it shut behind us.

'You worry too much.' He pats my arm. 'It'll be me looking after her the whole time. You get yourself home.' He pauses, then adds. 'The cops. It's me has to sort it when they go to the cops. He don't want to see. Soft-hearted. Good-night.'

I'm outside, on the street. My whole body aches.

The car is a few metres along the road, parked at an angle behind the bulk of the Mercedes. I get in and open my hand and read the words and close it. I drive down the road, round a corner, then another and onto a third road, and turn off the lights and park, the thoughts rushing through my head like a river in spate. I wait half an hour and get out.

The Mercedes Maybach has gone and the shop is in darkness. Nothing moves on the street. As I turn the corner into the side-street, I hear something above the rumble of the traffic on the A2, a noise like a sack being dragged across a warehouse floor.

I take off my shoes and move silently to the gate and peer through. My shoulder throbs and I can't make anything out. A figure moves near the Portacabin, the light from the window catches him. It's Syker. I shrink back against the wall. He reaches down and heaves at something on the ground, not a thing, a person, slumped forward. Syker sits him against the wall and reaches for the tap. I hear water splash down and flinch back. The thug bangs on the hut door with his cage fighter's fist.

A crack of light appears as the cabin door opens. A figure slips out and another. Someone turns off the tap. The man on the ground starts to groan. The others quieten him and lift him to his feet. Syker folds his arms and stands watching, taller than any of them, while they help the injured man inside. He slams the door and locks it.

Dear Christ, what should I do? Trust you, Yasir? The police? I steer round a cyclist, black jacket, earphones and no lights. Nic's face is before me, the colour of whey. Is it this she's been working for all these years? When she was at school on the edge of the playground and they wouldn't let her join in the football, what did I do for her?

Only one person I can think of who can help, and it's too late to go to him.

I drive back slowly, driving-test style. It's as if it's midnight and Cat's beside me. The kids are in the back, asleep, and I'm the guardian, both hands on the wheel, watching over all of them.

Thomas

Parliament House, next morning. I've queued for three-quarters of an hour for security and now I'm waiting for someone to come down and escort me upstairs. My skin feels tight across my chest. I'm doing the breathing they taught me, counting between breaths.

It's all open plan and you can see dust motes in the air. The atrium is four storeys high with a self-service cafeteria, leather armchairs and a bar at the far end, but we're cut off from it by a glass wall. We can watch democracy in progress but we can't get near the coffee.

It'll be OK. I'm not going to the police, I'm not telling anyone about Nic, I promised. I'm going to make damn sure she's OK.

I've got my best suit on, the dove-grey one. I've done this kind of thing before. No-one ever made me wait for an hour when I was with Dance and Fitzhugh. Would you trust Yasir? Would you trust a snake?

A polite young woman in a black headscarf and robe comes up.

'Mr Morlan?'

In the lift she asks me 'Have you got everything ready? He's very busy today.'

She leads me along a corridor panelled in light oak

and lined with portraits of distinguished politicians, all men. I recognise none of them. She stops at a door and knocks. The nameplate reads 'Mr Caldor, Senior Adviser'. She opens the door.

'Good luck.'

I swear she winks.

Thomas rises from behind a dark wood table strewn with papers. His suit fits him perfectly. I think of Yasir and his boardroom table – and Nic's office. You can just see the river out of the corner of the window behind him, grey, indifferent.

He holds out his hand.

'Nice to see you! Do sit down. Jack's been asking after you, you know.'

'It's good to see you too. I need your help.'

I sit heavily, take the notebook out of my pocket, fumble and drop it. I'm on the floor grubbing for the pieces of paper I wrote everything down on last night. I didn't sleep much.

'Goodness! Are you OK?'

He bends over me and almost lifts me onto the chair, sweeps up the papers and hands them to me.

'Now, how can I help?'

I have to keep my voice steady.

'This is business, not something I could discuss on the phone. I'll be brief. Do you have access to New Scotland Yard? At the highest level?'

Thomas gives me his full attention in the way he has. I've prepared everything and I'm focused, but the words falter and I have to explain twice. When I've finished he scratches behind his ear.

'You're sure about the address?'

I pass him the paper with the address typed out on it.

He looks thoughtful, and suddenly I see it, what binds him to Jack. They are both at heart academics, they want to understand the world but that's not enough. If you ask them, they'll tell you they want to change it. What they really most desire is to play with it, and they're very serious about their play.

'This could work,' he says. 'Good timing for the Repatriation Bill. Nothing much lost if it doesn't. You're absolutely sure of your facts?'

'Of course. You know the police won't listen to me, after…'

'I won't mention you. The vote takes place in two days. We've contacted every MP who might shift. This could swing it.'

'And there's the by-election.'

He grins, suddenly boyish.

'Don't jinx it.'

For god's sake, he has Nic. I don't say it.

A wooden picture frame stands on the table. Jack gazes back at me, the slogan "Britain Welcomes the World" in ten-foot capitals above him. That's the main Lecture Theatre in Church House, Westminster. He's the only white face on the platform and he looks inspired. That's my son.

Thomas picks up the phone and taps at the keypad. He caresses the port-wine stain with his finger-tips. I overhear a series of brief conversations, he's being transferred between different people.

He leans back in his chair and smiles into the receiver.

'Commissioner. Sorry to trouble you when you are busy with the jobs demonstrations. I've come across something I think you need to know about. It's the kind of thing that'll get back to the Sec of State. Anyone with you?'

He motions me to the door with his free hand. I rise, supporting myself on the back of the chair. He waves, drops a hand onto the mouth-piece and says,

'We'll meet up later, OK?'

He turns back to the conversation and I close the door behind me. I close my eyes and lean against it for a moment. A voice calls out 'Excuse me'.

An older woman I vaguely recognise is striding towards me. Grey hair, light-blue jacket, heavy pearls. She's followed by a group of smartly dressed young women and men, solemn-faced, all carrying files as if they were precious relics. She says something into a mobile phone and hands it to the nearest aide. I can hear the caller's voice still talking as the aide slips it into her pocket. I press myself back into the doorway and they pass on.

'Good meeting?'

It's the young woman who escorted me up. I follow her down a staircase, and we're in the atrium, the smell of coffee and fresh bread and salmon and cream cheese rising all round us. It's crowded, mainly aides and assistants and researchers, greeting each other, drinking their cappuccinos and flat whites, networking. Four or five senior figures, all men, with creased suits and florid faces, sit together on the larger tables at the far end. They hail each other extravagantly and ignore everyone else. Reminds me of the lunch-room at the agency.

My escort waves to a blonde young woman balancing a tray with a bowl of salad, an apple and a tablet on it.

She turns to me.

'A coffee?'

I shake my head.

'You look as if you could do with sitting down.'

'It's OK.'

The blonde woman has moved on and is deep in conversation with a balding young man, who's holding the tray for her and has a file under his arm. Something glints on her shoulder and I see they are both wearing paperclip necklaces, intern-style.

My escort looks disappointed. She uses her pass-card to let me through the turnstile. I stand outside under the canopy, gazing out over the Thames. I inhale the cold, faintly salty air and tear the wrapper off a Paradise Bar, just one. I deserve it. Nic's got back-up now.

Later she rings.

'I'm OK. I have a room by myself.' Her voice fades. 'We had couscous, tomato salad and some lamb last night. They give me the papers – nothing about me in them.'

I think of her face, white as curd.

'God, if he hurts you.'

'No, it's fine.' Her voice quavers. 'Please, just keep cool. This is something I can do.'

Yasir's voice.

'Mr Morlan. I hope you are keeping well?'

I don't answer.

'OK. Let us keep to the bargain and you will see your daughter shortly.'

Thomas is waiting when I get there. The pub is off St James Street, all dark wood and the scent of cedar, full of nooks with arched windows. I'm aware of conversations I can't quite catch all round me. I prefer meeting in places like this. The surroundings take you seriously.

He takes our drinks over to a side table.

'Hope you don't mind a quick drink. My boss has a dinner later and she'll need me along. Let's do a proper meal again when all this is over. Cheers.'

He's a big man and he leans forward over the table.

'Yes, let's – but is everything OK about Yasir?'

'Ninety-nine per cent. If you're right they cannot ignore it. As soon as Yasir makes clear he is a people trafficker, they'll go in.'

'Thank goodness.'

I take a good swig of the beer. Lovely. Thomas is on our side, I have to tell him.

'Thomas, listen. I have to tell you something. Yasir, it's not just going to be a live-stream debate on Facebook. It's more than that. He's got Nic.'

He frowns. I'm gripping his arm. I take my hand away.

'Nic, she got carried away, she went there and challenged him and he kidnapped her. That's why I can't go to the police. This debate, it's his idea, it's meant to be a big secret. God, I'm so frightened for her.'

'Jesus.' Thomas has his phone in his hand. 'I'll tell them, they'll go in straightaway.'

'You don't understand. He's a slaver, he runs brothels, drug factories, he has Nic and I don't know where he's holding her.'

I'm shouting. People glance at us and look away.

'He wants this debate – can't they track that down, find out where it's coming from?'

Thomas stares at me. He slips his phone in his pocket without looking at it.

'Good grief. Your daughter is the bravest person I have ever met.'

'Please help her. Please get her out.'

Nic versus Yasir

I put the carrier bag down as soon as I enter Jack's flat. He's standing by the window staring out. He hugs me. We stand there together, looking out. I feel his heart beating in his chest.

'Is this really happening?' he says. 'I'm scared.'

'I couldn't stop it, it was too late. Nic… she gets carried away.'

'Oh Dad, it wasn't your fault. It just happened.'

I take the carrier into the kitchen and serve it out, the best Thai food I could buy. He eats hungrily and finishes off what's left over. I gather up the containers. It's good to see him eat like that. I have no appetite and leave half of mine.

'It'll start soon.'

'I know. I wish this wasn't happening.'

The laptop's on the coffee table with a bowl of Russet apples, smelling of summer, placed next to it. He taps at the keyboard and clicks a couple of times. The screen shows two figures: Nic, her face grim, and Yasir, smiling like a priest at a church-door, immaculate in pin stripes. Nic's got her hair tied back and she's wearing the new jacket, with a double silver chain round her neck.

I think of her when I dropped her off on her first day at school, her face open, as if she trusted the whole world.

Yasir smiles into the camera and my hair bristles.

'That oily toad looks like he's CEO of Barclay's Bank, not a people-trafficker. Why on earth did Nic get into this?'

'She's who she is. Besides Thomas has got it sorted.' He glances at his phone. 'He said he'd call. This has to work.'

'I trust Thomas.'

He grins and for a second he reminds me of Cat. He reaches over and touches my hand.

Nic and Yasir are side by side, some distance apart, deep shadow behind them, and that's all you see. They could be anywhere. An alarm clock, a traditional bell and hammer model, stands on the table, its face reflected in the polished surface. Suddenly, I know where they are. It's the board table at *Workforce International*.

It's hard to keep my voice steady.

'Nic, call Thomas. It's definitely the address I gave him. Burgess Park.'

He talks briskly into his phone.

Yasir makes a movement with his hand, the speaker hisses and he addresses us, as if he's introducing a Radio 4 documentary.

'Good evening. I am a people-trafficker. Your government says I am a criminal. I hope that by the end of this broadcast you will understand that I have much to offer this country.'

He pauses.

'My friend Nic and I want to talk to you about two subjects that matter to all of us: immigration and forced labour. Who knows? Perhaps we will find something on which to agree.'

Nic doesn't smile. She addresses the audience.

'Remember: your MP will vote on the Repatriation Bill tonight. The new laws are a humanitarian disaster. They encourage people trafficking and force people into modern slavery. We offer you something which government has abandoned: reasoned debate. Fifteen minutes each.'

She turns to Yasir, who leans forward.

'Which of you trusts a politician? I'm a businessman. I ask you to trust me.'

His eyes are fixed on the camera. I know he's a crocodile but when he looks at you it's hard to doubt his honesty. There's an absolute self-belief in his face, and at the same time an absolute valuing of the person he's addressing. I find myself thinking this can still turn out OK.

Nic's gazing at him. She blinks, turns to the camera and speaks with confidence.

'Slavery is wrong. It's cruel, it's illegal, it's treating people as things and it's hateful. It's banned throughout the world. Yet forced labour flourishes in modern Britain, in plain sight. That man,' she indicates Yasir, 'is a modern-day slaver.' Yasir inclines his head. 'The Act will simply drive immigration underground, giving the traffickers more power to exploit and enslave people. Let me explain.'

Jack bites at his lip.

'Surely people believe her. She's obviously right.'

'Let's see how it goes.'

Nic talks easily and with enthusiasm, as if she's a college professor, an expert on her subject. I think of how she presented Salma's case in the tribunal. She explains all the pressures that force immigrants to seek lives in the west, all the evidence that choking off legal immigration encourages people-trafficking.

She pauses for breath and reminds people of terrified children forced into prostitution, of domestic servants with scars all over their bodies, of labourers surviving on one meal a day, of building workers who sleep on the site and are never paid, of agricultural workers frightened that if they protest the police will beat them up and send them back home.

She gives people a moment to think about it and quotes chapter and verse: arrests you read about in the newspapers, things you see out of the corner of your eye, that everyone knows about but wants to ignore, a list of crimes that takes minutes to recite, that she knows by heart.

I relax and remember the coffee. Don't like decaf but I can't taste the difference.

Keep going Nic, you're doing great. But don't keep glancing at Yasir like that, you don't need his approval.

Yasir, his face grave, nods from time to time.

Nic finishes.

'I urge you, never buy when it's too cheap. Email your MP. Tell them to vote against the Bill. Join the demonstration outside Parliament tomorrow. Kill the Bill! A vote for me is a vote against modern slavery!'

She doesn't smile but she closes her eyes for a moment and her shoulders relax.

Yasir gazes into the camera. His eyes soften.

'People call me a people trafficker. My work is everywhere condemned. Civilised people despise me.

If they arrested me, I would spend many years in gaol. But remember,' his voice grows stronger 'every leader of a movement for change is persecuted – Emmeline Pankhurst, Martin Luther, Nelson Mandela – all on the side of the future. I accept persecution.'

He bows his head. Nic's watching him and there's something in the tilt of her head I don't like, as if she's deferring to Yasir.

'And yet… I ask you to hear me out. This country believes in market freedom. Nic, you and I and many civilised people believe in the free movement of people, that you should be allowed to go and work anywhere you choose. I simply help people who want to work in Britain travel here and meet people who want to employ them. I take a fee for my services. What is wrong with that?'

Nic gathers herself and breaks in. She looks almost apologetic, but her voice is firm.

'You're a people-trafficker. You take people's passports, you force them to work for nothing. Anything they earn, you keep. You cannot deny it.'

Something moves in the darkness behind her but I can't make out what it is. Yasir spreads his hands. He speaks as if instructing a student.

'I'm afraid you do not understand business. Your immigration service denies my clients entry and I must use unconventional and expensive means of transport. How could it be otherwise? I must have security and their documents are the only security my clients can offer. How could it be otherwise? I find work for my clients and take money to pay my debts. How could it be otherwise?'

He smiles as if Nic is his protégé.

'You are a passionate young woman.'

Nic frowns.

'But ...'

She stops talking as if confused.

It's going wrong, we need to act now. I turn to Jack.

'He's admitted he's a trafficker. Why aren't the police in there? We've told them where it is, they must be watching.'

Jack doesn't take her eyes off the screen.

'Thomas, what's happening? Where are the cops?'

He puts his hand over the phone. 'He got through to New Scotland Yard but they won't listen to him. There's a big demonstration about jobs somewhere and it's turning into a riot. Makepeace called everyone in.'

My mouth's dry. I can't swallow.

'Makepeace? But that smug bastard's confessed on video. Nic's there, in the same room, they've got to get her out.'

'As long as we can see her, she's OK.'

Jack waves his phone at the TV, but he's gripping my wrist so tight his hand feels like an iron cuff.

Nic takes a deep breath and she's speaking again, gesticulating with her right hand. Her words are so fast they are hard to make out.

'It's wrong, everyone knows it's wrong. You take away people's freedom. You take away their rights. You don't treat them with respect.'

Yasir smiles and I think of a crocodile I met once in the Regent's Park Zoo, only dressed in a thousand pound suit.

'All competent economists agree that the market makes us richer. I provide security in work – and which of you in my audience can say you have that? Accommodation

112

in London – and which of you can afford that? Social mobility, from Somalia to Whitechapel – who else offers that? Work, food, opportunity – all the things you desire. The world is rich. I am the true face of globalisation.'

He pauses.

'I am your future.'

Nic stares at him, aghast.

'No, no, no. Civilisation rejected the slave trade in 1833. We must not go back.'

'To the contrary. Where do my ideas come from? They come from you, from your western civilisation. Slavery built this city. Look at your fine buildings, look at your centre of government. Whitehall. Georgian architecture. Where did the money come from that paid for them? Britain became great on the profits of the slave trade and forced labour in plantations. My customers want to enter Britain. They do not wear leg-irons. No-one forces them.'

He speaks like a client setting out a business plan.

'When I come to your cities I find people working for a pay-packet no-one can live off. I find people on your streets desperate for work. I find your interns with no pay and little opportunity. I find people who don't know if they'll be thrown out of their home next week.'

Yasir reaches out towards the viewer, his hand open, smiling a serpent smile, and lying.

Something scalds within me.

'I offer work, accommodation, food, security. Believe me, I understand what I am talking about. I came to this country with nothing, hidden in a lorry from Calais. I worked hard, I am successful and now I help others. I ask you to vote for me.'

The alarm clock rings, clattering across the table. He stills it with one hand and turns to Nic.

'We are, I think, out of time. I do not penalise you for your interjections. You are young.'

Nic's biting at her lip. Please let her leave. Now, as we agreed.

Jack's phone rings. Yasir's still talking about how to vote in the debate, something called Survey Monkey.

'Thomas says they're meeting now in the Home Office. They've over-ruled the Human Trafficking Unit. No 10's involved.'

Nic thrusts her face forward, talking as if she hasn't got much time.

'Remember. Kill the Bill! Britain needs immigrants. Stop legal immigration and you simply make Yasir and the other people-traffickers,' Yasir frowns and makes a deprecatory gesture, 'richer. That must not be our future.'

She sits back. She looks very pale and she's swaying in her chair. Yasir reaches over and lays a hand on hers.

'You are my guest. Let us not part in anger.'

Nic shouts at him but the words are jumbled and the screen goes blank.

Fury burns in me. I can't control my breathing. I'm on my feet, standing there with nothing to punch.

'Jesus. Who was working the camera? We've got to get Nic out.'

Jack's tapping speed call on his phone.

'She's not answering. Nic, pick up!'

'I'm calling the police myself,' but before I can key in 999 the phone starts ringing and, like a fool, I answer it.

Corridors of Power

'Thomas!' The words come fast. 'Where are the police? You must help Nic.'

'I'm with Makepeace. He wants to speak with you. A car is on its way.' His voice has lost its confidence. 'Please. It's the best I can do.'

'But...'

'We...I need you. Please.'

I hear someone shouting in the background and he rings off.

Jack's got the police on his phone. He's arguing. He looks up and mouths the word 'Go!'

The car is black, sleek as an eel, and the driver ignores speed limits. Tomorrow's first editions are piled neatly on the back seat, something about "Dagenham Riot: Policeman Injured" on the front page, but I can't concentrate on anything. A police motorcyclist overtakes us, lights flashing, pulls in front and accelerates.

The driver grunts

'Check your seat-belt.'

He settles himself in his seat.

Seven minutes later, we're in Whitehall. We keep going, take a sharp right and halt outside a five storey slab, its design half fortress, half office block. A young man steps forward to usher me in. He doesn't speak and I see the flash of a paperclip intern bracelet at his wrist as he holds open the door. I stride up the stairs and he has to run to keep up with me. Thirty seconds later I'm in a large office with oak-panelled walls and a semicircle of wingback armchairs that reminds me of the smoking room in the Groucho club. The dark oak desk is bare, no phone, no computer.

The air is heavy with the smell of leather and cigarette smoke.

A silver-haired figure approaches me holding out his hand.

'We've met.'

It's Makepeace. Why on earth does he want to see me? His grip is no stronger than a child's. I want to crush his hand, punch him, I want him sitting on the floor tasting the blood on his mouth, his hands shielding his face, terrified of me. I want to stop being this person, the one I am, who reasons with people, who always wants things to work out.

He smiles his general smile.

'Where's Nic?' I shout at him. It's as if the room absorbs the sound.

Thomas rises from one of the armchairs. His tie's loose and his collar's unbuttoned. A computer tablet lies on the arm of the chair.

He pulls hard at his ear.

'Thank goodness you're here.'

I want to shake him, both of them.

'You've got to get Nic out of there. Now.'

'Of course. But let us first consider.' Makepeace is still smiling, in fact he smiles most of the time, as if he thought you might glance at him at the wrong moment when he's uneasy and catch him out. 'This is a national crisis. My police force is fully stretched. I have persuaded Mr Caldor that we should adopt a bipartisan approach.'

Thomas nods, his eyes on Makepeace.

'Mr Makepeace has promised to address the kidnapping, but first he wishes to discuss the riots.'

Makepeace continues:

'Very well. I'm unsure whether you are up-to-date with the news.'

Thomas holds out the tablet.

'Live streaming from Tottenham.'

The image on the screen jerks sideways, steadies, and focuses on a policeman in full riot gear. He runs forward, drops to one knee and aims a wide-muzzled gun towards the camera. The eye-pieces of his gas-mask glint like sharks' eyes in the blue flashes of the emergency lights. He pauses and touches something on the gun. Smoke bursts from the barrel and the screen goes blank.

I thrust the tablet back at Thomas.

'Why are you showing me this? You're wasting time.'

Makepeace raises his hand, palm forward. His eyes are sharp as a cat's.

'Please listen, Mr Morlan. We live in a divided country and we must choose, each of us, which side we are on.'

'What has this to do with Nic?'

'One moment. Good-night, Mr Caldor. Bipartisan governance can only go so far. Thank you for bringing Mr Morlan to my office.'

I smash the tablet down on the arm of the chair. The screen cracks and the casing bends back as if hinged.

'For God's sake. Yasir has Nic. Why haven't you arrested him?'

He draws the corners of his mouth down. Is that how he laughs?

'We will talk privately.'

Thomas holds out both arms, takes a step forward, hesitates and embraces me.

'Good luck.'

He whispers in my ear and I feel his arm trembling.

'Never, never trust Makepeace.'

He closes the door behind him.

'He'll go far.' Makepeace speaks, as if to himself. 'Ah, if I … but I forget myself. Do sit down.'

He's holding a silver cigarette case towards me. I feel I'm in a nightmare.

'No? Do you mind?' He lights up and exhales. 'I fight this habit every day. Sometimes I lose.'

I speak as slowly as I can.

'Mr Makepeace. Do you have children?'

'I am grateful to Mr Caldor for bringing you here. You understand the arts of persuasion. Your son will shortly be an MP.'

'What?'

Again the repressed laugh. 'My police force is overstretched, as you see. You will do something for me and I will help you with Nic.'

'Indeed?'

My voice is thick with anger. I've met people like

Henry Makepeace before, arrogant idiots who think they deserve to outsmart you because they went to Eton and you didn't.

'Very well. Naturally I am in communication with Mr Yasir.'

He talks into his mobile and passes it to me. Nic's voice is loud in my ear, as if I were holding her against me.

'Dad! Don't believe a word they say. I'm OK.'

It goes dead. I've only heard Nic like that once before, the first time she went to Yasir's, when she was trapped behind the board table, holding back her terror.

'If you do not send the police in now, you are abetting a kidnapper, a self-confessed people trafficker, a modern slaver. I promise you that is the headline you will read in tomorrow's papers. Your duty is to protect Nic.'

'Mr Morlan, please. Let us not be childish. I have many duties but my first is to my party. Sometimes I face difficult decisions.'

I don't say anything. I feel I'm no longer part of this, I'm somewhere to the side, watching two people arguing in a play.

'My party has a dilemma. My friends in the city, in business, those who finance us, know that Britain needs cheap workers, cheap as we can get, especially with all this 'real jobs' nonsense. We need immigrants. People vote for us through force of habit or because they are fools, or racists, or patriots. Many of them hate immigrants. Democracy requires I carry out their will. The man who can solve that dilemma will be party leader, perhaps Prime Minister.'

I don't think. I don't need to.

I pick up the tablet and fold it where the crack runs across the screen. It breaks in half and fragments of glass and plastic glitter on the chair.

'You must act to rescue Nic. Now. I have many friends in the media.'

He smiles as if at a child.

'Listen. For Nic. My Immigrant Repatriation Bill will be passed tonight and tomorrow you'll see pictures on Breakfast TV of the Border Force packing people onto planes. I will be the most popular politician in the UK and that phone will dance on the table as the money men ring to say they'll never give the party another penny.'

'Why the fuck tell me this?'

'I'll be honest. I need your help. I want you to run a campaign for me. I promise you it will be the largest and most challenging of your career.'

I blink but there's a tiny quiver of delight somewhere near my heart. I'm very, very good at campaigns. I slap my cheek, hard.

'That's impossible … you will guarantee Nic's safety?'

'Of course. Let me explain. Just suppose: we permit controlled immigration. The new immigrants work free from employment rights. They receive accommodation, food, perhaps pocket money. Job seekers, homeless people, zero-hours workers, the great army who don't know if they'll have a job next month, who hate their insecurity, will join them.'

He stubs out the cigarette.

'People prioritize security over rights, I am afraid. Yasir's methods are … squalid, but I must credit him with the idea.'

'What – you will make forced labour legal?'

'Of course not. I will make work … secure and certain. Workers will be peaceful and contented, productivity will rocket, the money men will queue up to eat their words and all will be sweetness and light. Your job will be to sell the idea. You have an excellent track record in persuasive communication. I want you to contribute to my campaign.'

I see Nic trapped behind the table. I see Elsa Dance's smirk as she explains the concept of "partnership" to me.

'No, you fool. Get the police in and Nic out now or I will use all my skills to make sure everyone knows you for what you are. "Home Secretary Backs People Traffickers".'

He looks straight at me, as if the most junior aide had answered him back.

'You refuse?'

'Yes. Get Nic out now. That is your duty.'

He gives a tiny nod.

'There is another way of putting it to you.'

I turn and reach for the door-knob. He brushes at the shards of glass on the chair.

'Consider your daughter's prospects. Rioting on the streets of London. Police officers seriously injured, perhaps dead. We both know that Ms Morlan set up that video broadcast. A disinterested person might believe that propaganda about modern slavery provoked the riots. A conspiracy charge. Perhaps ten years. She would not do well in gaol. She needs sympathetic friends.'

He has the phone in his hand.

'But she didn't – Yasir tricked her.'

'Perhaps. Prove it.' He looks directly at me. 'Regret is a terrible burden.'

The blood throbs in my head, I can hardly think. What would Cat do?

I know the answer. Twenty-five years ago in Whipps Cross Hospital, lying there, white as the bed-sheet, she held Nic in her arms and she was the most precious thing in the world.

'OK.'

'A wise decision.' He's back at his desk. 'If you could sign these.'

'Get Nic out.'

'Your signature first. I need reassurance that you will fulfil your side. It's a standard contract, no media contact without my approval.'

He uncaps a fountain pen. It's only a bit of paper. Who cares? A promise under duress.

I scrawl on it. Hope I've bent the nib.

'Excellent. Welcome to the team.' He fixes his eyes on me. 'Don't change your mind. And you will not discuss our arrangement with anyone. That includes your family.'

'She never meant this to happen.'

'Two policeman have been seriously injured. The public needs a scapegoat. Your daughter is capricious.' Again the inverted smile. 'She would not attract sympathy.'

He taps a number and talks into the phone.

'Yes, Commissioner. Operation Absalom. Please go ahead.'

He puts the phone back in his pocket.

'If you hadn't been so impetuous you could have watched the police action on the tablet. Perhaps Ms Morlan will thank her rescuers on camera. She may congratulate the police on closing down another people-trafficking operation.'

He takes another cigarette from the box.

'Tell me, Mr Morlan. Do you believe the end justifies the means?'

I can't think and I give him the only answer that makes any sense to me.

'I really wish I knew.'

He puts the cigarette back into the box.

'Good answer. Now I must return to the House.'

He waves me to the door.

I'm on a bench in the corridor. My heart flutters in my breast like a bird caged between cupped hands. The aide who brought me in loiters, dabbing at his mobile phone. Coloured shapes cascade down the screen.

The video monitor at the end of the corridor flashes, white on black:

"Immigrant Repatriation Bill: Ayes 321 Noes 318".

The boy punches the air and shouts 'Yes!'

He catches my eye and sits down.

There's a noise of doors crashing open, a babble of voices, people in the corridors, all talking, shaking hands, slapping each other on the back. An older woman in a dark suit, pink top and pearls is holding a file edgeways to part the crowd.

'Christ,' she's saying, 'now we've actually got to do it.'

The shaven-headed man with her chuckles. 'You'll find a way.'

Part of the team. I still have the pen in my hand. It fits snugly in my fist and the nib comes to a point. I could go back and smile and smile and stab it into his throat and twist it and wrench it back and watch him choke on his own thick blood.

I regret I'm not that man.

Sell Out

I've walked a long way from Makepeace's office, down from Marsham Street into Parliament Square, where I once crossed the road, and on up Whitehall, the sentinel pillar of the Cenotaph looming over me. The street-lights glare down. Armed riot police stand motionless inside the railings of parliament.

I don't look back.

Police minibuses with wire mesh windscreen guards are parked along the kerb in Derby Street and more armed police stare out from behind the steel gates of Downing Street. I hear the clamour echoing off the Whitehall facades:

'Real Jobs Now! Real Jobs Now!'

Demonstrators crowd together on the pavement outside the gates. The placards read: 'Real Work for Real Pay', 'Fair Pay is our Birthright' and 'Shit Government, Shit Jobs', the last one on a union flag background.

Nic and Jack should be there. I pray Jack's with Thomas and Nic's safe wherever she is.

I scan the faces in the crowd.

A young Asian man with a megaphone shouts out 'Gizza Job!'

Blimey, you've got a long memory.

The demonstrators tail up Whitehall for two hundred metres. Men and women, old and young, black and white. No problem with equal opportunities.

One young man has a toddler with a yellow anorak wrapped round him in a pushchair, head tilted back and sound asleep. Someone blows a wailing blast on a whistle and the toddler jerks awake, looks up at his dad and instantly falls asleep.

A figure with closely-cropped black hair with a white streak, dressed in a jacket and trousers that don't quite fit her, forces her way through. She taps the young Asian on the arm and says something. He claps her on the shoulder and hands her the megaphone.

'Kill the Bill! Real Jobs Now!'

The voice booms out, distorted, but I know it's her and it's like birdsong. I start forward, but then halt.

What am I going to tell her?

'It's so great you're here, I was really scared for you, so was Jack, so was Thomas, everyone.'

She'll throw her arms round me, and she'll be laughing so much she won't be able to talk properly and I'll press her against me and feel how frail she is, as if I were clasping a child.

And then I'll say,

'Oh, by the way, just so you know, I did a deal with Makepeace. Now I'm on his team, I signed up. We're going to make forced labour legal, but don't worry, it'll be OK.'

I think of her face, how her voice'll tremble as she takes a step back, as if she doesn't believe what I'm saying:

'You're working for that bastard?'

126

I move back, against the buildings. She doesn't see me. I need to think.

A black limousine turns into Downing Street, just as I pass. Is that Makepeace, the round pale face at the window? He stares right through me. The gates swing open and the police step forward, clubs at the ready, glaring at the demonstrators.

I'm on the pavement in Trafalgar Square. People shove past me. Nelson's column, picked out by floodlights, reaches up above us all. The traffic's nearly stationary. Bus engines growl and the stink of diesel fumes hangs in the air. No-one looks back towards Downing Street where the demonstrators are massed half a mile away. You have to listen hard to hear the slogans.

I thread my way between the taxis and buses to the central plaza.

A troop of young women and men, smartly dressed, are singing and squealing, swaying onto the parapets, spattered by the spray from the fountains. Someone's chanting, they're clutching at each other, kicking their legs out. A woman stumbles, lurches over the water for a second and they drag her back, laughing.

'Ay, Yi, Yi, Yi! Conga – Conga, Conga! Conga, Conga!'

This time I cross by St Martins. Another church built with conscience money from slavers' profits, and now they care for homeless people. The doors are still open. I climb the steps and enter the hall with the black oak gallery, the only light coming from the tall windows at the far end, the hush enfolding me.

So many people there in the darkness, mainly men, most of them huddled on the benches, silent. A woman in a red anorak kneels at the end of the back pew, her hands covering her face. She's muttering but I can't hear what she's saying. She moves her hand and her cheek is the colour of dough. As her sleeve falls back you see the scars across her forearm.

Someone's talking off to the side. A man with an immense beard jabs his finger at the chest of a priest in a black gown, as if accusing him. The priest has his head on one side, listening as the other talks and talks at him. He says something and rests his hand on the man's shoulder. The talker bows his head and falls silent. A woman in an overcoat comes up, takes the man's hand and leads him along the aisle, out towards the night shelter.

I kneel. I've never prayed in my life. Nothing there when I close my eyes, only my own thoughts, Nic and Jack and Cat, and, once, Salma. I look upwards. The lights are all out and I can't really see the ceiling high above me, only something darker in the shadows. The building's huge. It takes in all the shouting and the trouble and gives you back silence.

You could sit for a long time, looking upwards, resting yourself, and thinking. What good does it all do? I made a mistake. God's had his chance and he can't fix it. There's just us and we generally screw up. That's enough prayer. It's a warehouse, a great white shed for people to hide in.

What happens outside it is what matters.

I feel in my pocket:

'Excuse me.'

The young woman looks up, her eyes wide, as if I've caught her out. The scars reach up her arm. I hold out a bundle of notes, I don't know how much. She stares at it, reaches out and snatches her hand back. I leave it on the bench beside her.

The priest's waiting by the door. He catches my eye and I nod to him and he says something but I'm not listening. I carry on, down the steps, heading north. The pavements are crowded on Charing Cross Road and all the way up Shaftesbury Avenue, well-dressed people in twos and threes or little groups, talking and laughing, from the theatres and the clubs.

Memory snatches at me. Cat loved live theatre, especially shows that made her laugh. We strode down this street, hand in hand, after "The Secret Policeman's Ball". I forget what she wore or where we ate, but the laugh is still there, joyful, brazen, as if we'd go on like this for ever, us against the world.

No sign of a jobs riot here. They'd all be taking selfies in front of it if there was.

My Left Hand

I had to tell them. Screw Makepeace. I had to tell them.

We're in Jack's flat. Nic sprawls on the sofa. She stares at me.

'Jesus. You did a deal with him? Jesus.'

'I got you out.'

She's on her feet, moving from side to side.

'I hate it, being like this. Everyone on tip-toe, waiting for me to screw up so they can sort it all out. I'm a lawyer, I can look after myself.'

'Nic …' I reach out to her. 'Please, have you taken your pills this morning?'

'That's it! Have you taken your pills? Have you brushed your teeth? Do this! Do that! I hate being this person!'

She braces herself and beats her forehead against the wall next to the picture so hard it shudders. She grunts, shakes her head and jerks it back. I get my left hand between her head and the wall and the second time her forehead smashes into the back of it. I shout out. It's as if she's driven a spike into it.

'Christ,' she says. She touches my hand, very gently, as if she's not sure what she'll find. There's no feeling in it, none at all. I leave it where it is, let it be part of the wall.

'But you're on his team, you're helping him.' She pushes both hands through her hair and shakes her head. 'Are you OK?'

'I'll live.'

I haven't explained about Makepeace's threat, the fake conspiracy charge hanging over her head. I haven't the heart. I just told them Makepeace blames Nic for the riots and he wouldn't send the police in unless I agreed to help.

Jack doesn't move. His face is very pale, his eyes wide, his mouth half open and then tight shut, as if I'd placed a dish of stewed spiders on the table in front of him.

'God. I wish you hadn't gone to see that bastard. I wish it so much.'

They both stare at me. I want them to speak. I don't expect them to forgive me, I just need them to say something more.

My hand starts to hurt. I daren't move it.

I taste salt in my mouth.

'I didn't want to do it.'

Don't you get it?

'I couldn't lose you again.'

Nic's biting at her lower lip, like that day at school when they didn't want her in the football team and she couldn't work out why.

'Yeah. OK. Thanks for trying, but I never asked you to get involved. It was my idea, my big chance, mine, not yours.'

Jack puts his coffee cup down in the exact centre of the table.

'You understand, don't you? You're on Makepeace's side. I'm so sorry but you can't be part of what we do, Thomas and me and Nic, not now.'

I take the bleakness and crush it in my good hand, squeeze it tight. My left hand hurts now, pain juddering out of it as far as my shoulder. I can hardly keep it still. I stand there, my eyes closed.

'You OK, Dad?'

I can't tell if it's Nic or Jack. I open my eyes.

'Sure.'

'You're bound to screw up, anyway. Look what happened on *Overview*.' Nic grins lop-sided for a second. 'That was a joke. I'm going to put a bandage on that hand.'

She puts a white gauze pad on the back of my hand and starts winding the bandage round, her gaze intent on what she's doing, her lip gripped between her teeth. Jack puts a couple of paracetamol in my other hand and a glass of water on the table.

While she's passing the strip of cotton round my wrist, I get my next big idea.

'Jack, I can still help. The campaign? Maybe you should go for law and order.'

'We discussed that weeks ago.'

'I know what I'm talking about. People respect me, they invite me on TV. Trust me.'

'How can I, when you do deals with Makepeace?'

Jack never gets angry.

'I know what I'm talking about. I've got a track record.'

He bursts out laughing and immediately slaps a hand over his mouth.

'Sorry, didn't mean it like that. I know you used to be a big player in the industry.'

An ice-thorn, deep inside me. I can't get my hand to it. I can't pluck it out.

132

'Not a problem.' I get up. 'Track record, I know, bit of a joke recently.'

I put my good hand on the door handle.

'Dad, I don't want my politics to be about stunts and advertising tricks. I want to be honest with people.'

He rubs a hand across his mouth.

Nic won't meet my eyes.

'Maybe later, when all the fuss has died down.'

'It's OK.'

The flowers are still there, in the same jar. They could do with some water.

I pull the door shut behind me.

Cat

I'm on the street, walking like a machine. People make way for me and stare at the loose end of the bandage flapping at my wrist where Nic's knot has come undone. I don't remember much about how I get home, my mind's too full. Did you really mean that, Jack, not the laugh, the thing about being honest? My work was never just stunts and tricks, I always wanted people to see the truth, not just the facts but the real truth, what was inside them, what their heart most desired. That's my track-record. People, powerful people, people with money respected me.

Anyway I only worked there, didn't I?

And we needed the money, we had to have the money.

When I'm home I soak the hand in cold water and put ice on it. Then I take it in my other hand and bend the fingers backward. The pain's no worse. Dr Morlan says no broken bones. It's an almighty bruise, like a bubble in soft mud, purple-blue. Painkillers.

I take a double dose and get down on my knees and unlock the bottom drawer of the filing cabinet at the back of the study where the air always seems cold.

I reach in for the grey cardboard folder, no label. Not easy managing it one-handed, but I tilt it over the desk and let everything pour out. Certificates. I've still got the O-levels (that's what we did in those days) and the A-levels and the degree certificate from LSE. Bright little bugger I was, bit of a radical. That's how I met Cat, the free nursery care protests.

I sweep it all in the bin. I find the photo, the bride and groom on a flight of stone steps. My hair's slightly too long and Cat's is centre-parted with tiny braids at the front. The clothes are comical, a bit hippy – me in a purple suit with ridiculous lapels and flared trousers, Cat in a rainbow-coloured wedding dress. Huge bunches of lilacs, chrysanthemums, lilies and roses, white and purple and red. We look so young, so unguarded, as if we're challenging the world to take a swipe at us. Maybe Jack and Thomas will look like that.

I sit down at the desk. Cat and me, that day. The registry office in Islington town hall and the photos against its neo-classical façade, with the rumble of traffic and that bus-driver who blew Cat a kiss. We had our half-hour rationed out, a finance broker in morning dress and a fashion model queued up behind us for their turn in the central chamber.

For some reason I turn the photo over and there's another one stuck to the back, the colours blueing with age. I recognise it instantly, sunshine on golden sands and two figures running away from the camera, Nic on her antelope legs and Jack with his sun hat and chubby knees, tottering after her. It was a good day, a holiday we thought we deserved but didn't expect.

I sit, staring at them. Then I lead forward and kiss them, the paper smooth, sticking to my lips, first Nic and then Jack. I turn it back and I kiss Cat in her wedding dress, like I did twenty-six years ago.

It wasn't yet dark, that day at Margate, apricot pink clouds against the sunset in a pale blue sky. We had the road more or less to ourselves, just the occasional truck. The car swept round them so smoothly you hardly noticed they were there. Occasional trees, elms in those days, flashed by. Green fields reached down to the road on both sides.

Cat had the children singing, "Ten little fishes" and "My mum's an engine-driver" and she kept swinging round and pulling faces in a way that made Nic chuckle.

'Want to wee! Want to wee!'

Jack's wriggling in the car-seat.

I pull up, half off the road, and we all get out. Cat holds Jack while he pees on the verge. Hooves drum on turf and a chestnut mare pokes her polished brown face over the fence. Nic is already clambering up on the bottom rail, a tuft of grass gripped in her outstretched hand. The mare sniffs, puckers her lips over giant's teeth and opens her mouth.

'Careful! Fingers flat!' but she pokes the tuft forward and I snatch her back, just as the teeth clamp shut, an inch from her fingers.

'Daddy. She's hungry.'

'She'll nip, she's got big teeth. Come on. Back in the car.'

'Nice horse.'

I hold her up in my arms and reach out, my fingers round her hand, holding it flat with the grass in her palm. Hot breath and the tongue slobbers it up. Nic chuckles.

Golden meadows both sides, now. A line of elms like candy-floss soldiers marches down to the road.

'Snack time,' says Cat and doles out half a tube of smarties each to them. I switch on the headlights and start singing:

"The mummies on the bus do the higher maths, the higher maths…"

Cat bursts out laughing.

Jack wheezes and gives a little cough. I glance back at his face, smeared with chocolate.

'One Smartie at a time, they'll stick in your throat.'

Cat turns her head.

'He's OK.'

She unclips her belt and reaches back to tickle his tummy. The lorry's slowing down in front of us, a cattle truck, with wisps of hay round the tailgate. I pull out. The sunset blazes in my eyes and the sports car hurtles out of it, straight at me, leaping from toy size to fill the road in an instant, the headlights glaring brighter, brighter, impossibly bright, into my eyes. Cat screams and the air bag hits me in the face and …

I lie there, as if I have all the time in the world, not opening my eyes, resting, listening to a truck passing by, to the metal ticking as it cools, a horse neighing in the distance.

A man's voice speaks, somewhere above me:

'The children were lucky.'

I guess I was lucky too. The police report gave details of the Benzedrine in the other driver's blood-test and didn't bother with the alcohol in mine. The coroner recorded misadventure and delivered a homily on the importance of seat-belts.

I couldn't write proper fiction any more. Myles was generous and I found a way through it and focused on the children and the agency. They paid well and they let me do a lot of it from home the first year.

A droplet of water falls onto the glossy surface. I put my thumb on it and wipe it away. I put the photo back in the folder and lock it up safe in the drawer.

I've got a decent pension, Myles saw to that. I've got the flat. I need to find something to do. I tried one thing and it didn't work out, but I don't let that knock me back. I could maybe think about the novel again, but I know that's not going to happen. Or non-fiction – "*The true story of Paradise Bars*". Sure that'd sell. Or I could offer my services to someone who runs a big charity – that US guy, Bill Gates?

I could take up Pilates. Lots of things I could do.

I sit for a while, then I turn on the lap-top and watch Henry Makepeace's statement. After all I'm on his team now, though no-one's actually asked me to do anything. This is his bid for party leadership, Jack reckons. All about the war against immigrants ("illegals" he calls them now) and law and order and trafficking and his duty and how Britain will rise up proud and independent when it relies on its own free people. Etcetera.

It's the bit at the end that catches my eye.

'What people need is security. My Immigrant Repatriation Act stops illegal foreigners coming here to steal our jobs and our health service and riot against our police. That's only half my task. We must heal our divided nation. We need a New Deal for Work. I will guarantee jobs, real jobs, for everyone willing to work and work hard. No more worries about the rent and the bills.'

The camera closes in on him and he smiles his broadcast smile:

'A job you care for, that cares for you.'

My fingers tingle.

"Jobs Guarantee", "New Deal", maybe "New Beveridge" those are politician's slogans, I've heard them fifty times before. They're what the smart young special advisers, Eton and Oxford, who've never been in a pub in Dagenham, let alone Hartlepool, think people want to hear.

"A job you care for, that cares for you" isn't about policy, it's not about rights or work or citizen duty. It's about you and your desires. It speaks to your fears, your self-doubt, and your insecurity. It's part of my world.

A creative wrote that, someone from an agency with political contacts. Only thing, it's a bit clumsy, it lumbers and puts you on your guard. I can do better. They've given me a way in.

I get out my mobile and make a call. Takes twenty minutes. I ignore the promises: 'The Minister is in a meeting. He will be available shortly', 'Mr Makepeace's assistant will call back when she's free' and keep talking. I find that my name has some effect, but it's when I say 'Tell him I'm on his team. I signed up, it's about the campaign', that there's a whispered conversation with a hand over the mouthpiece and finally I get through.

I shave and get out my powder blue suit and brush it down. I put on a blue business shirt and the Harvard tie. A lot of people go through Harvard. No-one can be sure you aren't one of them.

Everything moves more slowly when you can't use one of your hands. You get time to think. There are two

Ritchie's now, the one standing here, checking his tie-knot, the one on the team, and the other one, who remembers how Makepeace used Nic as a bargaining counter and then asked "Does the end justify the means?"

The guy in the mirror has lost weight. You can see tiny creases all round his eyes if you look closely. The tendons in his neck are beginning to show, but he looks the part. He makes a phone call, keeping his eyes on the mirror. He always treated the staff in the office as he'd like to be treated. He knows people who'll tell him things about other people's diaries.

He doesn't smile. He picks up an empty attaché case.

I can make this work. My hand throbs. I don't have time for that, it's part of the background now. I keep it in my coat pocket, out of the way.

Makepeace is standing by the door of the office when I arrive, an unlit cigarette in his hand.

'You're confident about this?' he says. 'Completely confident?'

'Of course.' He keeps his eyes on me as I walk across the room. 'One rule in advertising. People have to trust the brand. That's you. And one rule in politics. You must offer a better future. You've proved you are trustworthy, you've ended immigration as you promised. Now you offer hope – the Jobs Guarantee. The Right to Work and the Duty to Work.'

'Perhaps... excuse me.'

I stand back and watch him as he smells at the cigarette, sighs, lights it and draws in the nicotine. He paces back to the door, then to the desk.

'I need this to work, Mr Morlan.' He blinks and shakes his head as if afflicted by something he can only see out of the corner of his eye. 'And the British people need it.'

I'm still watching him. You'd watch a polecat if it invited you back for a whisky and soda. I start to speak. That other Ritchie will explain things and Makepeace will believe him.

'My plan is simple. Sincerity, trust and hope. Now is your moment. Your speech will take the party conference by storm.'

He's not really listening. He holds up his hand.

'I don't suppose you have any idea how heavily the burden weighs. Ordinary people are like children. So … easily misguided. And they forget so quickly.'

He jabs a hand towards me, the cigarette between two fingers:

'They need someone to take command, to watch over them. There isn't anyone else. It is a matter of duty.'

'I am completely confident.'

He glances at the wall behind him.

Churchill, of course, and is that Gladstone? Sombrely-dressed figures, their faces marked by the habit of authority.

Chin forward. Take a deep breath and look him in the eye.

'This speech will bring you everything you deserve.'

'Those policemen. One of them died, you know. I had to go to the funeral, I made the oration. I didn't know him of course.' He puts the cigarette to his mouth. 'So great a sacrifice. For all of us.'

He continues, half to himself.

'My only regret is that we were unable to arrest the people-traffickers themselves.'

I clasp my bandaged hand into a fist and feel the jolt of pain rush up my arm, and say nothing.

'I asked you once, do you believe that the end justifies the means?'

'If you ask the question, you know the answer.'

He thinks for a moment, and grinds the cigarette into a glass ashtray.

'Another good answer. I must play out the game as best I can. I have a duty to the people who elected me, and to the party that put me in this role. I will lead them.'

He taps the cigarette box and places it back in the desk drawer.

'You may go. You'll send me a draft of the speech? I have another appointment.'

He pauses.

'Thank you for your service.'

An Idea with Legs

Fire still smoulders at my heart. I see Nic trapped behind the boardroom table, I see Jack's face as he says 'Go!'

I see Makepeace with his cigarette, holding up his palm and saying 'One moment'.

In the flat Jack laughed at me, that hysterical laugh, his hand clamped over his mouth but he can't stop himself.

And Nic's judgement:

'Later, after the campaign, when the fuss has died down.'

I'm still here for you. Me and Zephaniah Ted.

I need to rest.

I sit down, on the dark oak bench in the corridor and think of the benches in the primary school in the village. Chestnut Lane School. Chrissie sat next to me, brown hair in bunches, and a scent of apples, always brilliant at spelling and she let me copy her work, but she'd never let me kiss her.

I sit there. I can wait.

Heels click further up the corridor and Elsa Dance strides towards me. Elsa, with her heart-shaped face, her sculpted silver-gold hair and her thousand pound suit, her attaché case gripped tightly in her hand. I wish I was back when I was ten and I knew the rules. Chrissie let me hold her hand under the desk when Miss Roe shouted at me because I'd got my sums wrong again. Neither of us was any good at sums.

'Elsa, this is a surprise. Good morning.'

'Ritchie Morlan. Good to see you looking so well. We must have lunch. Excuse me, I am pressed for time.'

She opens Makepeace's door without knocking and enters. There's a tightness across my chest. I sit on the bench and take deep breaths to ease the tension in my shoulders. Team-players, both of us. I know who wrote that slogan.

I've known Elsa since she joined the agency. She started off with the old Sprint bars account – straightforward snacks: "For when you've got to dash". She checked the demographic for that kind of junk food: social groups D and E, male, the left behind, the ones who don't vote and think all politicians are the same. She changed the colour of the filling and sourced the sugar from Norfolk beet. Then she renamed them "White Heart" and put them in a George Cross wrapper. Her budget didn't stretch any further. She came to me for help and I didn't cost my time on the video. I should have thought it through.

I did the George Cross images with a flag on the roof of the Shoreditch studio. We spent hours on the lighting, sunrise worked best. You can't help feeling just a touch of pride when you see it. It's the colours, you can never make up for a routine image however much time you spend on the computer afterwards. Elsa told me how grateful she was at least twice. She didn't tell me about the tag-line: "Pure Chocolate Outside, Pure British Goodness Inside". Her team added that in and I only found out about it after the launch.

In the first week sales were low. Then a newsman snapped Makepeace eating one on his way to a cabinet meeting. They were the official snack-food at the party conference and they sold by the truckload. I got the biggest bonus I've ever had that year. I gave the lot to *Refugee+* and took White Heart off my CV.

She never looked back. When Dance and Fitzhugh went public Elsa was CEO, no-one knew why. A couple of months later, Rob, my PA, stopped me in the corridor and showed me his phone. Girls, all of them white, in cheerleader dresses handing out White Heart at the big anti-immigrant demonstration that morning. He thought it was funny. Then the news came through of the attack on the bus-driver. His face changed and he couldn't meet my eye.

I stood for a while at my office window, looking out at the rainclouds over Wapping. I wrote out my letter, longhand, and took it up to the top floor.

Elsa sat there in her top-floor office with the George Cross mock-ups, triple size, chromium-framed, on the wall behind her. Floor to ceiling windows and London laid out like a garden with the river snaking through it. The air tasted of nothing.

She looked up at me. Her eyes are the grey-blue of deep water on a dull day.

She smoothed out my letter on the oak desk.

'Ritchie, you're our leading creative. We need you.'

'I can't be part of this.'

'But you are. Everyone knows you did that image. Besides it's just advertising. Study the market and give them what they want.'

I shake my head and she drops the letter into the attaché case by her chair.

'You're an adman. You'll always be an adman. Let's talk this through.'

'There's nothing to say. You tricked me.'

'But you'd never have done it if I hadn't. Think about it. It's branding and it's win-win. They like the idea of pure British chocolate and you get your bonus.'

'You made a fool out of me.'

'I can offer you a salary review. We would be generous.'

'There's nothing to say. I'm finished.'

'Without you, Dance and Fitzhugh would still be middle rank. I'm thinking of setting up a media futures team. You could be director. A seat on the Board.'

'Goodbye.'

'Ritchie, if you leave here, where are you going to go?'

The door closes behind me, cutting her off. I've chucked in a job I love over a bar of chocolate, and I feel as if spring's come three months early in Canada Square.

I walk past the lift and take the stairs three steps at a time.

Peters stands in his usual place by the street-door. He's short, well-built and needs a hair-cut. He looked after me on my first day when I didn't know my way around.

'Do you like chocolate?'

'Chocolate, Mr Morlan? I most certainly do.'

'What kind?'

He looks at me as if he's concerned for me and answers:

'Paradise Bars. Used to go for Sprint, but I've gone off it.' He reaches into his pocket. 'Would you like one?'

'Thanks. Lovely.'

I shake his hand and stride through the doors, and

leave him staring at the twenty pound notes in his palm. Paradise Bars, nothing special about them, they're just sugar and chocolate, you know where you are. I haven't seen Elsa since then.

And then it comes to me. My next big idea. That other Ritchie places his briefcase on the bench, knocks, and, without waiting for an answer, opens the door and follows Elsa into Makepeace's office.

She's seated at the table next to Makepeace, showing him something on her laptop. The air in the room is heavy and the sound muted, as if overpowered by the curtains and the carpet.

He smiles at us both.

'Ah Mr Morlan. I thought we had finished?'

'Trust me.' I fix my eyes on him. 'I know my duty. I can help both of you.'

'Perhaps you are right,' he says. Elsa smiles at me, like a viper. 'Miss Dance is presenting an idea to me. You should hear it. Miss Dance – Mr Morlan.'

She snaps the lid of the laptop down and places her hand on it. 'We've met. People usually call me Ms Dance'

'Please continue, Miss ... Elsa.'

He takes a cigarette out of the box and lights it, sucking in the smoke. She waves it away from her face, and opens the laptop.

'Very well.' She glances at me. 'We have brought immigration to an end, now we face the Jobs Crisis. All those people out on the streets rioting for jobs. That is the challenge, Mr Makepeace.'

He nods.

'What do you propose?'

'A bonfire of regulation. We are a trading nation. We will move to WTO standards for labour protection.'

'Sorry,' Makepeace draws on his cigarette. 'I understood WTO did not concern itself with labour standards?'

'My point. An end to paid holidays, parental leave, industrial tribunals, unions, all that rubbish. Your boss is your boss.'

'I foresee some resistance to this approach.'

'You're putting it mildly,' I say. 'It's crazy.'

Elsa raises an eyebrow.

'You've been out of the industry too long. No one talks about rights now, they want security. So many people are failed by the current system. You see them out of the car window, begging for money, sleeping in doorways, queuing up at the JobCentre, outside the food bank, you see them worrying where next week's rent money will come from.'

She opens the laptop and reads from the screen.

'All those people who live off the benefits that decent people pay for – the layabouts, the no-hopers, the marginal people – we make them the new national work-force. They get security – food, accommodation, pocket money – and a guarantee of employment for life. A Job You Care for, That Cares for You. That's what people want.' She looks directly at Makepeace. 'And labour will be docile and cheap.'

She pauses a moment.

'You'll have to ban welfare of course and begging, but WTO says nothing about them, either. No one likes scroungers, no-one likes beggars.'

She smiles at us.

I'm dumbfounded.

'But how will people live?'

'Join the national task-force.'

Makepeace nods and stubs out his cigarette.

'Excellent, Mrs Dance. Mr Morlan, you will put all this into my speech. I'm glad you have had the opportunity to meet another member of my team. Good-day.'

He takes a new cigarette out of the box.

Ideas whirl in my head.

'You're determined to do this?'

'Of course.'

'One moment.' I pull out a chair and sit opposite them. 'It's a big idea, but there's a better one.'

Elsa glares at me. Makepeace inclines his head.

'Tell us.'

'No-one's heard of the WTO. Everyone knows what it means to be afraid for the future. Three words: "Your Life Sorted". That's what people want. Cradle to grave they want their life sorted. "A Job That Cares for You" – what does that mean? Sounds like you're working in an old folks' home.'

Makepeace looks at me. He's forgotten his cigarette.

'I believe you're right.'

Elsa slams the lid of her lap-top so hard it sounds like a slap.

I'm back in the game.

'We need to introduce it gently. Have you thought of making it fun?'

'Fun?' says Makepeace. 'We're doing this for the British people. It is my duty.'

'Yes, but they have to like it. Everyone loves a prize,

everyone thinks they're lucky. And everyone loves an app. Just one click, you take a chance and it comes up for you and you get something and you think it's great. That's what we need.'

Elsa glares but says nothing. Makepeace nods.

'I think you have the germ of an idea.'

I'm on a roll, I can't fail now.

'We'll call it "Henry's Helpers". Interns for everyone. The right to work and the duty to work. Trust me.'

'"Henry's"?' he says.

'Branding. You want them to know who to thank, don't you?'

'I see.'

'One other thing.' I can hardly stay in my chair. 'We don't want too much tension – we need to pull the rug from under the demonstrators. We'll make it a National Apprenticeship Scheme and we'll pay them. They have to have hope, and they have to be better off than people on benefits.'

'Initially.'

'There's more. You've got to bring this home to people, to ordinary people, to the voters. They have to be part of it. They have to understand, it will make our country whole again.'

They sit and listen to me. Because I've had an idea, definitely my best yet – and I know Nic and Jack will like it, once I explain. It's an idea with legs, an idea that'll trip Makepeace up so he lands head first in cow-shit. It's an idea that'll plunge him in so deep he'll be caked with it for the rest of his life, and that's how people will remember him. Because I'm good at campaigns. I'm Ritchie Morlan.

Henry's Helpers

A week has gone by and I'm in the place we used to go to in Shoreditch. The price of a flat white is ludicrous and the croissants are, you could say, flaky. There are little booths at the back where you talk privately, away from the smell of stale coffee and people glancing up to scan the room and check who should be noticing them. That's why we come here. I set up at the back in my brand new dove grey suit with the top of the range laptop I hired that morning.

This is what I do, this is my world. I haven't felt like this since I shot that poster, the one I did for Nic and *Refugee+*, at the studio across the road. Makepeace won't believe he's getting quality if it doesn't cost.

I don't expect the staff to remember me. Tomas, slim, dark-haired and from Lithuania, has gone. A young woman with an east London accent takes my order.

'I'm meeting some people,' I say. 'Have one yourself.'

She doesn't smile. She's concentrating on foaming the milk.

'Later. Thanks.'

She scoops some coins out of the till.

Julia comes over first, with her cheekbones, and her hair dyed white and brushed straight back. She worked for

Myles when I'd just found something I could do, where people smiled at me and sometimes listened to what I had to say.

She sits down without asking and leans towards me.

'Look at you! The Ritchie Morlan!'

'Certainly am.'

As soon as she's there, the others feel it's safe to join us, all of them faking surprise, eyes wide, hands held out, cries of delight and amazement. No one asks where I've been or how Elsa's getting on.

I sit back, accepting their congratulations, not getting out of my seat. After all I'm the oldest person in the room, twice the age of some of them.

I give it five minutes so they can greet and size each other up and see and be seen and start checking their phones. I point to four of them: Anders for production, Hargreaves for the songs and the soundscape, Matten for graphics and Jimmy Rental for post-production. Not Julia. I've already got Otto Spencer for the App. I'll do direction and design, good fun. Think I mentioned I'm a creative, but I can do most things.

'Something that might interest you.'

They pull up their chairs and I wave to the girl at the counter for flat whites and neat blacks, sweet as a stolen kiss.

'This is big. You're on the team. You are going to change the world. You will redefine how people think about work, about their jobs, about their bosses.'

I swivel the laptop and show them the draft I did yesterday in twenty-three minutes, images of healthy young people with smiling faces, on your side, ready to help, and the text:

Henry's Helpers – Free For a Day.
Click the App – and you're in.
Anything you want – taking the kids to school, sorting the shopping, painting a window, looking after granny, giving your garden a makeover, fixing your TV, being your friend.
The Only Limit – Your Imagination!

'The Henry's Helper Lottery. The prize – someone who'll work for you for a day. No questions, they'll do whatever you want. Your job is to sell the idea – get people to click the App. Click and you might win a Helper for the day. Local papers, radio, leafleting, Facebook, anything you can think of. This is just the pilot, if it catches on, we go national, maybe international – and you're on the ground floor. We'll start in Dagenham and roll out across London.'

They look puzzled and Jimmy asks:

'Where's Dagenham?'

'Lot of journalists in Dagenham these days – first the Great Jobs Riot, now a by-election. We'll give 'em something to write about.'

Makepeace sits in a darkened room with cigarette-smoke in his nostrils and dreams of a future where people work for food. He talks of the public interest, of his duty. He thinks he can use Nic as a bargaining counter. Let's see how his ideas work out in the real world. He wants forced labour – that's what his Jobs Guarantee is – and he thinks I'm going to make it fun. Sure I am. I'm going to bring it home, on your street, in your house. Henry loves the idea of people on the dole working for free. So does Elsa. Will anyone else? People aren't fools. Just so long as they know who to blame.

We did the post-production in Shoreditch in five days. Same suite as I did the George Cross work in, when I thought integrity was the easy option.

There's something I need to do while they check and sequence and shave and re-light and whatever else they do to all those images with the courteous middle-class voiceover so you know it's all respectable: willing young women and men, black, brown and white, pushing lawn-movers and cleaning windows and wheeling your children to the nursery and shopping and nipping up a ladder to sort your roof-tiles and cooking your lunch and carting your rubbish down to the tip in a wheelbarrow.

I prise open my penknife, the bone-handled one Grandad gave me for my tenth birthday. Don't think he asked Dad first. I jab the point down into the wood at the edge of the desk and score it along. I've practiced and I reckon I don't do badly: Ritchie and a flamboyant swirl of underscore. Just so they've got something to remember me by, when they've all forgotten about Dance and Fitzhugh.

Hargreaves comes along with his hesitant walk and his tablet to show me something I know he's really proud of. I drop a sheet of mock-ups on my art-work. Then the phone buzzes; number withheld, but I know who it is.

I'm not Ritchie anymore. I'm the other one, cold, venal, driven. Someone like Henry Makepeace.

'Mr Morlan. Everything underway?'

'Of course, Mr Makepeace.'

'I take it you're aware that there is no statute of limitation for criminal conspiracy?'

'I shall do what we agreed.'

'Remember. You're doing this for the British people.'

I don't say anything and he rings off.

'Mr Morlan!' Hargreaves is staring at the desk. My knuckles are white and the knife-point is half an inch into the wood.

The Henry's Helper Lottery takes off. We run it from offices in Barking, in a new block across the road from the District Line station. Beige carpets and the sharp smell of paint and cleaning fluid, like a school on the first day of term. I can feel the shiver going through the staff when I make my entrance and walk through the main office, shaking hands, greeting them all by name. This is my world. Otto and his team have a separate section where they can eat pizza and drink whisky and Red Bull and play tricks on each other. I know the software is mostly borrowed from existing apps, but who cares? Makepeace is paying. I've got a transport and logistics manager, an accounts section, an administrator, a clothing team and a press secretary.

Laurie manages the human resources side. I met him when he worked for *Democratic Answers*, at that time the biggest survey firm in the UK. Dance and Fitzhugh commissioned analysis and reports from them. Their bread and butter was the big voter surveys. I didn't have much to do with that, it was always Elsa's territory, and the firm grew fat on it. She had good contacts with the money men, the people who knew which party they wanted in government and were willing to pay for it. Her dad ran a derivatives consultancy in the City, she never talked about what he did.

Laurie dealt with the free-lance interviewers, mostly women, over two hundred on a full sample national survey with face to face interviews before everything went on-line, and each of them on zero hours and desperate for a decent wage. He did it every day for seventeen years. He's a short, stout, balding man with a Pickwick face and a jovial manner. He always listens and then he tells you what will happen. And it does, only slightly over budget.

We meet up in a pub off Gracechurch Street. He doesn't say anything disloyal about Elsa but when I tell him it's a whole new venture, face to face, and I'm running it and he's in if he wants, his eyes light up and he chuckles.

I attend the Helper briefings in a church hall off the Woodward Road, hired by the day, cash in advance. The room's cold and smells of tea. No-one knows who I am, and I keep quiet. We advertise round the night shelters, "Big Issue" and on Facebook, but mostly word of mouth. Get it on Facebook, tell a few key people and it runs by itself. We contact the benefit offices and give them the big sell, I do it myself. They can't wait, they're so keen to get the claimants off their books you'd think it was Christmas. They haven't worked it out yet. When we're in business all they'll need is a sign in the door telling people to try Henry's Helpers, then where will their jobs be?

Nine out of ten of them are younger people, men and women, some of them quite decently dressed, with anoraks or coats and hats. They look straight at you, as if they're weighing you up, not that voiceless appeal with the furtive eyes, when they're squatting on the pavement with a cardboard sign. You can tell who they are by their footwear: trainers, too thin for the weather, or broken-down boots that don't fit. Not one of them, and there are more than a hundred, is overweight.

They crowd into the room, some of them standing in groups at the back. The coffee and biscuits run out in the first ten minutes and I send Abdi, Laurie's assistant, out for more. Abdi almost runs, he's anxious to get everything right. They mostly wait, not talking, not committing themselves, as if they've been disappointed before. Some of them stuff the biscuits in their pockets. They don't care that Laurie can see them doing it.

Laurie leads. He explains the scheme, going over everything twice. He doesn't actually say they are going to be prizes in a lottery. There's uproar.

'What the fuck! It's crazy.' A grey-haired man breaks in before Laurie's finished. His face is red as crushed mulberries and he keeps his overcoat on. 'You got me here for this?'

A young lad in a Union of Precarious Workers T-shirt with the clenched fist logo who sits in the front row is on his feet shouting at us:

'I ain't doing that.'

'It's a joke.'

'When do we get the food?'

'Who the hell are you?'

Laurie hears them out. He doesn't laugh at them. A black woman with tight curled hair in a green jumper and a black skirt, who keeps her coat folded over her arm, asks

'Is it legal?'

He looks over at me.

'100 per cent,' I say. 'We've checked it out with the police.'

The Home Secretary runs the police doesn't he?

She sits down.

Laurie holds up his hand and doesn't speak until he's sure he has their attention. This is the bit I didn't mention to Makepeace and Elsa. They think people'll be happy to sign up as Helpers in exchange for food and a bed, when they find they can't get their benefits any more. Big mistake.

'Don't forget we're paying you. £100 for the first day – 8.00am to 6.00 pm. Think of it as super-charged bob-a-job. We'll pay the first day and see how it goes from there.'

Someone whistles and the rest go silent. More than minimum wage: no-one's used to that. They don't understand it, most of them don't trust it, but what choice have they got? Wait for day two.

Laurie holds up his hand again though he doesn't need to.

'You need to sign up if you want the work. Start in three days. We'll bus you round to the lottery winners. Remember: best behaviour. Any problems, no money. Let me repeat: any problems, no money. And wear the T-shirts. You can have anything you like on under them.'

Abdi's handing them round.

A young woman wrapped in a red hospital blanket waves a hand.

'Why's it say "Henry's" on the T-shirts?'

'No reason. Just a bit of branding.'

I find a chair. We've got a bullet-point checklist: not much use to a lot of the Helpers, you have to go through

158

everything and then go through it again. This is going to work. I feel good about it. It's a big operation. Quite a while since I ran something like this, but it'll go so smoothly you'd think it was greased with goose fat. Trust me.

Laurie gives me a thumbs up.

Breakfast TV

Three days later. I wake at 6.00am and I'm at the window before I realise the hiss of rain woke me up. It's pelting down, too much for the drains. I hate it, not today, today matters, it's the big day, day one for Henry's Helpers. This'll kill it. I sit down, as tired as if I hadn't slept, and my thoughts come slowly. I did my best. What use is that?

The roadway is awash. The streetlights gleam on dark water, flicker and go out as one, leaving a glow on the back of the eye. Only a couple of people on the street, their umbrellas up against the downpour. It's no use, their feet will be sodden.

A bus butts its way into the flood in the dip opposite, nearly makes it through, and stalls, blocking the road. Its lights dim as the starter motor engages but the engine won't fire. One of the passengers, a young woman in a shop-worker's tabard, stands in the road by the door helping people down, ignoring the water round her knees. The bus is still there when I look out later.

No fun trying to get over to Barking, and no need. I make coffee and take up the remote. On second thoughts I put a bowl of porridge in the microwave. My hand aches and I massage it.

I hate early morning TV. I'd rather sit in the living room in my dressing gown and eat porridge and watch what's happening in the street. A breakdown vehicle is trying to get to the bus, but there are too many cars in the way and no-one can move. The clamour of car-horns rises faint through the double glazing. It's warm in the living room.

I can't make much sense of the news. The first item shows a plane coming in to land, no, it's dropping something black that spins and stabilizes. A gout of fire whirls out along the runway, engulfs a hangar and blazes up, orange and red. The running titles across the bottom of the screen say something about arms sales.

The picture cuts to a ship tied up against a quay in the rain. It could be a channel ferry but rust streaks mar the paintwork and I can't see a logo on the funnel. Guards in black uniforms are standing along the quay, arms folded, "Immigration Enforcement" across their shoulders. People file up the gang-plank, young and old, men, women and children. They're carrying suitcases, bedrolls and stuff in carrier bags. Almost all of them are black. Not one of them has a raincoat.

A man in a Fair Isle jersey, a shopping bag in each hand, slips on the damp wood and rests there on one knee as if he's forgotten how to get up. A red plastic fire-engine, the brightest thing on the TV screen, slips out of one of the bags, tumbles down, bounces off the edge of the dock and disappears into the water between ship and quay. The woman behind him gets her arms round him and pulls him to his feet. She's wearing a throwaway yellow poncho. He leans against the side rail for a second then moves forward again, the rain glistening on his hair.

The decks are crammed. People stand against the rails and stare out, not caring that they're soaked.

The picture changes again. People sit round a table, men, all of them white, in suits. That's Makepeace talking and they all gaze at him as if he's Henry V the day after Agincourt. The headline strip at the bottom of the screen reads "'Send home illegals and end the riots,' says Home Secretary'.

The voiceover announces:

'It's party conference season and we'll be discussing the possibility of a leadership challenge later in the programme.'

The host sits on a plump pink sofa, wearing a yellow tailored suit. She talks as if she's more interested in the weather, which is the next item. The younger man sitting beside her is much more animated. Bet you a Paradise Bar against a peanut he thinks he's chatting her up.

We're on to the weather. Dark clouds, rain, footage of fire officers in gleaming rain jackets hauling a Dalmatian into a rubber dinghy. Its paws slip on the wet plastic and one of the officers jumps in, water up to his waist, and pushes it aboard with both hands. The outboard coughs and starts up and the dinghy moves forward. The officer shouts something, you can't hear, but his lips move and he's waving his arms. He trudges after it, ripples spreading on the dark water as he forces his way through.

It might as well be in black and white so far as I'm concerned. I'm enjoying my porridge. I pile on the chopped dates and add a spoonful of sugar. Maybe I'll have a banana. I can't see what the couple on the pink sofa see in each other, they're neither of them interested in the news.

The man remarks 'Looks like the Dagenham West by-election's hotting up', and the woman looks bored.

I lean forward and turn up the sound. Jack's in the studio dressed in a navy blue Marks and Spencer suit, his tie dark, his back straight, despite the sofa.

The young man smiles winningly:

'Everyone loves repatriation. People say Makepeace's Act will swing it for the government. What's your answer?'

'This government stands for the politics of retreat. Britain has so much to offer the world. Why cut ourselves off?'

'And here's one of our viewers from Dagenham West on the line.'

A voice cuts in. 'There's no jobs round here. My son's on the credit. They told him he has to work for these Helpers. What you going to do about that?'

'Henry's Helpers. It's slavery under a different name. My party offers real opportunities. We want a proper National Apprenticeship Scheme, paid apprenticeships with training, so you can get a decent job with a future. This chain-gang government has no answer to the jobs crisis.'

I settle in my chair.

'And here's another viewer.'

'My daughter was mugged at knife-point, now she's scared to go out, she's missed her benefit's interview.'

'I'm so sorry to hear that.' Jack says. His concern comes over in his voice. That's my son, he knows what he's doing.

'We must make the streets safe for our families. We will only solve knife crime if we stop the cuts in police spending. We must invest in real jobs and proper training for young people. I visited a project for young offenders yesterday and I met Jamila, who's working hard to make our streets safe for all of us. How much money does this government give her project? None.'

A film clip of Jack comes on the screen. He's shaking hands with a young woman with close-cropped hair, wearing a leather jacket and dark blue jeans with turn ups. The young woman laughs at something Jack says. A group of young men and women gather round a stripped down car chassis behind her. One of them grips a screw-driver as long as her forearm.

The woman on the sofa breaks in with a new liveliness in her voice as the next item comes up.

'And now – a day when two legs are better than one. These commuters are getting a leg up in the city!'

A young man, head down against the rain, trousers rolled past the knee to show naked white calves, plods along the pavement. He's got a soaking wet T-shirt on over his jacket and you can make out the word "Henry's". A man, suited, overcoat, umbrella held high, is astride his back, knees jutting out, one arm clutching at his neck. A young woman, hatless, in a red anorak overtakes them. She's limping already and she's carrying a college student, in scarf, raincoat and boots. They're everywhere, a man in a flat cap urges his mount to go faster with blows to the shoulder, his mouth gaping in excitement.

'It's the Ministry of Funny Walks, only this time it's really happening.'

The camera zooms in as two bearers collide and fall backwards, their riders spread-eagled on the pavement, briefcases flying open, hats rolling away. If that wasn't staged I'll never touch another double cappuccino.

I should celebrate. Jack's on prime time and Henry's Helpers is taking off. I wanted it all to be fun. It is, people love watching other people get soaked to the skin and then fall over.

Jack cuts in

'It looks like a joke, but it's what this government wants for anyone who's down on their luck. That's what the Jobs Guarantee means. If you can't make ends meet, you work for food, same as if you're the victim of people-traffickers.'

'Some people would say that a job – any job – is better than the dole. Anyway, Henry's Helpers is just a bit of fun isn't it?'

'Not if you're like Claire, whom I met in Dagenham yesterday. She's a hard-working single parent with three kids to feed. She's a trained nursing assistant but she can't find a job that pays enough to cover her nursery fees, her food and her rent. Are they going to put her on the chain gang? I …'

They've cut him off. You need me there, Jack, in the control room, sweet talking the producer.

'Thank you Mr Morlan. Good luck.'

I'll let you into a secret. You may find this hard to believe, but in the Henry's Helper lottery, everyone's a winner. Well, not quite everyone. The Helpers in their white T-shirts are standing on doorsteps and pressing bell-pushes in all the middle-class semi-detached streets in Upminster and Chingford.

The voters'll love it won't they? Your very own free worker for the day. Here's the trick. They don't go away.

There's no budget to pay them for day two and they've got nowhere to go. You asked for them, you look after them.

What's it like, ordering people around, when the gloss has worn off? Do you feed them? Same as you eat? What if you like them? What if you don't? How do you get them to do things they don't want to do? Because you can, you practically own them. Will they have the same expression on their faces as the girl I once saw in a *Refugee+* poster when you ask them? How are you going to feel afterwards?

There'll be a couple of day's confusion but it'll be worth it. Henry Makepeace will take the blame as the man who tried to save the government money by billeting benefit claimers on the middle class. I don't think anyone will vote for that.

I've got a few ideas for Jack's by-election too. This is my time. It's hard to concentrate, I'm fizzing with it. Ritchie Morlan made it happen, Makepeace will lose his chance of leading the party and Jack and Nic will know it's all down to me.

Who are those two men playing dice in an angle on one of the tunnels you walk along at Monument tube station where you change for the District line and it's always either too hot or too cold? They're in jeans and white T-shirts, but they're squatted down opposite each other and I can't read the logo.

Most people ignore them but a black youth with a silver nose-ring and a rainbow striped Rasta hat tosses a pound down. The nearest man plucks it out of the air, bites it, and tosses it back. Someone bursts out laughing. I'm swept on by the crowd.

Your Life Sorted

The sky's clear at Barking, a pearly blue with snowdrift clouds and a washed-clean smell. The street noises sound crisper and the windows gleam on the office block over the road, my offices for my lottery, right in front of me.

A megaphone booms out over the roar of the traffic: 'Shit Government, Shit Jobs'

I've heard that one before.

They're lined up with their placards outside the main entrance, where the brass plate says "Helpers' Lottery", young men and women, black, white, dressed in jeans, coloured sweaters, anoraks and a medley of woolly hats.

I cross over and a young man with a beard like Ben Gunn's and a paint-stained denim jacket thrusts a leaflet into my hand.

I read: 'Who's Stealing Your Job Now?"

"Don't blame immigrants. Henry's Helpers work for food. They'll be doing your job next. You can't trust this chain-gang government! You can't trust Henry Makepeace!"

The picture shows a Helper in a white gown with a T-shirt over it and a nurse's cap. A stethoscope hangs from her neck. She leans over a tiny child, its face pink and puckered with crying, in a hospital incubator cot. It's plain from her tight lips and the way she's standing that she has no idea what to do.

The young man shouts 'Don't trust Henry Makepeace,' half at me, half at the street. His placard carries the slogan "Who Helps Henry's Helpers?" The T-shirt under his jacket reads "Union of Precarious Workers" with the clenched fist symbol. He patrols backwards and forwards across the pavement offering his leaflets to anyone who'll take them.

I push my way past him. The speaker with the megaphone shouts "Henry's Helpers" and the protestors respond "Out! Out! Out!"

You can't see her face but her hair's black and flops over her forehead. She pushes it back and catches sight of me.

'What the fuck!' Her voice roars out like the bellow of a bull. 'I should have known!'

Everyone looks round.

I grab the megaphone and force it away from her mouth.

'Turn that bloody thing off!'

My voice echoes off the office wall. Behind me people are laughing. I find the switch.

'Are you behind this?' she yells. 'What the fuck are you doing?'

'Cool down.'

'No way.' She shouts to the street: 'Henry's Helpers, close them down!'

'It's not what it seems. Can we talk?'

We're in the lobby. She's got the hood of her sweatshirt up and she thrusts her hands down into the pockets. She bites hard at her lower lip. Outside the demonstrators still hold their placards up but they've stopped leafletting to stare at us through the glass door.

'Let me explain.' Look her full in the face. Don't talk too fast. 'It's like I told you. Makepeace thinks I'm on his team. That was the deal: I do this and he sends in the police and they get you out.'

She screws up her eyes and shakes her head from side to side. She's mumbling something. I can't hear what it is. I touch her shoulder but she shoves my hand away.

I'm still talking.

'I had to do it. I couldn't lose you, I just couldn't. I'm sorry.'

She stares at me. She starts to talk, then hesitates.

'Wow.'

She's thinking. I press on.

'It's going to be OK. Makepeace thinks the Henry's Helpers stunt is to get people used to the idea of forced labour. That's why I branded it Henry's Helpers – pin it on him. I'm betting it'll backfire, especially round here. I'll make damn sure it will. "Your Life Sorted" sounds good, but not if it's working for nothing and being ordered around. And I think most people will be uneasy when they're face to face with how divided our society has become. The lottery winners won't thank Makepeace. And Henry's Helpers will hate him.'

'Jack's by-election,' she says. 'You cunning bastard.'

She punches me in the ribs. I rub at it, over my heart.

She strides across to the other side of the lobby and back.

'By the way, how's your hand?'

'Still works.' I keep it in my pocket. I bound it up tight this morning. Take the pills and don't think about it.

She's still talking.

'Great idea – show 'em what forced labour really means – for both sides. Choke 'em with cake. I'd better talk to the gang.'

She's off, through the doors. I drop into the nearest chair. It's going to be OK. She swings round to talk to one then another of the demonstrators, gesticulating with the megaphone. The young man with the beard is arguing with her, jabbing his finger at Nic's chest. I want to go up to him and tell him to pick on someone his own size.

A couple of the others lower their banners and start across the road towards the tube station. A delivery van skids to a halt and the driver jams the heel of his hand down on the horn.

For answer the demonstrators hold up the placards. Some of the others follow them. Nic gives a thumbs up and the bearded protestor starts shouting at the van driver.

I can breathe again.

Nic's back in the lobby.

'Let's get this show on the road.'

She's off, leaping up the stairs ahead of me.

'I'll catch you up. Let me sit down a minute.'

One thing I didn't tell her: the real deal, the conspiracy charge, always there, the wolf in the shadows, with its yellow eyes fixed only on her. I'm the guardian, between the camp-fire and the forest. At least I can do that for her.

Nic and I are in the main office on the third floor. I watch Laurie through the glass partition. He's listening to someone on his mobile, his eyes fixed on the view towards the towers of Canary Wharf. Grey clouds mass over the Olympic Centre, spreading out towards us.

I get the packet of chocolate biscuits out of the desk drawer.

'So you think I got it right, for once?'

She grins sideways, like she always does.

'Cool.'

Laurie enters with a free newspaper in his hand and a couple of tabloids under his arm.

'What you wanted, isn't it?'

He points to the headline:

"Your Life Sorted?"

A picture of a young black man in a Helper T-shirt fills the front page. He pushes a wheelchair with one hand and tows a buggy with the other.

> *"The Henry's Helpers lottery gets the thumbs up today, as thousands of lucky winners make full use of their prize person. Helpers – just for today – dig the garden, shop, do the school run, look after granny or paint your spare room, you name it. Shrewd citizens put their Helpers to work – and why not?"*

Interviews, more pictures, a cartoon of the PM's Helper answering the questions for her in Parliament, favourable but jokey editorial comment. "Cut-price bob-a-job week"; "Henry's Holiday – London lets the Helpers take the strain"; "Everyone a winner".

'Seems good to me.'

Nic grabs at the paper.

'God, can't they see what's in front of their face? They all think it's a joke. Same old story, nobody makes the connections, nobody takes it seriously. Slavery's always somewhere else.'

'Wait. We haven't had the pay-off yet.'

"Drivetime News: London gripped by Helper holiday. A new fun lottery lightens up the winter gloom with a novelty prize as Londoners make the most of their Helper for a day..."

Nic's busy on her laptop. She's checking on Jack's campaign, looking up at me from time to time, as if she's not sure I'm still going to be there. I check the time – 7.30pm. That's when the Lottery ends and everyone goes home.

'There's a lot on what to expect from the party conferences. Makepeace is getting a lot of coverage. Jack's still hammering the Helpers. "Real jobs with real pay, not fake jobs for one day". He's in with a chance.'

'He's got more than that. He's Jack.'

I know he'll win. Don't ask me how, I know.

By 8.30pm the news feeds have stopped treating it as fun:

"We're getting reports of incidents in suburban areas as Helpers refuse to leave their winners' homes. The way

the rain's coming down, who can blame them?"

The main evening news makes it a law and order problem, first item. A film clip shows a police constable, his cape glistening in the rain as he leads a Helper out of the front gate of a Chigwell semi. A small dark-haired child in Wonder Woman pyjamas stands in the porch and waves goodbye with one hand. She clutches onto her father's leg with the other. The Helper is tall and thin and her hair is matted on her head. A door slams at a house up the road and the camera swings round to show another Helper pressing the bell-push to get back in. A woman constable takes him by the arm and pulls him away. A third Helper stands by the gate waiting for them, his T-shirt sodden and clinging to him.

A superintendent, an older woman with red hair tied back and the green eyes and pale skin that sometimes go with it addresses the camera:

'We will enforce the Vagrancy Acts. There will be no beggars on the streets of London. But this is not a policing issue. We are receiving complaints about Helpers remaining in people's homes at the end of the Lottery. We can ask them to leave, but there is nothing we can charge them with.'

The screen shows footage of Helpers being released on Hackney Marshes, on the verge of the A13 and in side roads off the North Circular. Camera crews must be following the police vans. And the Helpers? Some of them just stand there, shoulders hunched, arms wrapped round their chests, but most of them set off the way they came. Bet you they're trying to find their way back to the people who won them.

And then it's Makepeace. His aide, a young man with an intern paperclip bracelet, holds an umbrella over him on the House of Commons steps while his own best suit is soaked.

'I take full responsibility for the Helpers scheme. Rest assured everything is being done to contain the small number of unfortunate incidents. We all of us have a duty as well as a right to work. That applies to me, to you and even more to Henry's Helpers. We need a stronger business model. I am bringing the "Your Life Sorted" lottery to an end. I have established a partnership with a leading provider of skilled labour, HelpCo, to ensure discipline. HelpCo centres will provide food and beds for Helpers and hire them out to local businesses. Individual citizens will not need to deal with Helpers.'

'"When Helpers go bad".' Nic laughs. 'It's like the horror film when the birthday party clown kidnaps the baby. Calling it HelpCo won't solve anything – he doesn't know what he's doing.'

Laurie shrugs, 'Maybe. I'm just here to do a job.'

'Sure,' I say. 'Look at his hand, he's desperate for a fag.' But I don't trust him. No-one said anything about HelpCo when we talked this through, Elsa, Makepeace and I.

The TV presenter continues:

'We understand HelpCo is wholly owned by Dance and Fitzhugh. We contacted them but the Chief Executive, Ms Elsa Dance, is not currently available for interview.'

I blink and stare at the screen.

Nic pats me on the shoulder.

'You OK? You look as if you've seen a ghost.'

'It's nothing.' I can't take me eyes off the screen. She yawns.

'Let's go home. Nothing to do here and I bet you the cops'll be round at some stage. I need a drink.'

'No you don't.'

HelpCo

Next day's different. Breakfast TV can't make up its mind. The first item is a heart-warming report about a school-teacher who's taken her Helper in as classroom assistant. The mini-people with serious faces in their pink check dresses and brown cardigans and jumpers and grey shorts squat round in a half-circle. They ask the grey-haired man in cracked boots what he did before he was a Helper. He says something that makes me sit forward and spill three drops of coffee on my carpet.

'I was a bit lost. Now I think I've found my way.'

He looks up at them and a small boy in a red home-knit pullover starts clapping and the whole class cheers and he smiles and bows his head.

The host, in a blue jacket with wide lapels and a thin silver necklace for today, puts on her serious expression, mouth straight, and looks directly into the camera.

'Henry's Helpers. We reported problems with Helpers who remained in their winner's homes last night and expected to be looked after. Now the new government agency, HelpCo, has stepped in.'

The film-clip shows a group of Helpers, men and women, perhaps twenty of them, in uniform blue boiler suits under canary yellow T-shirts, clustered on the

Heathway in Dagenham just along from the station. The T-shirts bear the one word "HelpCo" in green italics. At least the rain's stopped. They stand with their backs straight and look round them.

A neatly printed sign reads:

"For Hire: Willing Workers, Ready For Anything. HelpCo Accredited."

A young man with wavy gold-brown hair holding a yellow computer tablet stands to one side, scanning passers-by. He wears a silver-grey three-piece suit, Jack's got one like it. He turns to face the camera and I stare at the screen.

'Local businesspeople are organising Helpers and hiring them out. Our reporter, Jane Tompenny, is on the scene.'

A young woman in a green jacket steps forward and holds out a microphone. She addresses one of the Helpers.

'My viewers are curious. What are you doing here?'

The Helper, in his twenties, with dark eyes and a rose tattoo on his neck, laughs.

'You ask the boss. He looks after us.'

The young man steps forward.

'I'm sure I can help. Perhaps you could use someone to carry your equipment? Organise your schedule? We've a range of skills available here. Jed has a clean driving license and Melody here has level 1 secretarial skills. We're quick learners. I'm sure Winston has experience of video editing.'

'But these are Helpers. Everyone wants to know: how much do you pay them?'

'I am accredited by HelpCo. I assure you I look after my workers.' He turns. 'That's the truth isn't it?'

'Certainly is,' shouts the guy with the tattoo and the others cheer.

'Remember, these are the people society left behind. They have nothing, some of them not even a bed to sleep in. Now I offer them food and a roof over their heads. They are part of society.'

He turns to the workers and raises his voice: 'Our lives are Sorted.'

They shout back: 'Sorted! We are Sorted!'

A van drives up and the driver beckons him over. They talk briefly and shake hands. The gang-master nods to the interviewer.

'Excuse me. Business.'

The Helpers shuffle slowly forward, their heads down. Deep within me something shifts, uneasily. Images of other scenes, other times flash into my mind. The lines of slaves dragging the blocks for the Pyramids? The Coliseum? Stonehenge? A chain gang trudging towards the Louisiana cotton harvest? Captives forced to toil for war-lords in the gold mines of the Congo? I blink and shake my head to clear it. None of that could happen here.

He slaps the side of the van with a riding crop. He must have been holding it along the edge of the tablet.

'All aboard! Chop chop!'

The Helpers file past him and crouch to pack themselves inside, he slams the rear doors, climbs in beside the driver and they're off.

The stream of people on the pavement checks as an older man in a powered wheel chair halts to stare at the camera.

Back in the studio, the presenter looks puzzled.

'Are we seeing the first steps towards a new workforce? Or is this just a one day wonder? Phone our number and tell us what you think.'

I flip to the other channel just in time to catch the lead item:

'The Real Jobs demonstrations in Whitehall continue. We're informed that all police leave is cancelled and that officers are being bussed in from as far away as Sheffield."

The film clip is shot from behind police lines and shows the officers in close-up, grim behind their visors, and almost all of them under twenty-five. The demonstrators are glimpsed through the riot shields and you can't make out their faces. The shouted slogans blur into a baying roar, and the banners are a muddled smudge.

Someone blows a blast on a whistle and the mob falls silent for a second and then the chant sounds out clearly:

'Real Jobs, Real Pay. Real Jobs, Real Pay.'

The young officer next to the camera tenses, closes his eyes for a second, and flicks them open. The wall of shields parts. Mounted officers armed with truncheons charge through, the hooves of the lead horse striking sparks from the road. I glimpse the "Real Jobs" placards held up by men and women, some of them in white T-shirts, terror in their faces. A woman with long fair hair in the front row screams and ducks down, her hands over her head. The chestnut stallion rears up as the officer strikes down at her, and the screen cuts back to the studio.

'And now we have Mr Henry Makepeace.'

Makepeace has dark stains under his eyes and his cheeks are flushed. He smiles his general smile and speaks as if he wishes to educate the viewer.

'The subversives and illegals in our society are still seeking to make trouble for ordinary law-abiding citizens. They claim that there's a job's crisis. There is no such thing. Our police force has the situation well in hand.'

'Mr Makepeace, we're getting reports of heavy-handed policing. Seventeen demonstrators were admitted to Emergency Care at Central Middlesex Hospital, many with head wounds consistent with a beating by mounted officers.'

'Exactly. Our police are highly trained and use the minimum necessary force. The statistics you mention show just how far these rioters are prepared to go to incite violence. We must stamp this out. The Repatriation Act allows us to expel all illegals. My Jobs Guarantee will make sure the trouble-makers are put to work where they can be of use to the community.'

'Thank you. And are the Helpers all volunteers?'

'These people are carefully selected. They need discipline. Our focus must be on what is in their best interests.'

'I see. And now Jenny Gallagher with the sport.'

It's the same for the rest of the day. More on HelpCo mobilising the Helpers across London and demonstrators clashing with the police. Half the time it's fun, half the time it's law and order. No-one interviews a demonstrator.

HelpCo, gang-masters with riding crops, that was never in the plan. There's a snicker at the back of my head, just at the threshold of hearing. Elsa. Elsa laughing at me.

It's the same the next day. I'm getting used to Breakfast News.

My mobile rings.

'It's gone pear-shaped.'

'What?'

It's Nic. I can barely hear her.

'They've adapted.'

'Who've adapted? Nic, have you had your pill yet?'

'Pills don't solve anything. People get used to things, you never thought of that. They find somewhere for the Helper, a shed, the back of the garage. Your own little household slave – thanks to Henry.' The phone rattles. She's dropped it. 'Now business has moved in. Why pay wages when you can get free workers? You see gangs of them for hire, on street corners, dead cheap. HelpCo's taking over. Fucking brilliant!'

'Nic, have you been drinking? Are you OK?'

'Just a couple.'

'Half past nine?'

'Christ, Dad, what do you expect? We've just done – you've just done – it's the biggest fuck-up in history.' Her voice recedes then booms back 'You've brought back slavery and everybody loves it.'

'I'll be with you ASAP. Just hang on. Where are you?'

She's laughing, she's laughing at me, as if she isn't going to stop. Something squeezes at my heart. I start to ring for a taxi. It'll be quicker from the main road. I slam the front door behind me, still tapping in the destination, and step off the kerb without looking. The vehicle that nearly knocks me down is on its way to the rank at the station.

The door of her flat's standing open and there's no sign of her. I find her in the nearest pub, "The Artificer's Mate", brand-new and fitted in on the ground floor of a twenty-storey block next to a supermarket. Inside, it's like a glossy shed, everything faux, everything wipe-clean, from the varnished wood benches to the plastic cushions to the beer-engines to the sporting prints on the wall.

It's 10am. The door stands open. Three customers lean against the bar, glad of the entertainment.

'She yours?'

A brown-haired woman with blue-grey eyes and delicate features leads Nic forward. She stands swaying until the woman gives her a push and she collapses into my arms. She's a dead weight, her head on my shoulder, breathing heavily like a sleeping child.

'Wake up, Nic.'

Over her shoulder I see the woman fold her arms.

'How can I thank you?'

'Take her home.'

I take a pace backwards and collapse onto a bench. Nic flops sideways, the lop-sided grin across her face. I pinch her nose. She shakes her head like a baffled spaniel and mumbles something. The woman looks to the loafers by the bar.

One of them, an older man, shrugs.

'Henry'll give him a hand.'

The woman nods and the man whistles.

Henry's been behind the bar all the time. He's at least as old as the man on the bar-stool. He's dressed in trainers, jeans and a yellow HelpCo T-shirt.

I take one look at him

'Aren't you cold?'

He looks at me, blinks and looks down. He fails to get Nic on her feet at the first attempt, but the woman helps us up and we totter forward, all leaning on each other. The rain has started again and we're on the pavement when the taxi comes. I offer him a twenty and he looks at it, turns and goes back inside, his T-shirt soaked.

The driver's got the door locked.

'It's £125 if she pukes.'

I show him my wallet and he opens the door. I give him my address.

The radio's playing some tune I've heard before, all about Henry and his Helpers. It's the jingle Hargreaves was so pleased with.

The driver points to a vehicle ahead of us with a yellow pennant fluttering from the aerial and "HelpCo" in green italics across the back window.

'Glad I get my pension next year. This business has had it.'

Nic fiddles with the window and I reach over and open it. She sticks her head out and vomits and falls back on the seat. My bruise aches and I press on it with my other hand and there's a stab of pain that stops the thinking for a few seconds.

'I love you, Nic.'

She doesn't answer. She's asleep, curled against me.

Speech of a Leader

The *Sun's* headline is 80-point: "*Helping Me, Helping You*" alongside a picture of a smiling Helper hooking a bin onto the back of a rubbish truck. The *Mail* goes with: "*Pregnant Helper Delivers Own Baby.*" The Mirror has: "*Henry's Chain-Gang.*" The *Guardian* headline reads: "*Controversial Helper Scheme Denies Human Rights, says Archbishop.*" The *Financial Times* comments: "*No-wage HelpCo Boosts Service Sector.*" The *Times* has a full-page interview with Elsa Dance "the ethical advertising guru." *Cosmopolitan* runs the entire issue on sex-slaves and celebrity fashion.

Nic's tucked up in my bed and I'm outside the newsagent at the corner of the road. It's still raining. You think it's just drizzle but it's the kind that soaks you through a raincoat.

Makepeace's speech opens the party conference this afternoon, the one I wrote for him. Maybe it won't quite play the way he thinks it will. We're in with a chance. I coached him enough times.

There was a short piece on the Breakfast News about Helpers with placards in Trafalgar Square "Shit Government, Shit Jobs" and "Helpers Are People – Just Like You". The young woman leading them addresses the camera:

'Most people I meet support us. We want to work but we need a wage we can live off, not a bunk in a HelpCo warehouse and bread and soup.'

Then the police arrive and the interview ends.

Jack's been on TV again, on *Overview*, arguing for a decent youth service, jobs with better prospects, training programmes, real apprenticeships, anything to give young people a future where they can succeed. All the other side can talk about is the duty to work and HelpCo and lock 'em up. By-election next week.

I'd help if he let me. I walk on.

Helpers in T-shirts, most of them the yellow HelpCo ones, keep bustling past me, most with shopping bags or push-chairs, one or two pushing loads in wheelbarrows. A white van parks by the building site up the road. A tall woman in a trench-coat, yellow helmet and work-boots stands by the gate, her umbrella sheltering the yellow tablet in her hand. A riding crop dangles from her other hand. The van driver flings open the back doors and the workers get out and trudge through the gates, no helmets, no boots, just trainers or plimsolls. The yellow T-shirts stick to their backs. The one at the end sucks at the palm of his hand. There's a weal across it, as if someone's struck him with a whip. I hold my hand up and point to the bandage round it. He stares at me and doesn't grin. The woman taps his shoulder with the riding crop and lets the tip of the shaft slide across his cheek like a tongue.

I pass the Waitrose at the corner. A couple of older men chat over their trolleys, blocking the aisle. The rest of the customers, in yellow T-shirts with "HelpCo Shopping

Service" on them, are grouped behind them, shopping lists in their hands, silent, waiting. I keep walking. My feet are soaked through, the water squeezes through the uppers in tiny bubbles. Don't know why I put Nic's trainers on when I came out. Because I wanted to find out what it's like to be her when she's out in the rain.

My hand aches. I stop by a bin, uncoil the bandage and drop it in. The back of my hand's yellow, mottled with grey. I hold it out and let the rain wash over it.

I should get some food and go home, see how Nic's getting on. She likes bacon, she's never said that but you should see her with a bacon butty. Or two. What if she's right and HelpCo catches on and becomes part of the scenery?

I walk past the butchers and keep going. It's not until I get to Archway Road and nearly walk into a Helper half-running towards me, pushing an older man with no hat slumped sideways in a wheelchair, that I turn round. Doubt if Nic's woken up yet. I go into a café and order a cappuccino.

Opposite me there's a poster half the height of building. Henry Makepeace smiles down, looking as if he's just heard they're putting him up for Archbishop. The slogan reads "Your Life Sorted" in block capitals. One of mine.

The doormat is covered in yellow flyers – HelpCo gardening, home help, education, taxis, pizza delivery, financial advice, anything you can think of – and the flat smells of burnt toast. Nic's sitting in front of the TV in her pyjamas with the batteries from the smoke alarm on the table in front of her. She dips a spoon into the marmalade jar.

I put the package of bacon on the side table and get her a glass of water.

'Good to see you up. How are you feeling? Do you want a tray?'

She's hunched forward, the knobs of her spine showing through the material like sugar lumps. I get the rug from the other sofa and wrap it round her. Her hand, with the spoon dripping marmalade, quivers with excitement

'Look, it's that bastard. Hate him. Big speech in two minutes.'

'Yup. This could turn out OK. No one in their right mind will go for HelpCo.'

'God, I hope so.'

I hand her the glass. She stares at me.

'Careful, you'll spill it. Are you OK?'

My good hand's shaking.

Makepeace's speech opens the conference. It's a prime slot, always gets a lot of coverage. The hall's packed and they delay the start so they can get everyone in. Henry's near the front, standing, chatting to the leader. She laughs at something he says, both of them conscious of the cameras. He touches her elbow while she's still talking, turns and walks rapidly up the steps, leaving her to return to her seat in the front row. The audience applaud and a ripple of excitement runs through the room. I have a bad feeling about this. I sit down.

He stands centre stage and holds up both hands, half-bowing to the audience. He's wearing a three-piece suit, half-eye glasses, his hair brushed back and his hands clasped in front of him. He doesn't smile. Gravitas. No jokes. This speech matters, they are going to have to pay attention. People find their seats, the rustling in the hall dies away.

No auto-cue, none of this slick modern stuff, just an oak lectern, like a pulpit, and a sheaf of notes. You're trustworthy, the same way that politicians were once, you're a statesman not a chancer. I explained it all to him and he sat back with a cigarette in his hand, not smoking, and didn't interrupt.

He hits them with the patriotic stuff. That's standard, they're used to that – comfortable applause. He's good at it, his rubicund face glows with passion, he shouts out:

'Make Britain great again! Make the British people great again!'

I talked him out of 'Put the Great back in Great Britain'. The PM used that one last year, and the year before.

Some modest references to the Immigrant Repatriation Act – only once 'my Act' – and of course the line 'Now we stand alone – and proud of it.' That gets them on their feet.

Now you make your bid, Mr Makepeace, like I told you. This could still work out.

'Watch this, Nic. This is the bit.'

Nic glances at me, as if she'd forgotten I was in the room. She goes back to the screen. My mouth is dry, but I don't leave the TV.

The next line is about security. We rehearsed it in his office, keeping it slow:

'I tell you, in all honesty: if you want the future you deserve, you must work for it. That's what my New Deal for Workers does. No nanny state rules to hold you back. No one dodging off just because you've had a baby. No interfering lawyers going on about equal pay or double time or the minimum wage. It's up to you, the only limit is your imagination.'

He rests one hand on his notes and surveys the audience.

'The right to work. Yes, everyone should have a right to work. We also have a duty to work. What no-one has is a right to be paid for doing nothing. And no-one has a right to be paid more than they're worth. If you don't like what you're paid, go and work for somebody else.'

The money men might fall for that. I don't think voters will, when they find out what it means, especially the ones with jobs.

Nic's out of her chair, she can't stand still.

'You bastard. Tonypandy, Grunwick, Orgreave, people fought for those rights.'

Makepeace'll talk about the Jobs Guarantee next, a.k.a. Henry's Helpers, because that's what people will think of as soon as he says the word "Guarantee". I've made sure of that. It's simple. You want to live, you have to work – and maybe you just work for food in a HelpCo barracks.

The Jobs Guarantee solves everything: unemployment, layabouts on benefits, street homelessness – the problem of getting cheap, docile workers when you need them. It started as a joke that turned into forced labour for the Helpers and an embarrassment for the citizens who have helpers in their homes they feel they have to look after. Now it's people in white and yellow T-shirts who steal your job and demonstrate in Whitehall. He can't wash his hands of it, however much he tells people it's nothing to do with him. HelpCo is just a front for modern slavery, anyone can see that. Can't they?

It's a good speech. One of mine, but by the end he thought it was all his idea.

'Now's your time Mr Makepeace,' I told him. 'Tell people what you really believe. Honesty. Trustworthiness. A track-record of success. That's what people want above everything in a leader. They think politicians are out to cheat them. That's the number one finding of every focus group, every survey we've ever run.'

He looked up at me and nodded slowly. He forgot about the cigarette until it burnt right down.

'Tell them what you really, truly want for Britain. Freedom to work, for what you're worth. They'll be no more workers' rights, no more minimum wage, none of that nanny state stuff. Work will be a duty. That's what the Jobs Guarantee means. The simple truth. Speak from the heart, so everyone knows you mean it. You want to live, you have to work, and you get paid what the boss thinks you're worth. Your life sorted.'

I take a deep breath and let it out slowly. He's going to tell them he's solved all their problems by making slavery legal. He thinks they'll like the idea.

Makepeace looks straight into the camera. For an instant it's as if he's staring right at me. He snatches up the papers and flings them in the air, so the sheets sail out over his audience.

Nic's hopping from one foot to the other.

'What the fuck?'

The blood pulses in my wrist and my hand aches. Say it, Makepeace. Say it. "Your Life Sorted." Tell them what it means. You haven't got a job, you work for food.

Makepeace walks away from the lectern and stands right at the front of the platform, hands open, arms wide.

'Let me be honest with you. That's the speech they wrote for me, the clever people who wear posh suits and go to private schools and run focus groups. It's not my speech, it's not who I am, it's not what I believe in.'

He bows his head a moment and I stare at the screen. This is not the script. You bastard, you lying bastard. We had an agreement.

'I came into politics for the same reason that many in my party did, because it seemed the right thing to do. Yes, perhaps it sounds naïve. I wanted to make the world a better place, a kinder place, a freer place. I wanted ordinary people to be able to choose – who they live alongside, who they work for, who they want to help. I wanted all of that.'

He pauses and brings his hands together, almost as if he's praying.

'Many of my colleagues in this great party, all those who serve, on councils, for the voluntary groups at the heart of our communities, for their parishes, their firms, their towns and villages, in our army and navy and air force, will tell you the same thing. And those who serve as MPs, as Ministers of the Crown and as our leader and our Prime Minister. We are proud to serve you, to serve the people of this great nation.'

The hall is completely silent. He lowers his voice so that it thrills into every corner of the room. Even on a TV screen you can sense his ardour. I coached him in that, but not these words, never these words.

'Honesty. The simple truth. No politician has ever stood on this platform and told you this. But it is the simple truth. I want to serve.'

He raises his voice and shouts out:

'I want to lead our great party. I want to be Prime Minister. I want it so much I'll work every hour of the day and night for you. I will do this. I will do it for you.'

Someone in the front row gasps and a great roar of sound surges forward from the body of the hall.

Makepeace raises his hand.

'In all humility I offer the only thing I can offer. I offer leadership.'

He bows his head again, sucks air into his lungs and bellows, so loud that the TV vibrates:

'I will serve!'

Everyone in the hall, men and women, old and young, is on their feet, waving fists, membership cards, programmes and union flags. An older man, right in front of the camera, leans forward on two sticks, shouting, his mouth wide open and his eyes screwed shut. A younger woman in a pinstripe trouser suit shoves past him, joining the press of people crowding the gangways and forcing their way towards the platform.

Someone shouts out above it all 'Makepeace!' so loud it echoes in the hall. You think that's spontaneous? Not many people can shout like that. That's one of Elsa's tricks, I know it. He's earned his five hundred.

The rest of them, the rank and file, take it up:

'Makepeace! Makepeace! Makepeace!'

The camera focuses in on the PM in the front row. She's gaping at the platform, her mouth wide open. The person next to her, the Chancellor, Galton, white hair and black-framed glasses, has a hand on her shoulder.

I can't breathe. My throat's constricted and my heart is swelling, pounding, filling my chest.

Nic holds the water out to me.

'Dad. Are you OK?'

Makepeace has both hands in the air. He shouts the words as if he'd just thought them up.

'There. I tell you the truth, nothing but the truth. I want to be Prime Minister because I can do it better. Together we will build a nation that you, that we all, that Britons will be proud to live in. Immigration is at an end. Britain stands or falls by itself unaided. We are alone in a world that hates us. Let it fear us!'

He pumps his fist into the air.

'We will stand!'

Nic's staring at me.

'What the fuck? They believe him? That toe-rag?'

I don't answer her. Henry's Helpers? Forced labour, in plain sight, on the streets of London? He didn't mention it.

Nic shakes her head and bursts into tears. I want to throw my arms round her, fold her against me, keep her there, keep her safe. I want not to be this person, not to be doing this. I want everything to be easy and simple.

My phone buzzes. I think it's Hugo but I'm not sure. He's one of Makepeace's aides. They all have Eton accents and immaculate casual suits, I can never tell the difference between them.

'Mr Makepeace asked me to contact you. He wanted me to say how grateful he is for your advice about sincerity, about speaking from the heart. He apologises for altering a few words. He will not forget what you have done for him and for Britain.'

'But ... he butchered my speech. Put him on the line.'

'Sorry.' Someone's shouting at him in the background. 'People are rather excited here, I have to go.'

The phone goes dead.

Nic's right – I screwed up. Touch pitch and be defiled. Whoever said that probably didn't have children.

'I can't begin to explain. I'm going for a walk. There's some bacon here if you feel like it.'

I have to find a way out of this.

Margate Sands

I walk fast, head down, keeping in the road. A bus-driver hoots behind me. I keep going and he swings round me and shouts 'On yer bike!' out of the side window of the cab. A cyclist pelts along right behind him. No lights. You're too young to take that kind of risk.

I'm walking up Bloomsbury Street, one foot in front of the other. The city's too crowded, people everywhere, cramming the pavements, shoving past each other, all busy with nothing. How many of them care about job riots five miles away, about Makepeace and Yasir and HelpCo and people so wretched they'll beg to work for food?

I want to walk until the air's clear, until I feel clean, somewhere I can breathe and see the night sky. The British Library looms in front of me and I'm across Euston Road, into the station and on a train heading east out of the city. Everyone else seems to be drunk or asleep. The man next to me, my age, with a paper in his lap, lolls onto my shoulder, dead to the world. I smell the curry on him and reach over for the paper, fold it into a pad, tilt him sideways and slip it between his head and the window. The headline reads:

"Another Jobs Riot: Illegals Attack Police".

I'm not part of it, I've been hollowed out inside. I'm floating away from my body, it doesn't matter where I am, up there, in an empty sky, no stars, looking down. The roof peels back off the carriage, by itself, without any sound, like the lid of a sardine can, and I peer down into it. Someone's arranged lay figures on the seats, except I'm one of them and my eyes are open, I'm awake and looking upwards and my face is blank, no way you can tell what I'm thinking.

The train jerks to a halt and a chubby young ticket collector comes round, tapping people on the shoulder, shouting 'All change!' I shake the curry eater and he mumbles something and drags himself to his feet. I follow him across the station forecourt. No Helpers here. He gets into a taxi and I cross the road next to the roundabout and keep going along the promenade.

The railings feel damp to my hand, an ancient undersea coldness. The beach is below me, the sand rippled by the ebbing tide. Beyond it, there's nothing, just the salt smell of the sea on the breeze and the sky up above, black, with one star gleaming through a rift in the clouds.

I halt and take the air into my lungs. There's a cleanness in it, it's the same as it's always been, it couldn't care less about forced labour or Cat or my sordid pact with Henry Makepeace.

The seafront's changed since the day Cat took that photo on the beach. The esplanade has been extended out onto the beach, a squat new building with lights on it stands at the foot of the quay, and a poster saying 'Stop the Marina' flaps in the wind.

I could go on walking, I could walk for ever, but suddenly I'm tired and there's no point to it and I'm down on the sand, trudging away from the promenade, the harbour wall to my right. After a while I kick off my shoes as if I'm on holiday and sit down. I've walked too far already.

Early morning. The sun's rising away to the east and a vast pale blue sky arches up above me, but the harbour wall casts a dark shadow onto the beach. It's cold as midnight down here. I'm chilled to the bone and pain stabs into my neck every time I move. I'm exhausted and my legs are stiff as builder's planks.

About two hundred yards out a bank of mist hangs thick on the sea swell. You can't see the lighthouse at the end of the quay. The fog-horn booms, lost in the mist. Everything smells of salt and stale sea-weed. I watch the dark foam-edged water advancing a little further with each breaker.

I want to be here, it's a place where I can settle accounts, where I can get clean at last.

There's money in my pocket like there's always money in my pocket. I could find an all-night café, eat black pudding next to the radiator and think of Nic and Jack and the bargain I made with Makepeace.

I sit unmoving on the sand and the cold seeps into me. I wonder how long it takes the tide to get this far up. A gull flies over, barely a foot above my head, and lands a little way up the beach.

I shift my leg. Cramp grips my thigh. The gull flutters its wings and settles, eyeing me. I stretch, forcing the cramp back, crushing it down into a ball small enough to hold in one hand. I roll myself onto my knuckles and get to my feet. It's a new day, no different to the one before. I watch the waves rear and break and diminish and heave up again. The mist thickens into fog out on the water. I should get on.

Cold water surges past my feet and hesitates and falls back, sucking the sand away from my toes. I could walk further, I could keep walking, out to where the water's cleaner. The swell tugs at you, the undertow drags you out, into the fog, where the waves suck back and crash down and close over your head. I could enter that quiet world, smooth sand below, chill water above, dim shapes around me like shadows in a deeper darkness. Everything silent, everything peaceful, only the boom of the fog-horn and the rustle of sea-weed, no-one to question you, no-one staring at you, no-one telling you how clever you are, no-one asking you what you sold and what you got for it.

Back then we were on the quay, right at the end by the lighthouse. Everything else has changed, but the quay endures. We walked out together, the three of us, with the wind blowing hard from the sea. Nic held the canister, she wouldn't let anyone else take it.

I don't think Jack really understood what we were doing, not then. He wouldn't take my hand, he kept his eyes on the water and held himself upright, like a guardsman, except for the tears on his face.

I take a couple of steps forward and bend down and plunge my hands in, up to the elbows. The water swirls chill round my fingers. I scoop it up and rub it into my face. My eyes sting and I wipe away my tears.

The sun's high enough to warm me now. I glance back at the promenade. Someone jogs by in a grey tracksuit, brown hair tied back, swinging her arms, dodging among the dog walkers. I'm no cleaner than I was. Nic and Jack. And Cat. And Henry Makepeace. When you get close to it the mist seems warmer, safer, you could be in your own world.

The sun burns at me. There's salt in my hair.

Someone splashes through the water behind me. I swing round. A figure in a red hoodie, spray glittering in a silver arc around her. Her legs thrash out, almost sideways and she flails at the air with her arms to keep balance. She's making straight for me.

'What the fuck are you doing?'

She smacks me open-handed in the chest, hard as she can. It's like being hit by a snowball packed with ice.

'You scared me.'

I stagger backwards and she's got her arms round me as if she's stuck to me. She presses her forehead against mine. My breath mingles with hers and comes back to me, warming my cheeks.

After a long time she stands back.

'Knew where you'd go, worked it out. Here, I've got something for you.'

She's got it in her fist and the chocolate is starting to melt. I rip off the paper, break it, stuff half into my mouth and give her the rest.

'Thanks.'

She's wearing her trade-mark grin and we're standing with our arms round each other's shoulders and the waves breaking round our ankles, cramming Paradise Bar into our faces.

You can trust a Paradise Bar, they've never changed. You never see a zero calorie Paradise Bar or a Paradise Bar with chilli extract or protein supplement. Don't need to, it's the taste. Sugar.

'Tide's coming in,' she says. 'We should maybe move?'

'I'm OK. Could stand here for ever.'

'You're shivering. Here. Dry yourself on this.'

She's right of course. She passes me her hoodie. We clamber up the steps onto the promenade and she starts tapping at her phone. An older woman muffled up in an overcoat with a pink and orange knitted hat steps aside to give us a wider berth. Her Jack Russell definitely wants to sniff my trousers. I reach down to pet its muzzle and she hauls it back on the lead.

I look out to sea. The fog hangs over the water, dull and grey, and you still can't see the far end of the quay. A red glow swells and fades within it from the beacon. The fog horn bellows. I feel comforted. I hand Nic her hoodie. She starts speaking before she's got it properly over her head.

'We ought to get going – lot to do today. Hey, great you got me out of there after the debate – you and Jack and Thomas, all of you.'

Yeah. That's what we did. And Makepeace of course.

We start up the slope back to the roundabout. A figure comes out of the station, walking fast, and Nic runs ahead, waving both hands at once.

'It's wonderful to see you, both of you,' he says. 'Got your message on the train.'

It's Jack, of course it's Jack. Nic's got her arms round him, round me, both of us. She keeps making little chuckling noises. Jack's laughing at her and hugging her. And someone else joins in, grinning at both of them, and it's me.

'God, you're frozen,' she says. 'Let's eat.'

The café over the road's got a sign saying 'All-day Breakfast'. Nic notices things.

'You go.' I say. 'I might take a walk on the quay first.'

'On the quay? OK.'

The wind blows cold enough to make you wish you'd remembered your gloves. We've come past the parked cars, the fishing boats, all three of them, swaying on their mooring ropes as the tide lifts them. The cables on the masts clatter in the wind. We've got the place to ourselves. No-one's thinking of fishing today, I don't blame them.

The mist is thick and clammy. I feel the dampness coating my face and taste it on my tongue. Nic and Jack are with me, one on each side of me, holding my hands. We're in our own world, cut off from it all by the mist, everything muffled, everything distant. We could be anywhere, we could be twenty years ago. The fog-horn moans again, very close and somewhere above us, and the red glow sweeps across and is gone.

The stones under our feet are wet. You can hear the waves crashing in at the end of the quay, withdrawing with a rasp of gravel and crashing in again, the salt spray thickening the fog.

'Look out!'

Jack's hand tightens on mine. Nic's feet skid out from under her and she falls backwards tugging at my arm and

I stumble but don't let go. She's right on the edge, her legs kicking out in thin air and I'm on my back next to her, holding on to her. Jack gets his arm round my waist and we haul her back. She lies flat out on the cobblestones, gasping for breath. I kneel down beside her. She looks up and grins and gets to her feet and offers me her hand to pull me up.

We none of us say anything.

This is the right place. We stand there, all three of us, heads bowed, a metre back from the edge.

Nic puts her hand on my shoulder:

'You remember? I stood just here and you held me, you had your hands on my shoulders. I couldn't get the lid off the canister at first, but I wasn't going to let it beat me and in the end it came. I held it out, far as I could.'

She holds out her arm.

'I shook it. Don't know what I was expecting, maybe something that smelled of her, but all I found was that grey ash and it wasn't Mum at all. I wasn't going to cry. I didn't cry. But I knew we were on our own and I was desolate.'

I remember. The ashes whirling away in the wind, down into the water, a dark patch, spreading like a stain, washed back and forth by the tides, sinking down, becoming part of the ocean.

Jack's still holding onto me, gripping my sleeve. He's looking out to sea, his cheeks pale and wet with mist. The wind's taking his words but I can still hear him.

'No-one would smile at me, you all looked down as if you were searching for something you'd lost. You wouldn't look at me, you'd only touch me. That's what I remember most, the way you held my hand, too tight so it hurt, and I took my hand away. I thought it was some kind of gloomy game, and it would all get better, only no-one was laughing.

We had lots of games on the beach, Mummy loved them. I tried to join in this one, not to smile, to walk with my head held down. There was fog just like today. I hated it, you couldn't smell things in the fog and the sound went funny like you had something in your ears.'

He shakes his head.

'I remember all that. Mostly I remember you, Nic, I was trying to keep up with you, but you kept on walking, too fast, and then you remembered me and you waited for me.'

He rubs at his face.

'Mummy wasn't there and you were both so serious, I knew I had to play the game by myself. So I did. It was called "Being a Robot", you had to walk like a robot and keep your face like a robot and think like a robot. It made you a bit clumsy.

I followed you to the end and watched that thing with the canister. I wasn't any good at being a robot. I was just empty.

Let's get breakfast.'

So we go to the café and have breakfast with fried bread and two cups of tea. The Oxfam shop up the road next to the homeless centre's open. Nic treats me to a nearly new pair of trainers that I probably won't ever wear again.

You can see the beach from the café, you can see where I was sitting when I took that photo, the one I keep hidden in that file. The mist's gone and the fog horn's silent. A family gathers together and stakes their claim with windshields, all shouting instructions to each other. The mum's brought a garden spade and they're still in their anoraks, they're going to build the biggest fortress against the sea ever. Should I tell them the tide's on the turn? Find out for themselves pretty soon.

I grin at them, Nic and Jack, grown-ups now, maybe one day there'll be another child digging in the sand and I'll be sitting in a deckchair with the camera.

'Anyone want to build a sandcastle? We used to build brilliant sandcastles.'

Nic laughs and starts choking, her mouth full of toast. I slap her back. Heimlich? She sucks in a huge shuddering gulp of air and her cheeks are red.

Jack takes a deep breath and expels it, as if he didn't need it, he just wanted a moment free of talking.

'That was then.'

Nic takes a packet out and slips something in her mouth and washes it down with hot tea and catches my eye.

'Remembered. Yeah, that was then.'

They're both looking at me. After a moment, Nic says

'The accident. Wasn't your fault. The coroner said. He was right, OK?'

'OK,' says Jack. 'That's cool. The coroner was right.'

He closes his eyes and opens them again.

'We should maybe get back.'

We catch the train back with the early morning commuters, half of them asleep, the other half tapping away at their laptops. Nic and Jack get seats opposite each other and chatter away non-stop, mainly about indie box sets. They keep glancing round to include me but it's not my world. I know the words they're using, but I can't understand more than half of it and neither can the bloke opposite, judging by his expression. They're laughing and talking and showing each other pictures on their mobile phones, like teenagers, and we're on the train together and I'm stupid with love for them.

The train slides in past canals and gas-holders and warehouses and factories, all converted into flats and shops and cafes, as if people want to live here and go shopping and drink coffee and never do anything else.

Jack glances at his phone and he's on her feet.

'I must get back, breakfast meeting. See you soon.'

He's off, dodging through the crowd, half running half walking down the stairs onto York Way.

I follow Nic down the platform. She pats my arm.

'Yeah. See you soon.'

She's off, striding lop-sided towards the escalators.

Makepeace's face beams down from the giant screen news feed above the departure board. I stare up at him. I know you. People push past me. A young woman in jeans and a green padded jacket murmurs

'Don't look at him. It only encourages them.'

The picture switches to the images of a jobs protest, this time it's a sit down by the yellow T-shirts, blocking all entrances to the Stock Exchange. The strapline reads:

'More riots. Makepeace blames illegals.'

There's more on the repatriation programme, another rusty ferry-boat crammed with people. Then it's Makepeace again, Makepeace mouthing words about his duty to the British people, Makepeace shaking hands with the outgoing Prime Minister, Makepeace with his general, platitudinous smile.

Bastard.

People stream past into the tube station across the concourse, people with plans, schedules and other people waiting for them. A gang-master herds his Helpers past me and people back away leaving a little space round them. I wrap my coat more closely against the cold and move to the side where I can't see the screen any more.

There's a café I know tucked away off the Euston Road, with the windows steamed up and the smell of fried bacon everywhere. I need to think. I need to stop thinking.

Bring on the Clowns

I'm on Archway Road, a couple of days later. It's a good day, chill breeze with high dark clouds, but the sun's warm on the skin. Nine a.m. and the traffic rolls past like the waves on a beach, everyone except me has somewhere to go.

A bow-legged man in a yellow T-shirt comes towards me. His lips move but I can't hear what he's saying against the noise of the traffic. He bends forward, arms akimbo. He's wearing shorts and trainers, but he doesn't seem cold. I smell the tobacco on him.

'Got a job, mate? Anything, anything you like.'

Someone sniggers.

'Tell him what you're offering.'

A group of them stand at the kerb, smoking roll-ups. Helpers are everywhere, and no-one takes any notice. HelpCo, I never thought of that. Perfect business model. You buy a franchise, sign them up for food and shelter, guaranteed, and you hire them out for what you can get. The market goes round and everyone's a winner.

'Sandwich?'

He's dark-haired with wrinkled skin and round shoulders and a stoop that makes him look shorter than he is.

He shuffles his feet and glances down the street.

'I'm OK. Supposed to wait here, 'til someone wants me.'

'No, I'll get you one. And a coffee?'

'It's our job, mate.' One of the others has come over, a well-built man, early middle age. 'No snacks on duty. Take a pride in your work.'

'How much do you get for this?'

He laughs. 'It's not like that.'

'But it's crazy. You can't like living like this.'

He stops laughing and thrusts his head towards me.

'What do you know?'

'Yeah,' says the first one. 'Your sort never understand. What else I got to do?'

'Why do the bosses have those riding crops?'

The one with the stoop straightens his back.

'Leave it. They look after us, food and that.'

'You work for food? They're making fools of you.'

'We have a laugh. Who asked you to stick your nose in, anyway?'

He spits tobacco-juice into the gutter and squats down with the others on the edge of the pavement. None of them say anything. They keep their eyes on me as I walk away.

I'm not part of this anymore, I can't be. I'm a bystander, watching it happen.

A 210 bus draws up at a stop a few metres down the road. If I move fast I can catch it. I want to know what's going on in Dagenham. By-election tomorrow.

I've always liked buses, there's something warm and leisurely and sociable about them, they look after you and they take you where you want to go. I sit back in the front seat, top deck, ace seat on the school run. The yellow T-shirts are everywhere, on both pavements, serving in the shops, on bikes and on the building sites. Some of them drive vans or yellow taxis. I feel uneasy, I can't get comfortable on the seat. The T-shirts are so general that if you look hard enough you can't see them at all.

Two of them are on the other seat across the gangway from me, a thin man in yellow trainers and an older woman. I swear he's chatting her up, love on the dole.

'Down there, the Red Cap, that's a nice pub, used to go there Friday night. When the good times come, I'll take you.'

A young man leaps up the stairs. He doesn't say anything, he just grunts and they're on their feet, although we're halfway between stops. He sits and dumps his coat on the spare seat and starts tapping at his phone. When I get down the stairs the Helpers are squatted in the push-chair bay. I nod to them but they ignore me.

More yellow T-shirts outside Finsbury park station. The bus halts a hundred metres short of the stop because they've blocked the road, pavement to pavement. The buildings on both sides are grubby from a century of traffic fumes and dirty air. A banner hangs from the railway bridge. Bright sunlight picks out the words: "Real Jobs for Real Pay", and the placards and T-shirts of the demonstrators beneath it. Passers-by stop to watch what happens, someone cheers. Whistles hoot and a guy in a yellow T-shirt with a top hat on his head bangs on a drum.

The car in front of us wants to do a U-turn but a post-office van coming the other way blocks its path. The car driver leans on his horn. The air stinks of diesel and my spirits rise. It's a Holloway Mardi Gras.

The bus-driver chuckles:

'Bring on the clowns!'

He opens the doors.

A man wearing polka-dot spotted red briefs and socks with suspenders shuffles forward in front of the demonstrators. His chest's pale, shrunken, like an old man's. Gold-brown hair flops across his forehead. Someone tosses him a bundle of clothes and he drapes a crumpled silver-grey jacket over his shoulders. He's the gang-master I saw interviewed on Breakfast TV a week ago.

He lifts his head.

'This ain't right,' he shouts. A whistle shrieks in his face. 'I paid HelpCo good money for the contract, that's my tablet. Give us it back.'

Someone calls out 'It's a free tablet now,' but a young man with an outsize T-shirt over a leather jacket holds out the yellow tablet. The gang-master grabs it and makes for the station entrance, clasping it to him, in front of his shorts. Someone throws the riding crop after him and it falls to the pavement. No-one picks it up. The demonstrators give him a round of applause, the whistles howl, the car horns blare and over it all the drum-beat hammers like a heart awakened. The shouting turns into a chant:

'Fightback! Real Jobs! Rights back! Real Pay!'

The boy in the leather jacket waves his arms for attention.

'Fightback! No Forced Labour! Real Jobs for Real Pay! Where's the next gang-master?'

'You got no pride?' A young woman in a green anorak and a HelpCo T-shirt shouts from the opposite pavement. She carries shopping bags in both hands. 'Time you got your life sorted.'

He laughs at her.

'Who taught you to say that? Join us!'

'Sorted, I'm sorted.' She yells, pitching her voice so it echoes off the station façade.

A woman in a purple woollen coat pushes forward.

'Leave him alone.' She got off the bus just behind me. 'All he wants is a proper job.'

A police siren wails, growing louder, drowning out her words. Two vans, mesh visors down over their windscreens, blue lights flashing, drive fast down the wrong side of the road and pull up.

A senior officer gets out of the first van, fits his peaked cap on his head and marches towards the young man. Other policemen spill out of the vans and form a double row along the pavement.

The demonstrator bellows

'Greetings! When are they going to have you wearing the Yellow T-shirts? Lots of room for a stab vest under them.'

The officer says something and the demonstrator shakes his head. The police raise their riot shields and take three paces forwards. All round me the on-lookers are pulling back. The woman in the quilted coat tugs at a lead and a spaniel looks up and trots after her. Only the woman in the green anorak and I stay put on the pavement. I feel cold inside my overcoat.

The officer holds up a whistle, polished like a silver teaspoon, and puts it to his mouth. The demonstrator looks at him, shrugs and spreads his arms to wave the other protestors back. The yellow T-shirts retreat onto the pavement. I count more than a hundred of them. The bus I was on drives past, followed by a stream of cars, vans, trucks and bikes.

I catch up with the man in the leather jacket. He's talking to a slight young woman with high cheekbones and deep-set dark eyes.

'Good for you.'

He grins. He's enjoying himself. 'Yeah, well. We try.'

'I want to know, how many of you are there?'

The woman interrupts.

'You a reporter? You got to print this. Henry's Helpers fight back. Gang-master dumped.'

'I'm retired.'

'It's catching on,' says the young man. 'No one'll look after you if you don't look after yourself.'

She nods,

'Yeah. You and your mates.'

'Sure – something for your funds.'

I slip some twenties into his hand and I'm off before he can say anything. The tightness in my shoulders slackens

I change to the Central Line then the District Line, east, out beyond Stratford. Jack's territory. Just want to see how it's going. I feel warmer here.

Dagenham West

Jack's face greets me from a sticker on the bus shelter. There's an openness about him I never really grasped before. He's the stranger you meet in a café and you find yourself telling them things you never meant to tell anyone.

"Together We Can".

The same sticker's on the next lamppost and the one after. Someone's been scratching at it but you can still read the slogan.

The weather's changed like it often does when you're underground. The sky presses down, grey and heavy, it'll rain again soon. The Heathway's full of people, all busy, all hurrying, heading for the station or the shopping centre. Nearly half of them wear the yellow T-shirts. Some of them have them on over jackets or jumpers, but mostly they're bare-armed. Very few with waterproofs. It's as if they didn't think they deserved to be warm or dry. One of the older Helpers leans on a stick. It skids on the pavement and I see it's a broken window-pole. A knot of them, teenagers, most of them black, stand aside for me, dipping their heads, not meeting my eye.

'It's OK, you've got as much right to be here as I have.'

They back away from me, the way they came.

A poster looks down from the crossroads hoarding, but it's not Jack. It's Makepeace with his best bishop smile, shaking hands with a young blonde Helper.

"Your Life Sorted" in letters two feet high.

Anger glows in my chest. Someone's spray-painted a line through "Sorted" and written "STUFFED" in untidy crimson capitals with paint streaks dripping below them. Like Nic said, Jack's in with a chance. The next poster is lower down and they've sprayed on a whip dangling from his hand.

I keep on walking, not going anywhere in particular. There's a side turning ahead. A large car with a double logo on the bonnet noses its way out, smooth as black oil, bringing the traffic to a halt. It moves off, away from me, with no more noise than the wind in the corn. I stand stock-still in the middle of the pavement and feel in my pocket for a Paradise Bar without thinking. Everyone stares after it. How many of those have you seen in Dagenham?

I take my right hand out of my pocket and press my left fist against the back of it until the pain bursts out and I can't think for a moment.

'Excuse me, sir. I don't want to disturb you, but my master needs to get home.'

It's a Helper with a child in a green hooded rain suit in a large push-chair. School's out. He's been waiting behind me for some time. I nod and step to the side. He passes and I shout after them

'Why do you call me "sir"? You don't have to call me "sir".'

'I'm sorry sir, how would you prefer me to address you?'

He waits for me to respond. The child ignores us and clicks on a mobile phone, using both thumbs.

'Let me get you a coffee. You look like you could use a break.'

'Oh no, sir. I mustn't be late.'

He takes a pace forward, stops and turns:

'Maybe I will have that coffee. Eddie here enjoys a hot chocolate.'

I get them some take-outs and tell him about the demonstration at Finsbury Park. He doesn't say anything but his eyes narrow and he shakes my hand and thanks me.

The side-road's a dead-end, filthy brick walls on either side. It opens out in front of a large building with a smooth modernist façade. The words "Paradise Gardens" sprawl across it in free-flowing script, "Health Club and Spa for Gentlemen" in smaller capitals underneath. A one-time cinema from the look of it, the original name "Xanadu" still visible. No sign of anyone. My skin prickles. The area in front of the building, where the side-road opens out, is cobbled. Someone's swept it recently.

I look at the cars parked against the wall on one side, a mid-range BMW, a Nissan sports car, an Audi roadster and others I don't recognise. The roadway narrows and leads on round the building.

Paradise. "Paradise Dagenham" was the name on the box-file in the dingy office behind the shop-front south of Burgess Park, where I tracked Yasir down, the word the man with the wire-rimmed glasses trembled at as he scribbled on my palm in the Portacabin.

Syker's face, with the scar at the corner of his mouth, so close I can smell the ketchup on his breath.

'Best take no notice.'

The façade needs painting but you won't notice after dark when the neon lights are on. Images of a girl and a boy outlined in pink and blue run the height of the building on each side of the name. Below them are posters: a young woman in tight-fitting black singlet and running shorts faces you, her hair tied back, the muscles in her shoulders standing out, a dumb-bell raised in each clenched fist. A lithe young man in similar white sportswear, blond hair, square chin, broad shoulders, holds barbells, arms extended, above his head.

Large bronzed metal doors with raised rectangular patterns stand open but the lobby is in darkness. I can't be sure whether someone is moving about inside but no-one goes in or comes out.

Anyone there, on duty or loitering in the darkness inside those metal doors, you couldn't miss me.

I walk on up the Heathway towards the station. It's beginning to get dark. The shopping plaza on my right is lit up for Christmas. People stream in and out. A family, mum, dad and a curly-headed eight-year old in a red duffle-coat, enter. The boy's full of excitement, he chants 'Pepperoni Pizza, Pepperoni Pizza' as if he's just learnt the words. He looks up and catches my eye. I wink and he falls silent.

The atrium of the shopping mall is huge and unheated. It's paved with flagstones and large enough to have a raised flower-bed with a ten foot silver birch in the centre. There's a café set back to the right. Yellow-painted cycle-rickshaws stand in a line just inside the entrance, adverts for lip-stick, box-sets and Disneyland plastered on the body-work. The traffic noise, the sound of people talking, of footfalls, of a trolley or a door slamming all have that hollowness you get in confined public spaces

I notice that the whole area is tidy, the usual squalor of tin cans, cigarette packets and plastic bags is missing. A Helper in a green hoodie, HelpCo T-shirt over it, bends to pick up a torn newspaper over by one of the plate-glass windows.

Helpers in yellow T-shirts squat round the bed, waiting for work. No-one shivers, despite the cold. Some of them are grouped together, playing the dice game they seem to like and smoking roll-ups, but most of them wrap their arms round themselves and hunch down and wait.

I buy a tin of tobacco and some cigarette papers from the stall by the entrance. The assistant, an older woman with pink mittens, asks me:

'Sure you're old enough? Stunts your growth.'

Her face reminds me of a mince pie.

I join the group of Helpers under the birch tree and squat down.

An older man, who looks so thin that I'm glad he's got his back against the bed to hold him upright, stares at me:

'Who might you be, sir?'

I take the lid off the tin and pass it to the lad on my right, a black kid, not more than sixteen with tiny stars razor-cut in his hair.

'Help yourself. Pass it on. And no-one has to call me "sir".'

I take a paper, crease it lengthways and hand the pack to him. I reach over to the tin, take a pinch of tobacco, spread it along the fold and twist the paper between thumb and fingers as I've seen the others do. I can't get the edge to fold neatly inside to make a cylinder.

'Here,' the older man says. He takes the paper from my hand, deftly rolls it one handed, licks his finger, runs it along the edge of the paper, seals it, and hands it to me.

'Thanks. Helped me out.'

I show him my injured hand, the colour of raw potato skin, dappled with blood spots and still slightly swollen.

I light up and pass on the matches. The smoke is harsh in my gullet. I can't stop myself coughing.

They're all watching me. The older man takes a drag on the cigarette he's rolled for himself:

'Not used to this, are you? Sir.'

'Yup.'

I wait until they've all made their cigarettes and lit them.

'You know what day it is?'

'Christmas?'

'Don't be stupid.'

'Your lucky day?'

'No.' I point to Jack's sticker on the glass door of the supermarket. 'It's the election tomorrow and that's who you're going to vote for.'

'Jesus, not another one.' An elderly black woman with a thick ragged jumper under her T-shirt and a cable knit bobble hat waves a finger at me. 'Only talk to us when you want to tell us how to vote.'

A young lad with blue eyes and a port-wine birthmark motions me to the side.

'Scuse me, sir, can you shift yourself? I can't see the TV.'

I look behind me. TVs are stacked in the shop-window, most of them tuned to a football match.

'Yeah, you're in the way,' someone shouts.

The Helpers are edging to the side. Only the thin man and the lady in the bobble hat want to argue with me. Another Helper, a young black man in a white T-shirt with a nose-stud and silver ear-rings like tiny hoops, stands to one side, watching us

I crouch down so they can see over me.

'Sorry, only trying to help. Jack Morlan, he'd do things for you. Get you training, decent jobs.'

'Don't need a job. I'm sorted, sir,' says the young kid. He goes back to his cigarette. He's more interested in the football than he is in me.

'Yeah, got me mates, me food, fag money, somewhere to sleep. I ain't greedy,' says the woman and everyone laughs.

'Doing the right thing, ain't we? For the country. Voting's not for us.' The thin man has finished his cigarette. He reaches for the tin. 'Should have known – free roll-ups, don't call me "sir".'

The man with the nose-stud speaks in a baritone.

'Leave him alone.'

'What's it to you?'

'My name's Luke. You know what I like about being in the Helpers? I've got mates, same as when I was in the army. We look out for each other.'

The thin man nods. The boy hasn't taken his eyes off the screen but he's listening.

'Not many people look out for you when it comes to it. Me mum and me mates. The bosses are laughing at us. We got to stick together.'

He takes a step back.

The boy looks up at him.

'Don't go.'

He surveys us, raises a hand in salute and walks away into the mall.

I take my chance.

'What kind of a life is this, sitting on the pavement waiting to carry someone's shopping home in the rain? Don't you want anything better?'

'What's it to you, what I want? You can get back to your posh house and your car and tell your rich friends to mind their own business. Call you what I want.' He takes a drag on the roll-up. 'Sir.'

The tobacco smoke hangs heavy around us. Myles in the pub, on his long lunch break, handing me his empty glass:

'When all else fails, Ritchie, tell them the truth.'

OK, but I'm not telling them Henry's Helpers was my idea.

'Fair enough, I'll tell you the truth. Jack's my son and I love him. I want to do the best for him. Please vote for Jack Morlan.'

Silence. Someone says 'Oh!'

After a minute the black kid tugs his ear. 'He's OK, he came round and talked to us, bought us burgers, but what good does that do?'

'Yeah, same old story, all we get is promises and we're still bottom of the heap.' The thin man pauses to cough. 'Now we're on HelpCo. We've got mates. Like it says, "Your Life Sorted". You don't know what that means. Your life's always been sorted.'

Everyone shouts out, their eyes on the screen. A young man in a red and white striped shirt and white shorts takes a run towards the camera, ducks at full speed and turns two somersaults and a hand flip. His team-mates crowd round, wrap their arms round him, slap him on the back or just reach out and touch him, as if they want to check that he's real.

'Had a trial for the Orient, once, junior squad,' the black kid says. 'I'd go in the army only they won't take me.'

The thin man's the only one left talking to me.

'No offence, but I don't vote. Don't matter who you vote for, you just get the government.'

I nod.

'It's like Luke says, only people help you are your mates. Stick with 'em.'

'But why do your bosses carry those whips?'

He thinks for a minute.

'Wouldn't you?'

He tosses me the tin. It's empty.

I've no idea what I should do. The sky is completely dark. People spill out of the shops, pull on their coats and hats, their breath forming little clouds in front of their faces. I wrap my coat tighter round me. A woman comes out of the café, tosses an empty paper coffee-cup towards the Helper in the green hoodie and walks over to the cycle-rickshaws. Her hair is dark and cut short. She carries a yellow tablet and wears a thick over-coat and calf-length boots. A riding crop hangs from her wrist. She claps her hands, like an infant-school teacher, pauses, and slaps the crop against her boot. The Helpers get to their feet and the older woman shakes the cold out of her legs. Some of them are there to carry bags but most form a line next to the rickshaws.

The woman shouts:

'Cycle-taxis here! Less than fifty pee a mile. Why carry your shopping home?'

She's busy collecting money and allocating passengers and riders to the rickshaws.

The woman in the bobble hat reaches the head of the queue.

'Not you, you're past it.'

'I'm as tough as the young ones.'

The supervisor beckons the black kid.

'You next.'

The thin man pokes his finger at her.

'That's not fair. Jen was next.'

'Leave it. The boy gets the job.'

''S'OK,' says the boy. 'I'll wait.'

The passenger, a young man in a Burberry jacket, has already climbed into the rickshaw. He takes a stick out of his bag and waves it from side to side.

'You lot need a bit of discipline.'

He flicks it across the side of the boy's face, like a switch. The boy ducks and someone gasps. A hand reaches in from the side, twists the young man's wrist and forces him to drop the whip. Without letting go of him, Luke scoops it up, snaps it against the rickshaw and hands him the pieces.

'Behave yourself.'

'You…' The passenger's cheeks are red as boiled ham.

The supervisor steps forward.

'I'm very sorry, sir. You, you, you and you.' She points the riding crop at the older woman, the thin man, the boy and Luke. 'You're all barred. Find your own food.'

The thin man glares at her.

'It's not fair. We want to work.'

Luke snorts and looks round at the Helpers, then at the woman with the tablet.

'I'm not part of your team. Let's try it like this. We're sacking you. We don't need you. We can run this and we'll share the money. Look out for each other. Luke's rules. OK?'

'Yeah,' says the boy. The others are in a circle round them, not talking. The woman raises the riding crop, holding it by the middle as if she's not sure what to do with it.

Luke takes the yellow tablet out of the woman's hand, turns off the power and hands it back. 'Off you go – oh, just a moment.'

He takes the riding crop.

'But…HelpCo gave me that. With the contract.'

'Tough.'

She looks round. The Helpers are closer now and there are more of them.

She waves the tablet at them, but they edge in round her.

'It ain't right. You work for HelpCo now.'

Her voice is uncertain, it's as if she's appealing to me.

I shake my head.

She blinks and looks round her. Her face is pale with blue eyes. She forces her way through the crowd of Helpers and makes off down the street.

Luke grins.

'Let's get on. Who's next for a trip? Co-op Rickshaws, friendliest taxis in town.'

I drop the tobacco tin in a recycling bin as I pass, thinking of the Maybach, of Nic's face on the television screen, as she shouted 'I never agreed to this'. I think of Yasir, calm as always, leaning forward to the camera, of Makepeace with his hand held out to welcome me into his office. I think of Salma and Ariam and a poster I once saw in the *Refugee+* office with a black child, her belly swollen, her face pleading, resentful, demanding, the child who knows with absolute certainty that it's you who are to blame, the question in her eyes:

'Whose side are you on – you, who have it all?'

Paradise

I'm not Ritchie any more, I'm that different person, the bystander, as if I'm watching it all on a film. It's spooled up, snug on the reel, everything that's going to happen. Only way you can stop it is to break the celluloid. I walk back along the Heathway, down the side-road, up the steps and through the main door. I must have walked too fast, I can't catch my breath.

A young man, who could have been the young man in the poster, sits behind a reception desk.

He looks up and smiles and I see tiny lines round his eyes.

'Can I help you?'

'Yes. I'm looking for gym membership.'

'Of course. Our introductory offer. The first session is free.'

I don't know how to do this. I avoid the young man's eyes. I see glossy colour photos of slender young people performing impossible exercises across the wall behind him and framed certificates with crests. I look away. The smell of bleach hangs on the air and signs point to "Changing Rooms" and "Squash Courts". A ball thuds against a wall somewhere nearby followed by the sound of running feet.

'I'm feeling a bit tense.'

The words are there in my head but they don't come out clearly.

'I'm sorry, I didn't catch that.'

I look up at him.

'You know, tense.'

I rest both hands on the desk as if to steady myself.

'Sorry, sir, are you feeling OK?'

The young man rises to his feet.

A deeper voice cuts in behind me:

'I'll look after this one.'

A man dressed in a dark suit like an undertaker's assistant steps forward and takes me by the arm. He's broad-shouldered and barrel-chested and his hair is greased back. He must have been standing in the shadows at the side of the lobby.

'You take a seat Glenn. Look after business.'

'The gentleman asked about gym membership.'

'Don't you worry, I know what he needs.'

He's squeezing my arm and it hurts but he doesn't seem to know he's doing it. I feel too tired to resist.

'Yes, Mr Jason.'

The boy sits down. The man lets go of my arm.

'You're all alone in the world, aren't you?'

His eyes are a soft grey.

I nod.

'You come with me. I'll find you something to set you on your feet.'

He opens a dark wooden door I hadn't noticed at the side of the room and beckons me through it.

'You need a nice relaxing massage.'

We're in another room, dark red wallpaper, thick carpet, dim lighting and a door in front of me, this one painted blood red to match. Two armchairs upholstered in white face each other across a low table. A man sits in one of them. He looks up and holds out a hand. He's balding and plump, with red cheeks and creases at the sides of his mouth.

'Take a seat. Now what can we do for you?'

'The gentlemen would like a massage.'

The man in the dark suit stands just behind my chair.

'To be sure, to be sure. Now what takes your fancy, young man?'

He's holding out a tablet. I think of the menu at a restaurant such as Marco's, heavy and leather-bound.

'Boy or girl? Black or white?'

The screen shows images of young women and men, like the staff page on a firm's web-site. They're in skin-tight black underwear, posing, submissive, smiling at the camera. I look away from them.

'He wants a boy.'

My mouth's dry.

'I don't know. Maybe both?'

'Excellent choice. I like the way you think.' The plump man rubs his hands together. 'Naturally, these things cost money.'

I lay my wallet, thick as a poetry paperback, on the table. The man riffles through it, removes some of the notes and hands it back to me.

The first man takes me through the red door. I have an impression of endless corridors, dull red walls and dust motes hanging in the air and a heavy smell of musk.

The sounds are muffled, distant, as if the air is too heavy to stir.

We skirt round the edge of a large room furnished with small tables and plush sofas, and a stage at one end. The curtains are drawn above it, maroon with a gold border. Most of the light comes from the bar along one wall. People stand against it, mainly men, youngish, white and black, all smartly dressed. Heads turn towards us, they're bored, on edge, waiting for something to happen. No-one says anything. The room smells of alcohol and dust and under it the musk.

I look round. I'm aching for a Paradise Bar.

The man leads the way to a door the other side. The men by the bar follow us with their eyes. I glance back at them and a tall man in a sharkskin suit nods to me and looks away.

The man stands by the door, holding it open.

We enter a room with a hand basin and a massage table, a white towel spread on it, a shelf with plastic containers of oil, brushes and flannels, and a row of hooks. A black velvet bag with something heavy inside hangs from the first hook and a black full-face mask, like an executioner's, and a riding crop, from the second. The man touches it with one finger and lets it swish backwards and forwards, like the pendulum of a grandfather clock.

He opens a door at the back and ushers me through.

"Number 10," he says.

I'm in a corridor, with doors along it. The carpet is deep-pile, magenta, and the paintings on the walls show men and women, half-naked, slender, entwined. Laughter comes from a room on the left. He gestures to a door further up the corridor. The corridor smells of cheap scent. Everything is wrong.

Somewhere music's playing. It's Wagner's "Forest Murmurs". I remember when I last heard it, at the Royal Opera with Cat. That was another life.

I take a few paces forward and I hear a different noise from a door on the right, number 8, an animal noise of muffled sobbing.

None of this is my business.

I open the door. I feel as if I'm coming to the end of a journey.

A bed almost fills the room, gold satin sheets and an elaborate plush bed-head with a mirror on the wall above it. A south Asian boy sits on the bed, naked, his face in his hands, yellow material clutched against his chest. He's so thin I can see the outline of the bones in his shoulders.

He's crying, sobbing so his whole body heaves.

'Ariam? Are you Ariam?'

He looks up. Something about his face reminds me of Nic, when she was a child.

He's been crying for a long time. His eyes are red and sore as if he's rubbed them. His face is terrified, like Nic's that time, at Yasir's place, trapped against the wall behind the table.

A shudder runs through him. He shakes his head.

'No. Who's Ariam? I'm not Ariam. Please, say it was good, you'll say I was good?'

The T-shirt falls back. His chest is covered in weals, red and angry. Blood-spots dot the sheet, like paint flicked from a brush. I reach out and he shrinks away from me.

Someone shoves the door open behind me. The boy screams, high-pitched, like a cat. The blood pulses in my head.

The barrel-chested man in the dark suit from the lobby seizes me by the arm.

'Out of it. You shouldn't be here.'

There's no strength in me. I slump against him and smell garlic on his breath. The boy screams again. The man twists me round, shoves me into the corridor and slams the door behind him.

I shout 'Salma! Salma!' but it comes out no louder than a groan. I force air into my lungs:

'Salma!'

A tall figure stands in the doorway of the massage room at the end of the corridor, watching us. I glimpse a distinguished face, black hair, greying at the temples, and a suit that fits him as if he was made for it. He holds the riding crop loosely in his hand.

He nods to the man holding me.

'Put him out with the garbage.'

He steps back into shadow.

The bouncer half-leads half-pulls me away from him, tugs open a fire-door at the far end of the corridor and thrusts me through.

I totter down some steps, my feet slip and I catch hold of a rubbish bin. Orange light shines down from a frosted glass window two storeys above me. The bin contains three yellow T-shirts, the top one with a streak of blood across it. Beneath them are crumpled towels.

The alleyway stinks of stale grease and rotting vegetables. My skin feels filthy.

I shake my head, trying to clear it. I need to drink water, cool and silken in my throat.

I find my way round the side of the building, leaning on the grimy brickwork and down another alley so narrow my shoulders brush the brickwork on both sides. The alley ends at an eight-foot metal gate topped with razor wire. I thrust my hand against a green plastic knob on a metal panel set into the wall. Bolts slam back and I'm out, between a betting shop and an estate agent, much further down the Heathway. It's raining, and I reach out and let it wash down on the back of my hand.

I step on something soft, a yellow T-shirt, streaked with grease, screwed up on the pavement. There are more of them, along the gutter to the shopping mall, in piles as if people have thrown them down.

I know what I'm going to do.

Pray for me, Nic. Pray for me, Jack. I'm Ritchie Morlan.

The Blade of a Knife

Early evening. The Helpers have gone from the shopping centre now, just people coming home from work, off out to eat, out for the evening. I push open the door of the pub, the "Elizabeth Fry", next to it. The room's cold and half-empty. The barman serves me a whisky, slaps down the change and goes back to the TV. It's football, same match as I saw in the shopping centre. Extra time. No-one looks up at me.

The whisky is harsh in my throat. I cross the room and push open the door to the loo. The room is ill-lit and painted the colour of tobacco juice. I lock myself in the end stall, flush it, lower the lid and sit down. I take out the small knife, Grandad's knife.

He had a tin with "Golden Virginia" on the lid, like the one I'd bought for the Helpers. He'd open it sometimes.

'Jarrow March,' he said. 'History to you, but I was just your age when they took us out to see them, under-sized men in broken-down shoes trudging past. They'd never quite meet your eye.'

'They came round after the march was finished. They'd stand at the door with their cap gripped in both hands, asking for work. My dad gave them tobacco in tins with shiny lids, the same as this one. They seemed to like the tins more than the tobacco, somewhere they could keep things. They all had

232

something, a letter, a photo, a medal from the war, a door-key, a hairgrip with a bow on it, they always wanted to show it to you. Useful thing, a tobacco tin. Airtight.'

Grandad had medals in his, dirty silver discs on rainbow ribbons. He had a black and white photo of Reenie, his wife, posed for the camera in her wedding dress, her hair waved, her face young, vulnerable, an absolute beginner, like Cat and me in our wedding photo. He'd look at it and sometimes he'd touch it, but all he said was:

'You should have seen her, that day. Pretty as a picture she was, pretty as a picture.'

Under everything was a photo of a baby in a white cap and christening shawl staring round-faced and incurious at the photographer.

'That's your Dad,' he said. He looked at it for a moment longer and closed the tin and put it away back in his pocket.

He trusted me with the knife.

'That's good steel, you'll always find a use for it.'

It's four inches long when folded and fits snugly across the tin.

I click it open and tilt it from side to side so the light flashes from the blade. I test the point against my thumb, I can hardly feel the prick but I see a tiny globe of blood. I raise my hand and lick it up, salt on my tongue. I close the blade and slip it back into my pocket.

Yellow streetlights shine down on the Heathway, but the side-road is lit only by the neon signs, everything pink and blue. People are talking in the lobby, laughter bursts out and subsides. I keep to the shadows at the side, crouching down in darkness.

A bus rumbles past the end of the side-road then everything's quiet again.

The Mercedes Maybach is in front of me. It's been backed into the alleyway where it swings round the building. I grip the hilt of the knife in my pocket, cold and perfect. The bonnet gleams, tinged with pink from the light. I reach out and touch it and slide my fingers along towards the radiator where it's warm, with an animal heat.

I flick open the blade and carve a long scratch along the side, peeling off a wafer of black paint as if I was carving a joint. It hardly makes a sound. I slide the knife back in my pocket.

I wait there, leaning against the wall, my hand in my pocket, my fingers touching the hilt. A group of men enter the club, talking loudly. The one in the lead has a fleshy face and wears a pork pie hat.

I tap at my mobile. Just the same digit, three times.

I hold my breath until my ribs ache, and, just as they answer, I gasp out:

'They've stabbed me.'

I force air into my chest.

'Please, it's the Heathway.'

I drop the phone, pick it up and mutter:

'Blood,' louder. 'I can't stop the blood. Paradise Club. Please.'

I hold it against my throat, gasp in another breath, drop it and ring off.

I rest for a few moments, then I make the second call, the one that counts.

No answer. I leave a message.

I stand up and turn the corner and walk forward, up the steps to the entrance. The reception desk has been pushed against the wall and the barrel-chested man is just inside the main door. He glances down and brushes at the sleeve of his jacket. Then he sees me. He takes a pace forwards and a thick-set man in shorts and a black T-shirt pushes past him, scowling. I pull my hand out of my pocket, the knife gripped in it, half an inch of blade jutting out. You don't notice it until the light glints on the metal.

'Thought I told you,' he says.

He seizes my elbow and pinches hard. His fingers are like rods. I can't move. I scream and stab upwards, my fist curling backwards into my own shoulder. The knife-blade jars against the bone.

Syker grunts and shakes me as if I'm made of sacking. Blackness swirls round me. I have to get into the lobby. I grab at his face with my other hand and my fingers slide across his cheek as if I'm slapping a child. He opens his mouth to laugh and my forefinger slips through something hard. I stumble and my weight jerks against the ear-ring. I hang for an instant and the ring tears free and I stagger forward one pace. He bellows and I'm past him and through the door and on my knees in the lobby. People crowd round, there's a hubbub of jumbled noise and lights flash, blinding me. Someone shouts and over it all Syker snarls like a chained bull that's broken loose. The ear-ring rolls away from me, bloody, glinting, unnoticed. I want to reach after it, but my arm won't stretch out. I gasp for air and something squeezes at my heart and the blackness rushes in. I tumble away from Syker, away from Paradise, from the noise and the lights. I'm swathed in the blackness, nestled in it, safe.

My shoulder feels as if it's on fire. I'm stretched out and the floor is cold under me. I'm grateful just to lie quiet, not to be part of anything. I count the bulbs in the light-fitting above me but it's a different number each time. I hear a siren in the distance, the sound swelling, getting nearer.

Footsteps at the entrance, someone running. The crowd opens up.

He's kneeling by me, pressing on my shoulder. I can feel his breath on my face.

I don't open my eyes.

'Dad! What's happened? Are you OK?'

I look up at him.

'Law and order. Your chance. This is for you.'

Blue light flashes across the entry. More noise, heavy boots on the gravel, someone shouting. A police officer leans over me.

'He OK?'

'Needs an ambulance. We have to stop the bleeding. Quick.'

Jack's in charge. He bears down hard on my shoulder with the palm of his hand.

The officer talks into his radio.

'One minute.'

He turns to the crowd.

'Back inside everyone. Through the doors please.'

The bouncer's arguing with someone, spreading his arms out. A group of police in stab vests push past him and into the club.

An older man in a green uniform kneels down next to us and Jack pats me and stands up. The man presses a pad down hard onto my shoulder. Someone else fumbles with my sleeve. A young woman with black hair connects something to my other arm. She smiles at me.

'What's your name, sir? Ritchie? You're fine. Nasty cut you've got. We'll get something on it and take you down for a check-up.'

They lift me onto the stretcher. Six of the police officers move out through the doors ahead of us in a tight group. Yasir, his hair untidy, his face grim, is in the middle and one of the officers grips his elbow.

Another group follows with Syker. Fresh blood streaks his neck and cheek where the ear-ring's been torn out. He's handcuffed between two officers. He sees me, swings round and opens his mouth to roar:

'You bast…!'

One of the officers elbows him in the stomach. He doubles forward and they half drag, half walk him out of the lobby.

I relax. The stretcher sways down the steps and Jack's beside me.

'You're in good hands. Gosh, that was brilliant. I'm praying for you.'

Someone's trying to get his attention. A reporter I've seen before in a smart suit holds out a microphone. ITV, and we're in time for News at Ten. Jackpot.

'Catch you at the hospital.'

He turns to the camera, his face serious.

'Modern slavery, here in Dagenham, now, on the high street…'

I can sleep now.

'Mr Morlan?'

237

A young black man with grizzled hair in a white coat smiles professionally down at me. I'm in bed, in a cream-painted cubicle, curtained across the end. The air smells of disinfectant and the familiar hospital clatter surrounds us. I've slept my way into A and E.

My skin itches. I'm dressed in a hospital smock. My shoulder's numb and a dressing like a huge sticking plaster covers most of it.

He touches the shoulder and I wince.

'Sorry.'

He smiles again.

'We'll keep you in overnight for observation. You need to get the dressing changed in three days. You're a lucky man.'

'You're absolutely right.'

'One thing I can't work out, why he went for the shoulder. Usually these people go for the ribs. Do more damage.'

'Maybe he slipped.'

He nods.

'That must be it. Anyway, let me give you some advice.' He sits on the edge of the bed. 'You're not a young man and your heart's not strong. You should stay away from these places. Eat properly, take things easy, a bit of exercise. Your heart won't forgive you.'

I stretch out against the coarse hospital sheet. I need to rest.

Later I'm awake. Something pricks at the back of my memory and I try to drag it forward, but Nic's waving her mobile at me.

"Candidate leads slavery vice den raid"

I read, scrolling across the tiny screen. Jack's talking to the camera, his face resolute. Two police vans are parked behind him. Uniformed police escort the men from the club bar past him and into them.

'He's going to win this,' she says. 'Who's the law and order candidate now?'

'Yup.'

'OK.' She grips my hand. 'Not hurting you? You're brilliant.'

It hurts like hell but my heart's singing.

She lifts the curtain and two Helpers in the yellow T-shirts push a trolley past.

'Excuse me!' she shouts.

She's off, after them.

Next time I wake Jack's there with his candidate's rosette on his lapel. A young woman stands next to him. She's smartly dressed, with an identical rosette and a shoulder bag with leaflets and a tablet poking out of it.

'Hi Dad, you're looking pretty good. Here's Katya, she's helping me.'

Katya smiles at me.

'I'll get some coffees. Cappuccino, latte, flat white?'

'Not for me, thanks. I'm on water.'

Jack grips my hand, the good one.

'I don't know how you did it, but that was great. All those poor kids in there, penned like cattle for men to rape them. It's dreadful. And they caught the traffickers – same people that kidnapped Nic.'

His eyes are shining.

'Thanks, Dad.'

And he blushes and kisses me on the cheek, and I blush too.

'Just lucky, I guess.'

There's something else, something I need to tell him.

Katya pulls the curtain open and shakes her head. 'Sorry. Only Henry's bloody coffee. It's everywhere.' She taps her wrist.

'Something to tell you,' I say. 'About Yasir.'

Jack rests his hand on my shoulder, the good one.

'I've got to get going, the count's already started.'

He bows his head for a second.

'I'm proud of you.'

I sleep and wake, troubled, and Salma's face, her eyes glowing, is in my mind, more real that the green curtains round the bed.

'He is a jackal ... You people know nothing.'

I think of her, walking away from me, her hand jammed into her pocket, her fingers on the photo of Ariam. We're on the Larkhill Park Estate with a phone box along the road and a long way away a girl in school uniform staring back at me. I sit on a low brick wall and I'm crying and Cat's there and she's always there with me.

227. Where people bring Yasir money. Where he keeps his records.

I breathe deeply and wait for my head to clear. Salma. I can do something for her and for Ariam. I check the address on the map on my phone and text it to Jack and to Thomas.

The grey-haired doctor enters. He glances at the monitor, warms the stethoscope between his palms and places it on my chest. The skin round his eyes is puffy and dull under the ceiling light.

'Good to go if you pass the test,' he says. 'Can you remember the advice I gave you?'

Saying it's easy.

'Your heart doesn't forgive you.'

'Don't forget.'

I get a taxi back (not HelpCo), eat second breakfast, turn on the TV and fall asleep on the sofa. I'm woken by the soreness in my shoulder. It's the morning news and Jack is first item, a clip from his acceptance speech, thanking all the people who voted for him.

'This government has failed. We can do better. We will heal our divided nation. That is the message from Dagenham West. HelpCo means modern slavery. The support you've shown me, all of you, that's what gives me the courage to go forward. Thank you for your votes. I pledge to do my very best for you, for all of you.'

The Tory's right behind him in her pin-striped suit. She looks like a kid who's dropped her ice-cream in a ditch. The Lib Dem's the only one to keep her deposit.

The expression on Jack's face puts me in mind of Makepeace when he took his stance at the front of the platform, but he's the one I trust. Absolutely.

I get up to open the curtains. I'm taking it easy, doctor's orders. The rain clouds are just passing over and it's going to be a fine day. To the east there's a clear blue sky and the tiny dot of an airliner far above. Maybe I should stroll to the end of the road and read the papers over a coffee. Think about a holiday somewhere warm. I know, I'll take the car, get used to driving again.

The presenter looks into the camera: 'And now, breaking news. The government reports further successes in its campaign against so-called illegals. Over to our Political Editor outside no 10.'

A large man with bushy eyebrows and moustache in a dark overcoat and scarf faces the camera, the Georgian façade of Downing Street behind him. Raindrops glisten on his bald scalp but it doesn't seem to bother him. He speaks as if addressing a school assembly.

'Mr Makepeace has announced that the Metropolitan Police have detained people traffickers and a large number of illegal immigrants in a series of raids in the London area. Charges of people smuggling will follow. My sources confirm that these are the same criminals who exploited illegals in the Dagenham vice-den.'

'Unusual for the Prime Minister himself to make this kind of statement, isn't it?'

'Unprecedented. We would expect this to come from the Commissioner or the new Home Secretary, Hilary Angel. Mass deportation is Mr Makepeace's signature policy. It brought him the premiership. We can only speculate that he wishes to reinforce his position in the face of the controversy aroused by his Jobs Guarantee and the unrest over workers' rights.'

'One other thing. I understand that the new MP for Dagenham West supplied the information on which the raids were based.'

'Yes. Jack Morlan's campaign against modern slavery is now centre stage in public debate.' He glances off camera. 'And now back to the studio.'

Warmth crowds into my breast. Time for a stroll to the corner.

The smell of coffee coils round me. A young woman with her hair in a plait and a yellow T-shirt with "Here to Help" in green cursive script across her shoulders sets the cup down.

'There you go, love.'

'Thanks. Table service is new, isn't it?'

'Don't ask me. Only yesterday I found my place here.'

The coffee's good, but all the staff and none of the customers are in the T-shirts. The Helpers that brought everyone here squat on the pavement outside with their cycle-rickshaws. A young brown-skinned man sits on a folding chair at the end of the rank under a golf umbrella, his riding crop across lap. He taps at a mobile phone. I watch the Helpers shrink back whenever anyone walks by. No-one else glances at them, hunched down against the cold, no-one seems to notice them, modern slaves, in plain sight.

Le Gavroche

A few days later a letter arrives. It's handwritten on thick, cream notepaper and signed by someone I've never heard of. "The Prime Minister, The Right Honourable Henry Makepeace, MP, asks me to invite you to no.10 for a gathering to celebrate British heroism in service to the community. Dress: lounge suit. RSVP."

I tear it up into small pieces and put them in an ashtray and set fire to them with a match. They burn well. I tip the ash into an envelope and seal it. It'll go in the filing cabinet at the back of the study.

Or maybe I should drop in. See how Makepeace is getting on. It's a nice day. I'll maybe go for a walk.

I love the view from the Victoria Memorial across St James Park. London seems like a continental city, the Georgian palaces of Whitehall framed in greenery and the outline of the London Eye beyond. I'm on Birdcage Walk looking for a taxi when a black Bentley Continental draws up beside me. The driver steps out, and comes up to me. He's wearing a peaked cap and a black jacket.

'I'm sorry, you've got the wrong guy.'

'Ms Dance's compliments. She would be delighted if you'd join her for lunch.'

He opens the rear passenger door and warm air gusts out. Elsa sits on the cream leather seat, her attaché case beside her.

'Ritchie!' she holds out her hand. 'So glad I found you at last. Where shall we go? Your choice.'

Elsa wants something from me. Greeks bearing gifts. I was never much good at Latin, either.

'Le Gavroche?'

Her eyebrow quivers for an instant.

'Of course. Do get in.'

She nods to the driver who is already talking on his mobile.

We cut silently through the traffic. The bigger the car, the more likely people are to get out of your way. Why's that?

'Congratulations,' she says. 'I see your face in the papers every time I look.'

'And how are you?'

'As you see me. Doing a lot of political work these days – I have an excellent contact.' She grimaces and I realise I've only seen her smile once before. 'You should help. Let bygones be bygones. After all you're a national hero. Always good for the brand.'

'So they tell me.'

The driver sounds the horn – I hardly hear it inside the car – and a yellow T-shirted Helper with a yoke across her shoulders shuffles sideways out of our way. A dozen shopping bags dangle from it on cords.

The driver and the doorman usher us into the restaurant, one on each side. Elsa talks briefly to the maître d' in his dinner suit, with his greased back hair and waxed moustache, and we're led across the room. He seats me on a green upholstered banquette facing Elsa across a table where the cream cloth reaches the floor. An elaborate display of cardinal flowers and red poppies stands in a niche opposite. I breathe in the rich summer odour of meat and meadow and blossom.

I've always liked Le Gavroche. It's impossible to ignore the splendour of the décor, but the food is excellent. You can see everyone looking you over, registering you, and looking away.

I order the lobster mousse with caviar (how long since I've eaten that?) and the steak because I assume they're the most expensive items. I pay no attention to what Elsa's having. The lobster tastes so rich it's almost sickly but I wolf it down and smile at Elsa.

'Nice food,' she says.

I answer with my mouth full:

'This isn't just because I'm a hero is it?'

'Mainly yes. You took a knock and we won't talk about that, but you've built up your brand. Resilience. I respect that.'

She raises her glass. As I tilt mine to my mouth, my elbow catches the end of my steak-knife. It slides sideways off my plate, falls, and lands on the carpet with no noise. The waiter is at the table with a fresh one and an apology before I can reach down and pick it up.

I stroke the handle of the knife. Silver, ridged and widened to protect your fingers where it joins the steel of the blade. The cutting edge is honed to a bright streak. The wine tastes full-bodied, heavy on my palate, overpowering the richness of the meat. I angle the knife and the light flashes across Elsa's face.

She blinks and continues:

'There's more. Henry's Helpers. You made that happen. I must admit I had reservations, I couldn't really believe it would work. You proved me wrong.'

She pauses as if she expects a response. I say nothing. The cinders within me glow as if caught by a draught.

'It caught on and now we're building it – a franchise operation under the HelpCo brand. My idea. Thought it might help things along. It's going to be very big business, perhaps the biggest in this country.'

'Really?'

My fingers are still on the knife.

'You proved that there are people who will trade a precarious job at the minimum wage for guaranteed meals and a bed in a barracks.'

'That wasn't my idea.'

She looks straight at me.

'You're part of the team. Henry, Mr Makepeace, believes in us. We've already got the concession for all benefit claimers, students with loans, disabled people, all the loafers and shirkers who expect to live off other people's taxes. Next we'll move gradually through the labour market as far as we can take it. Britain's lost the illegals, so we need cheap labour. Helpers are the answer.'

The bait is laid out before me. I've been here before, with the client and their adviser across the table and the adviser clearing her throat and suggesting we postpone any decision.

'You can't be serious. All those people I recruited had no choice – street homeless, benefit claimers. I was trying to get them an apprenticeship, a decent job.'

'Exactly. No choice. What do you think's going to happen when all the legislation feeds through – the banning of trade unions, the abolition of labour protection, the rolling out of instant dismissal and the dissolution of industrial tribunals? Your life sorted. In some ways Henry is an idealist. He sees a lot wrong in this country. It is his duty to sort out people's lives. You and I are the ones who will make it happen.'

She fills our glasses and raises hers.

'To you, Ritchie. Everyone in the industry knows you did it. I'm going to make sure you get your slice of cake. You're a hero in the fight against modern slavery. You're the ideal figurehead for HelpCo.'

'No.'

She nods. She thinks we're into a negotiation.

'Think of it. Retail, entertainment, leisure, care homes, transport, warehousing, all those routine jobs. We used to think they'd be taken over by robots and computers: the new industrial revolution. Workless malcontents would flood the streets. Not now. Henry's Helpers are cheap as chips, and it's all down to you.'

I stroke the hilt of the knife. I feel as if this doesn't really matter. Two people in a restaurant, talking about something of no importance. I know what's going to happen, and I'm not telling.

'The riding crops – whose idea was that?'

Elsa smiles, the smile on her face two years ago when she called us all together, that Wednesday. She announced that the Board had made their decision about the CEO, and I looked round and Myles wasn't in the room.

'Ritchie,' she says. 'The job is made for you. You can't ignore this. Besides, Henry is certain you'll take it on.'

She fixes her eyes on me, she scans every detail of my expression. She hates me.

'He said I should remind you you're part of the team now. He said: "Tell him regret is a terrible thing."'

The trap snaps shut. My hand's hurting where I'm gripping the knife. I release it and spread my fingers. They close back on the hilt without me thinking about it. Everything becomes very clear.

'I'm flattered. But I must say no. I'm going to spend more time with the family.'

She drains her glass.

'Remember what I told you. You're an adman, you'll always be an adman. This is an opportunity you can't deny.'

Something stirs. I know that traitor passion.

I smile back at her.

'I'm a hero. I think I'd make a very good witness in court. That video wasn't Nic's idea, it was Yasir's. He's under arrest for running a vice-den I'm told.'

'I don't think they've charged him.'

She flips open the attaché case. My head is cram-full of words. They slither past, but they won't make sentences. Elsa's still talking, '… press release … draft for your speech.'

I'm on my feet and she says very clearly:

'We need you, Ritchie.'

I start walking. The skin's too tight across my chest and I stop halfway to the exit and lean on the back of a chair,

I put my hand against my neck and feel the blood pulsing under my fingers. A waiter takes me by the elbow.

'Excuse me, sir.'

He takes me to the gentlemen's toilet, sits me on an upright chair and holds out a glass of ice water. The maître d' bends over me and I smell the greasy odour of his hair-cream.

'Are you feeling better, sir?'

'Just need a rest. A bit of a shock.'

I take a deep breath and drink down the water. My mind clears and everything becomes simple. Nic and Jack, Jack and Nic. You'll understand. I know you will.

'Please tell the lady I'm fine. It's not necessary to wait, she'll have my answer this evening. I'll find my own way.'

'I beg your pardon.'

He reaches down and takes the knife from my fingers. I flex them and rub my knuckles gently with my other hand.

Syker

Next day. I'm heating up some soup when the phone rings.

'Dad? They've arrested Nic.'

'What for? Where is she?'

I need to sit down.

Jack's voice, telling me things. I know what happens. Elsa talks to Makepeace. Makepeace talks to the Met. They don't waste much time.

'That video business – conspiracy, she could get ten years. Makepeace is behind it, I'm sure. Thomas is trying to get Adam to take it on.'

'Are you OK?'

'I need to get through to the Shadow Home Secretary – it's political. They've got her at New Scotland Yard. You get down there, I'll join you later.'

He rings off. I grab my coat and turn off the gas just as the soup boils over. I'll sort that later.

I'm on the stairs, jabbing at my phone for a taxi as I run.

We halt outside the anonymous block on the embankment. It looks like a budget hotel with a glass-sided atrium added to the front by a different architect. I'm still in the queue for the reception desk when Adam strides past.

He doesn't smile.

'You'd better come with me.'

He says something to the security guard by the gate who hands us passes and buzzes us in.

'Difficult business. They want to charge her with conspiracy. What we need is a reliable witness.'

'I was there. I'm very respectable these days.'

'Yes.' His shirt cuff is unbuttoned. I point and he halts to fasten it.

'Thank you.' He purses his lips. 'I'm sorry. You're compromised – the accused is your daughter.'

'Can't they see she's innocent? Yasir trafficked children as sex-slaves.'

'I know that. You know that. Can we prove it? Turns out when they raided that house on the Larkhill Estate that all the paperwork is in Syker's name. Yasir is a clever man. Remember: the forced workers never saw him, only Syker. No identification. He was visiting a gym club of which he is a member. They had to let him go. No charges, apologies all round. He's also suing for wrongful arrest. Through here.'

He pushes through double doors with a sign reading "No Public Access" above them and sets off down the corridor beyond. Again I'm reminded of a budget hotel. Beige walls, doors at regular intervals, light oak laminate on the floor and fluorescent light fittings. Everything smells of plastic.

He knocks at the end door. It bears a brass plate with the one word "Seton."

'Take your lead from me. Best if you keep mum. I've known Seton since college.'

The room contains a wooden office desk, two upright chairs in front of it for visitors. A balding man sits opposite us, studying a file. A window fills most of the wall behind him, with the venetian blind closed. A fluorescent strip-light glows down from the ceiling. I'm reminded of a police inspector's office I visited after the accident. A picture of a Victorian constable with prodigious moustaches and polished buttons hangs on the wall to the right.

The figure at the desk looks up and I recognise him as the large man in the grey suit who sat in on the interview after my slave stunt outside parliament. Brasenose, poshest college in Oxford. I check Adam's tie. Snap.

He doesn't get up or shake hands. He seems weary. I keep my eyes fixed on him. I don't trust him.

'Adam. Good to see you. I'm afraid I can't spare you much time.'

Adam rests his hands on the back of one of the chairs.

'I'm sorry to barge in like this, Howard. Something you need to know. Nic Morlan is entirely innocent. I am representing her interests.'

'Ah. My master believes that a prosecution will succeed.'

'The Shadow Home Secretary is also taking a personal interest in the case. I'm afraid it will attract media scrutiny.'

'Too much political involvement already. Nonetheless we believe we have a strong case. Syker is an obvious malefactor. Ms Morlan, I am afraid, instigated riots in which a police officer died.' He closes the file and slips it into a drawer. 'I'm sorry.'

He looks directly at me.

'We've met before. You don't look well.'

My turn now.

'I am here to confess to conspiracy to incite a riot, or whatever the charge is. You've got the wrong Morlan. May I sit down?'

I take the other chair. My mouth's dry and it takes all my strength to keep my back straight.

Adam glares at me.

'Please ignore my client.'

'I'm not his client.'

'Gentlemen.' Seton waves a hand in front of his face as if bothered by flies. 'You muddy the water. We have charged Ms Nicola Morlan and the papers go to CPS as soon as I've signed off on this file.' He points his ball-point at me. 'You are a hero. We are not about to charge you on your own unsupported confession. It's a pleasure talking to you, but I must get on.'

I lean forward.

'I've got a lot of contacts. Do your superiors want to read: "CPS Charges Wrong Man in Riot Case" over their breakfast?'

Adam stares at me. 'But…'

'We have our contacts too,' says Seton. 'I don't think any of us want this case tried by the media. Have you thought about what they'd make of your daughter? I believe she has a number of public order convictions.'

I get to my feet and turn to Adam.

'Come on. We need to talk.'

Seton's mouth twists as if he is suppressing a smile.

'You do.'

Adam is white with anger and there are dints at the corners of his mouth. He starts talking as soon as the door closes behind us.

'You are an idiot. Seton and I go back a long way. I could have done a deal, maybe a non-custodial sentence.'

I lean against the corridor wall. The solidity of the building comforts me.

'I was there when we set the thing up. It was my idea, but Nic got carried away, she wanted to take the lead. It was going to be about immigration, start off a rational public debate and mobilise people against the Repatriation Bill. Yasir outsmarted her. He wanted his trafficking operation to be made legal. The riots were nothing to do with it.'

'Sure. I worked that out for myself. Yasir is, as I said, a clever man. Syker is the fall guy. They're charging him and Nic. Yasir comes out as an innocent businessman who runs an employment agency and a health club. Syker supplied the workers, it was his job to check on where they came from. He also set up a brothel in a separate section of the building. Plenty of people to testify to Syker's brutality.'

'Great.' I wish there was somewhere to sit. Then it comes to me. 'Syker's our witness. Why doesn't he put the blame on Yasir?'

'Try to think what it'll look like in court. You have Syker on the witness stand. Everyone knows he's a violent thug. Yasir wears an Armani suit and is treasurer of the local Rotary Club. He gives five thousand a year to charity and goodness knows how much to the party of government. Syker says it's all Yasir's idea. Who wins?'

'But what about Nic?'

'I'm sorry. Think of Nic against Yasir. Nic is reckless, excitable. A clever prosecutor would make mincemeat of her. We'll try to use her mental health problems in a plea for mitigation but it won't be easy. A policeman died in those riots. Are you OK?'

He reaches out to pat my arm but thinks better of it.

'Only way we're going to get this to work is if the politicians do a deal. I'm sorry. I wish things were different.'

We start walking. I keep one hand on the wall. At the end of the corridor is a lobby with three purple armchairs arranged as if people meet there to chat about Netflix and photocopiers.

I sit down. Adam comes back and stands with his hands behind his back, looking down at me.

'You've got to try,' I say. 'Please. Nic won't do well in prison. Thomas would want you to try. Jack would want you to try. Syker is key to it. He was there.'

I think of Nic's voice on the phone. Adam sighs and sits opposite me.

'We'd better go over it all again. I can give it twenty minutes.'

So I tell him everything – the discussion in the boardroom, when Nic took over the idea and Yasir twisted it, the Portacabin in the yard, the debate on video and Yasir's intervention about job offers with full security at the end.

Adam listens carefully. He doesn't take notes. He asks one question.

'The video equipment. Yasir provided that, not Nic?'

'Yes, it came with the venue. They did it in the room with the polished board table. That's how I recognised where they were.'

'Come on.'

We're sitting on upright chairs in a small unlit room. A woman police constable sits at a desk to one side with a shaded light, taking notes. She ignores us. A one-way window fill most of the wall in front of us. The draught from the air conditioning chills my neck. Adam sits next to me. He leans forward in his chair and concentrates absolutely on the scene in front of us.

The interview room is the other side of the window. There's a grubbiness about it as if it's been used too many times.

Syker sits on the far side of a metal table. He has a dressing on his left ear which he rubs from time to time. He's wearing jeans and a camel-coloured jumper. He glances round the room as if looking for a way out.

A middle-aged woman, fair hair tied back, sits next to him. I assume she's a duty solicitor. She stares at the file lying open on the desk in front of her as if it contained the key to the case, but it holds nothing more than a single sheet of paper, a type-written form with a photo in the top right-hand corner. Two police officers, a woman and a man, sit with their backs to us. The man has a sticking plaster on the nape of his neck. The light is tinged with yellow. A tape recorder and clock have been placed at the side of the table.

'Mr Syker, Mr Yasir tells us that you supplied workers to his employment agency,' the woman officer asks. 'Is that correct?'

She sounds bored.

Syker closes his eyes as if trying to think something through.

'If Mr Yasir says so.'

'You realise that in saying that, you are effectively admitting to people trafficking?'

He shakes his head.

'We're partners. You ask Yasir. He's my friend, always has been. You ask him, he'll tell you.'

'Perfect fall guy,' Adam mutters.

'We have already done so. We are concerned with your role in the organisation. You provided ...children for clients at the Paradise club?'

'They weren't children.' He sounds resentful.

'I'm afraid they were. What do you mean?'

'You never met them. Dirty little bitches. Yasir don't know what it's like dealing with them.'

'Of course. But you do.'

'Yeah. I'm the only one who could make them do it.'

'Yasir. Your friend.'

'Yeah. We go back.'

Syker relaxes in his chair. Adam leans towards me.

'I wish they'd give me five minutes with him.'

The man breaks in.

'Mr Yasir, your friend, doesn't always call you Mr Syker, does he?'

Syker looks down.

'Calls me Sykes. Thinks it's funny.'

'It is. Do you know who Sykes, Bill Sykes, is, Mr Syker?'

'Why should I care? It's just a joke.'

'Sykes is a violent thug who beats his girl-friend to death.'

Syker meets his eye.

'Bitch must have had it coming.'

'He drowns his little dog.'

Syker says nothing.

'He kidnaps a young boy, but the cops get him.'

Nothing. The man leans forward, his face no more than a foot from Syker's. He grins.

'You know what? He's the fall guy. The boss puts everything on him, Mr Sykes, I'm sorry, Syker.'

'You bastard.'

'Don't you get the joke? You should be laughing. Yasir is.'

The policewoman has her hand over her mouth. She's giggling, as if she can't stop herself.

'What you laughing at?' Syker jabs a finger at her. He's half out of his chair. The solicitor takes hold of his arm.

'My client is unwell. I request a recess.'

The interrogating officer glances at the policewoman.

'Request denied. The accused is clearly fit to continue.'

Syker grunts and sits down. He places a hand on the table and curls it into a fist.

'I done everything for him. He had no right.'

The solicitor whispers something to him. He glowers at her and puts his hand in his lap.

'Something you should know. Mr Yasir will appear as a witness for the prosecution. He blames you for everything. He tells us he's shocked to discover you are a people-trafficker. I'm afraid people will believe him.'

'What do you mean? He'd never do that.'

'He's done it.'

The officer glances at the solicitor who nods.

'We reserve our defence.'

The man opens a folder and takes out a photograph. It's a shot from the video, Nic and Yasir.

'There's more to it. The video. You were present when it was made, weren't you?'

'Course I was. What was all that about that bloke Sykes? Who told you?'

'Please concentrate on the matter in hand. The video…'

'No! He never respected me. He set me up. The bastard.'

'I'm afraid the joke's on you. Now tell us about the video. Tell us about Ms Morlan.'

Syker glares at him and says nothing.

'Mr Syker. I ask again: why did Nic Morlan take part in the video?'

'You ask Yasir. He knows about all that.'

'So what did he do? Remember, he's Queen's evidence.'

'He set me up didn't he? His idea, that video.'

The officer smiles at him. Syker's solicitor intervenes.

'You don't have to say anything. Just "No Comment".'

'What do you know?' Syker glares at her. 'He just talked to her, always talking, that's what he's good for. I knew she was poison. It was me made her do it.'

'Ah.' The officer leans forward. 'What did you make her do?'

'Be in the video, I keep telling you. I had to push her around a bit. Yasir told me to. "Don't mark her," he said, and I didn't. That was before her dad got there. He never knew.'

My teeth are clenched so tight my jaw hurts. I dig my fingernails into my wrist and the pain makes me gasp. Adam glances at me and frowns. Syker's still talking.

'Two days. It was me kept her there, me who made sure she didn't get out, me who fed her. I swear I never touched her. Stuck-up bitch, kept saying she was ill. Yasir was busy, meetings, all the stuff he does. He kept going out.'

'So you kept Ms Morlan – Nic – on the premises when she wished to leave? You made sure she took part in the video?'

'Yeah. Not many people get past me.'

'And Yasir asked you to do this?'

'He was well pleased, said I'd done good.'

Syker sits back, looking pleased with himself.

'Nailed him!' says Adam. 'Well played sir!' He applauds and turns to me. 'I think that is a successful conclusion.'

The PC beside us looks round.

'Shhh!'

The woman officer shuffles her papers together.

'Thank you Mr Syker. You've been very helpful.'

'I done a lot for Mr Yasir. He relied on me. There was the flat in Larkhill Park, there was the van. I done all that, I used to get the letters for him. He always said thank you.'

'No doubt, Mr Syker. We will discuss these matters in due course.'

We're in the atrium just inside the security barrier. Seton joins us.

'I suppose I should say "Thank you". We have Syker's evidence against Yasir and Yasir against Syker. We can dispense with Queen's evidence and plea bargaining. If the video led to the riots, they are both responsible for it.'

I smile.

'A pleasure.'

Seton blinks.

'Ms Nicola Morlan is free from suspicion. We have the evidence. We also have the trafficked victims, but I am afraid they will not play well as witnesses in the current climate and they will shortly be repatriated. Nonetheless an excellent chance of conviction.'

Adam nods.

'Good. Let's just say you owe me one – as does Ms Morlan.'

'Don't push your luck. Good day.'

He shakes Adam's hand and ignores mine.

'Our political masters need not concern themselves further. We must catch up sometime.'

'Of course.'

I touch Seton's shoulder. He swings round, frowning at me.

'Was there anyone called Salma? Or Ariam?'

'I beg your pardon?'

'Among the victims, Salma and Ariam?'

'I really couldn't say. Now if you'll excuse me.'

He turns his back and we pass through the barrier. Jack rushes up to us and seizes my hand.

'Great to see you, Dad – and congratulations, Adam. Maybe we could have a chat about the new Right to Work Bill sometime? I'm on the committee.'

Adam pulls on his coat.

'Got to go, be in touch. Nic's free to go, all charges dropped. This chap,' he means me, 'was helpful. Regards to Thomas.'

Jack hugs me in front all the solicitors and their clients and the officials and police officers, in front of all the people passing by outside the plastic atrium tacked on the front of the Portland stone office block.

'Wonderful,' he says. 'Thomas said you were the only one could do it.'

'I'm so proud of you. You'll be Home Secretary one day.'

He tries not to smile, but I know he's pleased.

'We'll see. I'm not sure what you did in there, but thank you. We'll go over and meet Nic as she comes out. I bet she'd like a decent meal.'

'I'm sorry, there's an appointment I really mustn't miss. I'll catch up with you later.'

Downing Street, Whitehall and Parliament Square

We check in at the booth by the gate. Only twelve of us in the queue, that's enough for the group photo and the press release.

The guard stops me:

'I'm afraid you're not on the list, sir.'

'I'm absolutely certain I let you know. No matter. I'm sure the Prime Minister will want to see me. You know who I am, don't you? Tell them I'm Ritchie Morlan, I'm on the team.'

I show him my credit cards.

He makes a phone call, keeping his eyes on me the whole time he's talking. I look steadily back at him, my breathing under control.

'I beg your pardon, sir. Please go through.'

I step through the body-scanner and they find Grandad's knife.

'You don't see many of those these days, sir.' He squints at the blade. 'Sheffield. I'll make sure you get it back on the way out.'

We continue along Downing Street. A police constable holds the door open at number 10. An aide takes my umbrella, and furls it, revealing the paperclip daisy-chain at his wrist for an instant. We're led upstairs past giant portraits, staring across at each other above us.

I lag behind. I stop and catch my breath halfway up the stairs. Makepeace, leader of the pack, at the centre of everything. I guess you think I'm here to congratulate you, fall in behind for my share of the pickings, the bright sick fruit with the canker at its heart scattered before me.

I follow the others and we cram ourselves into a first floor drawing room which isn't large enough and smells of soap. A waiter with a ready-made black bow tie hands us our glass of fizz and cream cheese salmon canapé on a paper plate. We stand shoulder to shoulder, eyeing each other.

I've seen most of them before in the corridor outside Henry's office, answering his phone, showing him something on a laptop, once running out for a packet of Rothmans. They ignore me. The team. They're all in their smart suits, their black dresses and jackets, all of them neatly brushed, all of them white, all of them young, except me.

The door opens and Elsa enters, white-gold hair, and a blue silk dress. She scans the room for a moment, looks through me, waves at someone and starts talking to one of the young men. He tilts his head and listens to her, not saying much. I catch a couple of words and immediately know he's the one who rang me after Makepeace's speech. I can tell that he'd love to reach out for a second glass of champagne but fears she might think it was rude.

I push my way through the crowd and hand him my glass, untasted.

'Hi Hugo,' I say 'Ritchie.'

'I'm sorry, I didn't quite catch…?'

'Ritchie Morlan. Speech-writer.'

I turn my back on the pair of them.

The aide who took my umbrella pushes the door open and murmurs

'Good evening.'

We all fall silent and Makepeace enters. He smiles round at all of us. His gaze pauses briefly on me and I shiver as if caught in a draught.

'Good evening. Let me welcome you here. You know, in a way this house, No. 10 Downing Street, with the portraits of Britain's former prime ministers all round us, stands at the heart of the nation. You are all here because I wish to thank you. I am proud to stand here and thank you. You are all heroes, heroes of the New Britain, the nation that we will reclaim together. That is our duty.'

He makes his way among us, a handshake, a word with each of us, a special smile, to make sure we don't forget. We're on the team.

It'll soon be my turn. I look down at my hand to still the trembling in my fingers. Something burning presses at my ribs. I slip my hand in my pocket.

'Mr Morlan. So good to meet you again. A signal service in Dagenham. I am honoured to have you on my team.'

He offers me his hand. The flesh of his forefinger is reddened near the tip, he must scrub at the nicotine stain.

'Tell me,' he says. 'I asked you once, do you think the end justifies the means?'

He leans towards me and lowers his voice.

'We both know it does. I look forward to our continued association. I believe you made the right choice.'

Anger burns through me.

I grasp his hand in mine and my thumbnail digs into the sore patch on his finger. His eyes widen. He lurches forward and I hate him and the air in the room shudders and I'm that other Ritchie. The fingers of the hand in my pocket are wrapped round the cold, squat pen I used to strike the devil's bargain, when I sold myself for Nic. In my mind's eye I jab it upwards, towards Makepeace's throat. I see myself twist the smooth metal barrel and it slides in, like a hot skewer into raw meat.

But I stumble and cling onto him and we fall to the floor. That other Ritchie is no longer there. I've dropped the pen and I'm still holding onto his hand. He looks at me as if I'm someone he knew once, long ago. His mouth moves, he's trying to tell me something. I hear the words '… my people'. He slumps sideways and rests his head in my lap, like a weary ten-year old, and sighs.

I fold his hand shut and restore it to him.

People are all round us, reaching down to lift us to our feet. The aide helps Makepeace to a chair, talking softly to him. Makepeace stares at me, as if he remembers he's met me but can't place me. Then he presses both hands into the arms of the chair, rises, smiles generally at the room, and turns to Elsa and Hugo.

I'm outside, on the staircase. The sound of the people talking over each other in the room upstairs is far away, an argument on the other side of a busy road. Above me, Harold Wilson's sly face stares down at Tony Blair.

I'm filled with sadness. I did the best I could under the circumstances. I grieve for the illegals being herded onto ships, for the Helpers with their yellow T-shirts out on the streets in the chill rain, for the forced labourer in wire-framed glasses whose name I never knew, for Salma wherever she is, for Ariam, for all of us.

I wonder if Makepeace meant what he said, if he did it all for duty? If he'd rather have been comparing Christmas bonuses with his school-fellows in the city than dirtying himself in the grubby world of trafficking and poverty and homelessness and slavery, that ardent world, where Nic and Jack and Thomas struggle and suffer and seek humanity?

The rain's stopped. The policeman hands me back my knife:

'You be careful with that, sir.'

I pass through the gates. I move slowly. I need to find somewhere to sit down, to rest.

How long ago was it when I last walked away from Makepeace, along Whitehall, past the cenotaph, past the demonstrators, on to St Martin's, to Margate and to Nic and Jack?

The demonstrators are massed on both pavements now, some in the road. Hundreds, perhaps thousands of them, all in yellow T-shirts, a surge of gold flooding towards Parliament.

A young man in the front row with a faded blue denim boiler-suit under his T-shirt carries a small child in a similar all-in-one riding on his shoulders, his tiny hands locked in his daddy's hair. An older lady leans on a wooden walking stick on one side and on her daughter's shoulder on the other.

None of them talk, their faces, black, brown, white, are turned up to a tall woman with a megaphone. She wears a canary yellow T-shirt over a red jumper and blue jeans and stands on the plinth of the Cenotaph, the grey pillar behind her and the crowd in front.

'Who are we?' she shouts, so loud that her voice echoes off the Georgian facades on both sides. The crowd answers her.

'The left behind.'

'Yes, the rejected, the discarded, the ones they overlooked.'

Cops line the road, holding back the people on the pavement. The officer in front of me looks no more than eighteen. He has blue eyes and a thin black moustache. He keeps shifting his weight from one foot to the other. There's no traffic, they must be diverting it at Trafalgar Square.

The woman continues, her voice ringing out.

'How many are we?'

'Thousands, tens of thousands.'

'More join us every minute, every hour.'

She points towards Trafalgar Square.

'Look!'

She falls silent and the only noise is the tramp of feet resounding from the buildings on both sides of the road. No one shouts, no one cheers. A huge procession, everyone in yellow T-shirts, floods towards us like a river in spate, a torrent of gold, filling the street and the pavements, stretching back to the square and beyond. Black banners with the slogans 'Real Work', 'We Are Many' and 'Together' in red and gold float above it. The young cop stands to attention.

A figure runs ahead of the demonstrators, waving with both hands, you keep thinking she will trip over herself, but she doesn't. My heart skips a beat and I can't help grinning.

The woman hugs Nic and hands her the megaphone. Nic turns to the crowd. Her voice booms out:

'Brilliant, so wonderful to see you all here. This is a miracle.'

She looks round at us all.

'Henry Makepeace has done us a favour. He's brought us all together, all of us. We were trudging through life, looking for a real job, trying to live off what the benefits office gave us. We were in make-work jobs at the bottom of the pile. Then the bosses found they could call us Helpers and they could make slaves of us and didn't have to pay us anything.'

She grins round at them; she can't help it.

'Well that's all changed. Now we've got mates. We're there for each other. They're going to have to listen to us. It's time for the fightback.'

Her voice blurs into the shriek of the whistles and the throb of the drums. I can't make out the words. The demonstration streams on down Whitehall. It checks at the entrance to Parliament Square and the crowd in front of me opens up, just for an instant. I see them, both of them, a young man holding the arm of a woman with braided hair and colours sparkling in it, red and blue. She glances towards me and I wave and shout 'Salma! Ariam!' but who can hear me in this din? She smiles, open-mouthed, reaches towards me and starts forward. The procession gathers itself and surges into the square. The demonstrators on both sides press in and the gap closes.

I push towards her, but there are people everywhere, packing the street and swarming past me, so many I can't make out their faces. I need to rest, just for a moment. I sit on the pavement. The young cop in front of me turns. His face is very pale. He bends and reaches out. The darkness, the same darkness that's been there ever since I held Makepeace's hand and forced my thumbnail across his finger, swirls round and edges closer. A giant hand grasps at my heart, and the darkness rushes in from all sides like a river racing round a rock and I can't hold it back any more.

I need a damned good sleep. When I wake up, they'll be round my bed. I'll tell them all how much they mean to me. I'll ask Jack what he wants for a wedding present. I'll tell Nic how proud I am of her, of what she's done. I'll say something that makes them all laugh.

Because I'm Ritchie Morlan.

OTHER NOVELS BY PETER TAYLOR-GOOBY

THE BABY AUCTION

The Conrad Press, 2016

The law of the market rules Market World. No relationship is permitted but that between willing buyer and willing seller: no slavery, no exploitation, no charity, but no trust, no gifts, no self-sacrifice.

Anna, a successful business woman, falls in love with Dain, Captain of Enforcers, ardent in his service of the One Law. Ed, a tough, spirited and streetwise young woman, and Matt, unsophisticated but humane, also fall passionately in love.

Then, one day, Matt rescues a drowning child and they face the question: can love and compassion overcome the harsh laws of Market World?

ARDENT JUSTICE

Troubador Publishing, 2017

Ade is a tax-inspector. She hates the City of London. She hates the corruption, the casual sexism, the smug self-assurance, the inviolability of the men she deals with, and the cold certainty that nothing you can do will ever touch them. Then Webster, the tycoon, tries to rape her. She fights back and finds herself in the world of the rootless, marginal street homeless who live meagre lives in the shadow of the office blocks that house the rich.

She meets Paul, an Occupy activist who works with homeless people. Ade and Paul become modern-day Robin Hoods, striving to expose the scale of fraud in the City and help the poor and dispossessed, but the power of money to influence government and control the media defeats them. As their love for each other grows, they find real fulfilment in fighting for the rights of ordinary people, such as Gemma, a homeless single parent. Then Webster comes back into Ade's life and it's payback time.

Ardent Justice tells the story of Ade's struggle against the City and for her own integrity, and of her love for Paul, and how hard it is to live a morally good life in a corrupted world.

"Good to find a novel with a strong social message about the way we live now"
Polly Toynbee, *The Guardian*

 Matador